He's My COWBOY

Published by Kensington Publishing Corp.

He's My COWBOY

DIANA PALMER

REBECCA ZANETTI

DELORES FOSSEN

ZEBRA BOOKS
KENSINGTON PUBLISHING CORP.
www.kensingtonbooks.com

ZEBRA BOOKS are published by

Kensington Publishing Corp.
119 West 40th Street
New York, NY 10018

All Kensington titles, imprints, and distributed lines are available
at special quantity discounts for bulk purchases for sales promo-
tion, premiums, fund-raising, and educational or institutional use.

Special book excerpts or customized printings can also be created
to fit specific needs. For details, write or phone the office of the
Kensington Sales Manager: Kensington Publishing Corp.,
119 West 40th Street, New York, NY 10018. Attn. Sales Department.
Phone: 1-800-221-2647.

Zebra and the Z logo Reg. U.S. Pat. & TM Off.

First Printing: July 2023
ISBN-13: 978-1-4201-5532-7
ISBN-13: 978-1-4201-5533-4 (eBook)

10 9 8 7 6 5 4 3 2 1

Printed in the United States of America

CONTENTS

THE HAWK'S SHADOW

DIANA PALMER

CHAPTER 1

It was a miserable Monday morning. Undersheriff Gil Barnes was filling out a report from a local citizen about a robbery, one of the very few that had ever happened in Benton, Colorado. His boss, Sheriff Jeff Ralston, was out of the office. In his absence, Gil was in charge.

He'd just been given the new position of sheriff's investigator. He was crazy about forensics, and while working as a sheriff's deputy, he'd completed two certificates in this special field already at the local community college, going to night classes. He'd also aced a certificate through distance learning, and he belonged to two international forensic societies. But so far, he'd had no reason to use those skills.

It wasn't as if they had that many murders in Benton. Occasionally somebody got shot, but more often than not, it was accidental. Of course, there had been the recent excitement when a nearby rancher was targeted by his sister's murderous boyfriend. But that case was solved and there hadn't been a murder. This past year there had been a murder with a knife. What a mess that had been. And years ago, there had been a notorious murder involving the mentally challenged heir of a millionairess. That had long been solved. In recent times, there had been a couple of attempts. But just attempts.

He sighed as he went down the form, filling in the information for the files. At the front desk sat the new receptionist, a pretty brunette who was answering the phone. She was the youngest of three sisters whose family had been the wealthiest in town but had fallen on hard times. The other two were married. This one, Jane Denali, was the prettiest of them all and the nicest. The sheriff, Jeff, was sweet on her.

Just as well that she didn't do anything for Gil, he reckoned. He'd had his heart broken by a fickle woman a few years earlier, when he was in the military, and he'd never gotten over the humiliation of being thrown over publicly and insulted in the process as the woman transferred her affection to his drill sergeant. These days, he mostly ignored women. Oddly, that seemed to draw them. Go figure, he thought, amused.

He didn't notice Jane's quick glance at him. He was very attractive. He was tall, built like a rodeo rider, all muscle without any exaggeration. He had blond hair and dark eyes and a face like a movie star. Jane tried not to notice. He was obviously not interested in her.

He was just finishing filling out the form when the front door opened. He heard the receptionist ask who the newcomer needed to see.

"There's a body!" the man exclaimed, red-faced. He was wearing working clothes, and his shoes were full of mud from the rain. "We need the sheriff!"

Gil got up and moved out to the front office. "Actually,

you need me," he said, smiling. "Hi, Red," he greeted the city worker. "What've you got?"

"A body," he said. "We were repairing a water break, and there's a skeleton under the pipe!"

"Are you sure it's a person and not an animal?" Gil asked.

Red nodded. "Absolutely. And it's been there for some time. The clothes it was wearing are just tattered cloth, almost disintegrated."

Finally, a real crime to solve, and the body was skeletal remains. Gil muttered under his breath. Well, this one was going to require a forensic archaeologist, and he didn't have the credentials yet. That meant he was going to have to share the case with some hotshot from the state crime lab. It was a very specialized skill . . .

Gil followed the city worker back to the site, where he went through the routine procedure of cordoning off the area and securing the evidence. Luckily the water break was a few feet down from the remains, or there would have been more problems. It was right at the edge of the city limits, within throwing distance of the local elementary school, a florist's shop, and the big brick mansion where the town's mayor, Dirk Handley, lived with his wife.

"We'll need a forensic archaeologist," Gil murmured.

"Sure looks like it," Red said. He grimaced. "I guess I can't keep working . . . ?"

"Sorry. No. Not until I deal with the crime scene. You can patch the pipe, but that's all."

"That's something, at least. Everybody's raising Cain, especially Mayor Handley." He looked past Gil and groaned. "And speak of the devil . . . !"

"What the hell is going on down here?" Handley, a tall,

red-faced, redheaded, overweight man, glowered at the workers around the hole. "And why hasn't this water leak been patched?!"

"We have a problem," Gil said, pointing to the skeletal remains in the hole.

Handley scowled. He moved closer to the hole and looked down. He hesitated a few seconds and swallowed, hard. "My God," he said to himself. He took another breath. "Who is it?"

"We don't know," Gil said. "Body's obviously been there a long time, but I'll need help to excavate the remains and work the crime scene. This involves forensic archaeology. I'll have to get somebody here from Denver."

The mayor drew in a breath. "Poor devil," he said softly. "Any idea who he could be?" he asked.

"None. We don't even know if it is a man or a woman," Gil said. "It will take an expert."

"Then, how long until your expert can get here?" Handley asked abruptly. "And more importantly, when can I get my water back?"

Gil didn't say what he was thinking. "Soon," he promised. "I told them they could patch the leak."

"All right, then." Handley looked once more into the hole. "Poor devil," he said again. "Well, keep me informed." He glanced at the undersheriff. "Should we call the press? They might help identify who it is."

"Not just yet," Gil said diplomatically. "First things first."

"Let me know. Re-election is coming up soon," he said. "A little publicity never hurts. We don't let anybody get away with murder in our town."

Gil was affronted. "Mayor, we don't even know if it was a murder yet," he said.

Handley blinked. "We don't?"

"He could have fallen into the hole; he could have had a heart attack . . ."

"Right. And nobody noticed him."

"It's a very deep hole," Gil reminded him, "and if it was dark . . ."

"Okay, I see your point. Damn, it's cold out here," he muttered. "Going back inside. Fix that leak, please. My wife's raising hell in the house."

"We'll get right on it, Your Honor," Red told the mayor's retreating back before he made an unseen face at Gil and returned to work.

Gil left a deputy at the scene to make sure the body wasn't disturbed. Then he went back to his office and called the state criminal investigation unit for assistance.

"Oh, sure, we've got a graduate right out of college who's a whiz at forensic archaeology, and she's available right now!" the man said, a little too enthusiastically. Red flags were going up in Gil's mind. "Here, let me have her talk to you. Hold on!"

Gil sat at his desk. He overheard the man calling to someone.

"This is right up your alley," he told someone else. "His name is Gil Barnes. He's the sheriff's investigator over in Benton. He needs to talk to you."

There was a pause and then a perky voice. "Hello?" a female answered.

"Yes. This is Gil Barnes—"

"He already told me that," she interrupted. "What sort of problem do you have?"

"Skeletal remains," he began.

"You need a forensic archaeologist for that," she returned.

"I know what I need! Why the hell do you think I called the state crime lab for assistance?" he growled.

"Well!" she exclaimed. "If you're going to be adversarial, this will not be a pleasant association. No, not at all. You shouldn't speak like that to people who are just trying to help you . . ."

"You aren't, and I didn't," he muttered. "Look, I need someone to process a body. Can you do it?"

"Of course I can do it," she replied. "I'm a forensic archaeologist. There are very few of us, you know."

He ignored the comment. "When can you come?"

There was another pause, then a joyful male voice agreeing that she could leave the office immediately. That wasn't reassuring, either.

"You're in, let's see, Benton?" she murmured, as if she were looking at a map at the same time. "Yes, I can be there this afternoon about two, if that's all right? Do you have an airport?"

"Yes," he said with exaggerated patience, "we have an airport. Real planes land at it every day."

"Sarcasm will not win you points with me," she assured him.

"Hallelujah," he said. "I'll expect you at two. If you'll phone the office, someone in a real sheriff's car will come to the real airport and pick you up."

"Now, see here . . . !"

He hung up as she was speaking.

Sheriff Jeff Ralston, standing right behind him, was almost doubled up laughing. "You poor man," he exclaimed. "I wouldn't be in your shoes for bank notes! I'll bet she's fifty and skinny as a rail and has hair that stands out on both sides."

"And probably horns," Gil agreed heavily. "I'm going to study forensic archaeology in case we ever find another skeletal remains in my lifetime," he told his boss. "Just so I never have to deal with that person ever again!"

Jeff checked his watch. "While you're waiting, you might check the database for missing persons in town or in our county. Of course, we don't have an age or sex for the victim yet, but it wouldn't hurt to do a preliminary search. It's not like we have a lot of people go missing."

"That's true enough," Gil said. "I'll do that."

And he did. But nothing turned up. It wasn't surprising. A lot of missing persons cases never made it into the national database for one reason or another. This was one of those times.

In the meantime, Jane Denali finished the form she was typing and went to lunch while Jeff stared after her admiringly.

"Why don't you ask her out?" Gil teased his boss.

Jeff sighed. "I don't do anything for her," he said wistfully. "But she sighs every time she looks at you. Why don't you try your luck?"

"I'm off women," Gil said quietly. "Now, about this DB that Red found. That phone call you heard was about this forensic archaeologist I've got coming over from Denver to take a look." He made a face. "She's got the personality of a snapping turtle, but maybe she's good at her job. She's flying in today."

Jeff's eyebrows arched. "That's quick. I'd think she was much in demand, it being such a rare skill."

"That's what I thought. Her co-worker sure seemed

anxious to get her out of his office," he recalled. He shook his head. "After talking to her for five minutes, I understood why."

"Well, if she's good at her job, you can manage to get along with her for a day, right?"

"Sure," Gil lied, and mentally crossed his fingers.

"I wonder who the remains could be?" Jeff wondered out loud. "We don't have that many people go missing around here." He scowled. "That water line was put in just after Mayor Handley—well, he wasn't the mayor at the time, just a clerk at the hardware store—moved into that house with his wife." He rolled his eyes. "She married him for what he had. Poor guy. She never wanted kids or a family life, just money, and Handley's people were loaded."

"If his family had money, why was he working as a clerk at the local hardware store?" Gil asked, curious.

"His dad believed in the work ethic. No easy path for his only child, no, sir. The boy worked his way up from cleaning the floors at the family business to selling stock to delivering lumber. The old man was a hard taskmaster. He cowed Dirk."

"Shame."

"It happens."

"How many years ago was it when the mayor moved into that house?"

"Let me see, I was away in the military at the time, but my mother went to the wedding—she never liked Nita Handley—and it was the year the Autumn Festival was established in Benton, floats and bands and all. That was . . ." He thought about it for a minute. "Twelve years ago, roughly."

"You're a wonder, Jeff," Gil said. He grabbed up his hat. "Where are you off to?"

"The county office to look at copies of the weekly

newspaper. To see if it lists any disappearances from twelve or so years ago."

"I like the way you think," Jeff said with a chuckle.

"Pays to have a curious nature if you're going to investigate murders," Gil replied with a grin.

Gil went through pages and pages of the newspaper without turning up anything.

"Any luck?" Judge Garrett, the longtime judge of probate court, asked after an hour, her short gray hair gleaming in the light from the overhead bulb.

"Nothing." He sighed. "I wish there was a way to search these papers for key words."

"It would be nice," she agreed. "Maybe one day we'll get a willing volunteer to do that for us. It would be a tremendous help." She looked over his shoulder. "What are you looking for, if you don't mind my asking?"

"Anybody who disappeared between eleven and thirteen years ago," he told her. He glanced up at her and smiled. "We found a body when city workers unearthed a broken water line."

She was frowning, deep in concentration. "Marley Douglas," she murmured, nodding. "Yes, it was Marley. He disappeared quite suddenly twelve years ago. He was on his way home from church one Sunday evening, but he never made it. I remember because it was raining cats and dogs. We had the worst flood in Benton's history."

He was taking notes on his phone. "How old was he?"

"Marley? Let me see, he was in his forties."

"Married?"

She shook her head. "No. He never married. He lived with his sister. She's long dead. There was no other family. They never found a body. Someone said he ran off with a woman he'd met at a carnival that was in town, but that was just a rumor."

He stood up. "Judge Garrett, you should have been a detective," he said with a grateful smile. "You're super!"

She laughed. "First time I was ever called that, for sure. If it was murder, I hope you can find who killed him," she added gently. "He was a sweet man. Everybody loved him."

"I'll keep that in mind. Thanks again."

He went back to his office and stopped in the doorway. Jane Denali and Jeff Ralston were listening to a slender woman with curly dark hair that stuck out all over her head, dressed in a very expensive, perfectly fitting gray pantsuit with a spotless white blouse, holding a rolling suitcase.

"Well, can you have somebody find him?" She was raging as she pushed oversize glasses back up on her nose. "I don't have time to stand around waiting for people!"

Jane and Jeff looked over her shoulder at Gil with expressions of profound relief.

"That's Gil," Jeff said. "Sorry, work to do."

"Phone to answer," Jane mumbled, and ran toward her desk.

The object of their attention turned around and glared at Gil from gray eyes in a flushed face that was pleasant but nothing more. "So you're the investigator, are you?" she asked sarcastically, giving him a cold appraisal. "You don't look much like one!"

Gil's dark eyes slid over her with nothing more remarkable than indifference. "What are you supposed to be?"

She almost gasped. "I'm a forensic archaeologist!" She flared at him.

He shrugged, arms folded over his broad chest. "Don't look much like one."

They glared at each other while a visitor to the office smothered a laugh and took off for the ladies' room.

She shifted irritably. He had a hawkish look about him. Or a hawkish shadow look, she thought wickedly. "Can I see the supposed human remains you found?" she demanded.

"Sure," he said. "But who picked you up from the airport?"

"I decided to drive. Now, where is it?" she persisted, looking around, while Jeff, in his office, quickly closed the door.

"I had it in my desk drawer but people complained," he drawled. He looked down at her smart low-heeled, highly polished black shoes. "Want to go look at the body?"

"We refer to such things as skeletal remains," she huffed.

"Refer to it however the hell you like," he said with a blithe smile. "This way, then."

She left her suitcase by the door and followed him out to one of the deputy sheriff cars. He bypassed his own, spotless one, and ushered her into one that had been used the night before to apprehend two drunken brawlers. It hadn't been cleaned, and it reeked of beer and unpleasant intestinal fluids.

She made a face. "Don't you people know about Lysol?" she demanded as she fumbled her seat belt on.

"Sure," he said, starting the car. "It comes in a can and smells like a hospital. I think the sheriff has a can of it. Want me to go back and get it?" he offered, putting on the brakes.

She ground her teeth together. "Let's explore the crime scene first."

"Up to you."

He drove her to the broken water line, which was covered in mud. So was the pavement all around it.

She got out of the car by herself, noting that her companion wasn't offering to help, and almost slid down into the mud.

She grabbed the door handle, holding on for dear life while her feet did a hula.

"Sorry about the mess," Gil said. "Rain, you know."

She made a rough sound.

"It's right over here."

He'd deliberately stopped several yards from the site where the body was found. She slipped and slid and muttered under her breath. She wasn't wearing a raincoat. She didn't even have an umbrella. Gil was decked out in his yellow slicker, with another over his hat.

"Don't they have raincoats in Denver?" he asked.

She glared at him. "It wasn't raining there," she pointed out.

He almost bit his tongue trying not to mention the availability of weather apps on the internet.

She stopped just above the body, which had been covered by a tarp on sticks so that the remains themselves weren't disturbed.

She drew in a breath and wrapped her arms around herself. "Well, we can't tell much from up here," she murmured.

"Sorry. Want to go down into the pit?"

"You need to get the coroner out here and have him remove the body to the morgue, unless you don't have a coroner . . . ?"

Just as she spoke, a van drove up and a young woman with short curly hair got out. "Hi, Gil, nice day for it, isn't it?" she asked, and paused to light a cigarette.

"I do not smoke!" the forensic expert said pertly.

"Well, I wasn't going to offer you a cigarette," the coroner returned simply. "Good God, the price of cigarettes is outrageous!" She blew out a cloud of smoke and coughed.

"Smoking is for idiots!" the other woman muttered.

"Really?" the coroner asked, and sounded interested. "What's standing around in the pouring rain without a raincoat called?"

Gil got between them. "Cassie, we need to get the body to the morgue," he said.

"Sure. Worked the crime scene already?"

He nodded. "About three hours ago. Not much in the hole. A chewing gum wrapper and some sort of stick, like from a popsicle. We bagged it and sent it to the lab for analysis."

"Our lab, I hope," the archaeologist mumbled.

"The FBI lab," Gil replied with faint arrogance. "With so little trace evidence, we felt that the lab with the greatest expertise would be best."

She didn't try to argue with that. She sneezed and reached into her pocket for a tissue. "Can we leave? I'm freezing."

"No wonder." The coroner shrugged, snug in her hooded raincoat. "It's cold out here." She gave the woman's fancy suit a raised eyebrow. "Nice suit. I'll bet it looks good in Denver. See you, Gil," she added before the visitor could open her mouth.

Gil drove the woman back to town. She sneezed the whole way.

"Who are you?" he asked.

She drew in a breath. "Nemara Landreth."

He just nodded. Odd name. Odd woman. He kept driving.

She pushed back her wet hair and took a deep breath. It had been a long, painful week. Her new co-workers in Denver already hated her guts and had made their opinion of her crystal-clear. They couldn't wait to shoot her out the door into this hick town to oversee this hick case. She was an expert. Her grades had been phenomenal in college. She had the best education money could buy. And what was she doing with it? Looking at an ancient skeleton in a hole.

"I could have worked in DC for the FBI lab," she muttered.

"You sure could have," he said enthusiastically. "There's still time to apply. There are flights out of our airport all day. You could fly over to Denver and go straight to the nation's capital."

She glared at him. "No, I can't. I work for the unit in Denver."

"Poor damn guys." He glanced at her with pretended shock. "Oops. I didn't mean to say the quiet part out loud. Sorry."

She was flaming mad. Her lips made a thin line. She glared at the road straight ahead. "I spent years in college for this!" she growled, waving a small hand at the horizon.

"Yes, I'm sure it must be a real come-down, having to waste your brilliance on a cold case in the backwoods."

She glanced at him. He sounded pleasant enough.

She shifted in her seat, drew in another breath, and sneezed again.

"Any particular reason why you didn't check a weather forecast before you came here?" he asked.

She grimaced and stared down into her lap. "Weatherby."

He blinked. "Excuse me?"

"Weatherby," she repeated gruffly, averting her face. "I found him dead in his cage this morning."

He felt a twinge of guilt. He had a pet of his own, one that kept him mostly dateless. He wasn't sharing that with Lucrezia Borgia here, however. "What killed him?" he asked.

"Don't know," she said huskily. "Vet's doing an autopsy."

He stopped at a traffic light. "Had him long?"

She nodded. "Seven years."

Her voice sounded rusty. He could imagine she was grieving. If he lost Bert, he'd be grieving.

"Sorry," he said after a minute.

She drew in a breath. "Yes. Me too." She glanced at him from red eyes. "You got a pet?"

He nodded. "Just one. Bert."

"Had him long?"

He nodded again. "Nine years." He smiled. "He's a lot of company."

"So was Weatherby."

"Give it time. It's as hard to lose a pet as it is to lose a human sometimes, they say."

"You ever lost a pet?"

"No. But a friend, and a partner, yes."

"Oh." She moved again. "Sorry."

"Thanks."

She sat back in her seat, peering at him. "You ex-military?"

He laughed softly. "What gave it away?"

"Your posture," she said simply.

His eyebrows arched.

"There's a way military people carry themselves," she explained. "It's different from the way most people walk."

"Well!"

He sounded impressed. She felt a tiny skirl of pleasure.

Most people weren't impressed with her, despite her credentials. In fact, most people didn't like her. It was a fact of life that she'd accepted long ago. A lot of it was due to her relatives. The rest . . . well, she was shy, and she didn't really know how to interact with other people. She never admitted it, of course. She never showed weakness to the enemy. And the enemy was, pretty much, everyone.

Gil pulled up in front of the sheriff's office and glanced at the black SUV she drove to the precinct.

"Nice vehicle," he said.

She managed a shy smile. "Thanks. It's got a great sound system."

He raised an eyebrow.

"I like . . . music," she said hesitantly.

"Yeah. Me too."

He got out and opened his door. He started to open hers, but she made it ahead of him and walked into the sheriff's office. Her luggage was right where she'd left it.

"You didn't leave your gear in your SUV," Gil remarked, gesturing toward her bags.

"It's got a lot of specialized equipment in it," she explained. "I wanted it to be safe." Then she flushed, because it sounded as if she thought Benton was full of thieves. "I didn't mean that the way it came out," she blurted out.

"No worries," he replied.

Gil walked her into Jeff's office.

The sheriff had been on the phone, but he hung up. "Well?" he asked.

She moved a step closer. "The body was positioned as if it was tossed there, not as if it had been placed or fallen," she began. "There was a button missing at the neck. I saw a depression at the back of the head, which was slightly turned to the left, as if the body had taken a blow there or had fallen and hit something very hard. It wasn't a deep depression, so I don't think it was an assailant who put it there." She paused, aware of two pairs of very interested eyes. "The shoes were missing. That's curious, because I haven't seen such a thing in many cases of this sort. There were socks on the body, however. That's all I have so far."

Gil let out a soft whistle. He'd looked at the body longer than she had, but he hadn't noticed those things. She was extremely observant.

"When we get the remains to the morgue, I can do a more in-depth assessment," she added.

"I'll look forward to hearing about it," Jeff said, smiling and nodding.

"You'd better get to a motel, reserve a room, and change into something dry before you catch cold," Gil added, staring down at her.

"Good idea," she stammered, then turned toward the sheriff. "I forgot to introduce myself. I'm Nemara Landreth, from the crime lab in Denver."

The sheriff smiled. "Jeff Ralston, sheriff." He nodded toward her companion. "He's my undersheriff, Gil Barnes. And our newest crime scene investigator."

She just nodded awkwardly. "I'll go get a room and come back in the morning. About eight thirty?"

"Eight thirty's fine," Gil replied.

She nodded again. "Well, okay, then. Thanks."

She left the room. Minutes later, they heard the SUV pull away from the parking space.

"What do you think?" Jeff asked Gil.

Gil sighed. "I think we've got a perplexing case. And I hope she's what we need to help solve it."

"Time will tell," Jeff said.

"You got that right!" Gil agreed.

CHAPTER 2

The motel was at the edge of town. It wasn't much to look at, but the double bed was comfortable and the door had a solid lock.

Nemara stretched out on the bed after a bath and a change of clothes. She was wearing sweats, gray pants with a gray pullover, and her hair was curling like mad. She couldn't tame it, no matter what she tried.

She fought tears. It was so hard to realize that Weatherby wouldn't be waiting for her in her apartment in Denver. She missed him so much. The local vet was having his ashes put in an urn for her. She would place the urn on her dresser and hoped that would help her heal. She'd talked to several other grieving pet owners who said that they'd done the same with their deceased pets, and it did ease the pain. She wasn't sure. But she was willing to try anything.

It had been such an awful week. Weatherby's death was the last straw. Tears rolled down her cheeks. She knew she wasn't making a good impression here. She hadn't expected to. Men didn't like her. They always felt that she was showing off when she was just using the expertise she'd achieved in college. They shunned her or made fun of her. Occasionally, one would treat her as a sister and moan about whatever girlfriend was treating him badly. There hadn't ever been one who liked her for herself. She didn't expect it, anyway. She was too odd to suit most men.

She sighed as she thought over her day, reviewing the body in the water line hole and what she'd observed so far. Her pale eyes narrowed. It was going to be a tricky case, and she badly wanted to help solve it. In the months since graduation, most of her cases had been cut and dried. This was the first real murder she'd been asked to investigate. It was exciting and sad, all at once.

She got up, pulled out her computer, and started making notes.

The following morning, Nemara arrived at the sheriff's office in Benton at eight thirty sharp. But this time she was wearing jeans and a simple gray sweatshirt with a denim jacket. Her feet were in boots instead of spiky high heels. Her hair, as wild as it was, framed her face like a halo, and it was really pretty. Gil studied her with more interest than he'd felt the day before. It was as if she'd shed her skin, like his pet, and become someone, something, else.

"Good morning," she said to Gil. "Do you have time to go to the morgue and then the coroner's office with me?"

He nodded. "It was on my agenda for today," he said, pulling out his cell phone to show her the reminder app.

She laughed. He was surprised at how pretty it sounded when she did. She looked up at him with sparkling gray eyes that just matched her sweatshirt. She pulled out her own cell phone and showed him an identical app. Beside its icon were half a dozen weather apps, some earthquake and volcano apps, and a celestial events program.

"Well!" he said, surprised. He pulled up his home screen and showed her several that matched her own.

"A kindred spirit," she said, and then flushed a little.

He grinned. "I have air traffic bands and police bands on mine, as well as fire and state police and emergency services."

"I don't have those, but I'm learning Chinese on an app . . ."

He whistled shortly. "Me too."

Her eyes sparkled wildly. *"Ni hao ma,"* she said. *"Wo shi Chunguo sheashung. Renshi Ni hen gaoxing."*

He bowed. *"Wo ye hen gaoxing renshi ni."*

The sheriff was standing in the doorway gaping at them. "I beg your pardon?" he asked.

They both turned toward him at the same time. "Chinese," Gil said.

"We're studying it online," Nemara said.

"Well!" Jeff shook his head. "I guess I might try Spanish or French, but I'd be terrified to try and learn such a complicated language as Chinese. Trying to remember all those characters . . . !"

"It's not as hard as you might think," Nemara said. "And it's fun. There's this app called Duolingo. You can do quests with friends, follow other people." She cleared her throat. "It's sort of nice if you don't have a social life."

Jeff shook his head. "Then it would be perfect for me," he said with a sigh.

Jane, hearing him, laughed softly. "Me too," she confessed, and then flushed and moved away.

"Well, we'll be off to the morgue," Gil told Jeff.

"Good luck," Jeff said.

"Damn! I forgot to tell you. I know who it is!" Gil exclaimed.

Jeff was all eyes. "Already?"

"It was Judge Garrett, the judge of probate court," Jeff

said. "She told me that a man named Marley Douglas disappeared twelve years ago . . ."

Jeff put his hand over his eyes. "Damn! I should have remembered that! Mr. Douglas had been a Boy Scout leader when I was a kid," he said. "We all loved him. He was such a sweet man. Yes, he just vanished. Nobody knew where he was. He was on his way home from church at the time."

"His shoes were missing," Nemara commented. "It indicates, to me at least, that he was probably someplace where he felt comfortable enough to take them off. Somewhere inside, out of the rain."

Jeff sighed. "We never found that out," he said. "Our sheriff at the time talked to everybody who knew him. The mayor was one of his best friends." He grimaced. "This will hit him hard, if it is Marley. They went fishing together in the summer."

"Tough luck," Gil agreed. "It will take a little more legwork to ascertain his true identity, but it's a start."

"It is. Thank God for Judge Garrett's excellent memory," Jeff said, smiling.

"And I'll put an amen to that!" Gil chuckled.

The morgue was free. So was the medical examiner, a local surgeon. The three of them, gowned and masked, went into the autopsy room where the skeletal remains were laid out on a metal table.

"Such a sad way to end a life, in a hole beside a water line," the surgeon said. He was at least fifty, and he had kind eyes. "I knew him, you know. He was a fine man. Everyone dies, but I wish he hadn't ended in a ditch."

"So do I," Gil said quietly. "If you knew him, I may have some questions for you in a day or two."

"I'll be around. No problem."

"Thanks."

The autopsy began. Gil collected evidence in bags while Nemara went over the skeleton with quiet expertise.

"See this?" she asked, indicating the back of the skull. "It indicates perhaps a fall onto a hard surface rather than being struck with a blunt object."

"Yes, it does," the medical examiner agreed, having seen his share of bodies resulting from both sorts of encounters.

"The socks you bagged, Deputy Barnes, may give some idea of where he was, especially if there were carpet fibers or some sort of material on them that could be identified," she remarked.

"I sent them off to the FBI lab along with a paper wrapper." Gil hesitated. "I wasn't being insulting, about not sending them to the state crime lab. It's just that the FBI lab—"

"No need to apologize for that," she interrupted with a smile. "I would have done the same thing. A cold case like this needs all the expertise you can find. Poor man," she added, studying the body. "What a sad and lonely way to die."

"There are worse ways," he replied quietly.

She only nodded. She studied the remains for any breaks or fractures, but found none. There was a curious depression in the joint of the shoulder, as if a thin, blunt object had been pushed rather severely into the victim. Considering the depth of the depression, it would likely have gone through flesh very quickly. And the depression was charred.

"Look at this," Nemara said, intent on the wound. "This went through both flesh and bone, and the depression is charred."

"Ouch," Gil said under his breath. "That would have been immensely painful."

"Yes, it would." She frowned. "What sort of weapon would have made such a wound?" she asked Gil, remembering he was ex-military.

"I don't know of a weapon that would leave such a mark. It isn't a gunshot wound."

"No," the medical examiner seconded. "There would have been bone fracture, with the burn. It indicates a close-quarter wound. A gunshot at close enough range to leave charring would have shattered the bones."

"A fire poker," Nemara said, her eyes still fixed on the wound. "One that had been left in the flames for some reason."

Gil and the medical examiner gaped at her. She flushed as she realized she was being stared at. She ground her teeth. "Sorry," she said quickly. "I get these . . . impressions. I just blurt them out. I didn't mean to . . . !"

"But you're most likely right," the medical examiner said with a smile. "It fits the evidence very well."

"Yes, it does," Gil agreed, smiling.

She cleared her throat. "But that still doesn't give us a murderer."

"Somebody armed with a fire poker, and it went right through into the bone," Gil said thoughtfully. "An argument. A hot argument, pardon the pun, and one of the two was enraged enough to attack the victim."

"Usually," the medical examiner interrupted, "a close attack like this indicates someone familiar with the victim who was angry enough to inflict wounds at close quarters. The perpetrator knew the victim."

"Yes," Gil said. "We have cases like that occasionally. It's intensely personal when someone uses a knife or a club instead of a gun to inflict wounds. We had a victim last year whose killer took a knife to him. The crime scene was horrible. And it was in the summer," he said, shaking his head. "We used a lot of Vicks salve while we worked the crime scene."

"I hear you," the medical examiner said.

"At least I'm spared that," Nemara replied. "I only work with skeletal remains. It's a great deal less . . . messy." She chose the word carefully.

"It would be nice if my job was like that," Gil said. "But it's not."

"Neither is mine," the medical examiner added. "This was a change of pace for me, although I'm sorry for poor old Marley here. At least he wasn't barely dead and cut up," he added. "Poor old man." He shook his head. "Takes a monster to do something like this."

"He wanted to hurt the victim," Gil said.

"Yes. There must have been an argument," Nemara agreed. "A very bad one. Tempers were lost, and this was the result."

"The water line had been dug recently, twelve years ago," Gil was remembering. "The murderer likely panicked when he realized what he'd done. He carried the victim out into the rain and put his body in the deep ditch. I'd bet money that he shoveled a lot of dirt over him so that he wouldn't be noticed. In the pouring rain, when the workers came in the next morning, they probably just went to work filling the ditch with a backhoe and didn't even notice the body in the hole, especially if it was covered in dirt, or mud."

"That sounds logical," the medical examiner said.

"What can you tell me about Marley Douglas?" Gil asked him.

"Not a great deal," the surgeon replied. "He was well liked in the community. He taught a Sunday school class.

He was active in local politics. In fact, he was running for mayor at the time against Dirk Handley. It was a friendly competition." He chuckled. "Neither man was vehement about winning. They even joked about it."

"That helps," Gil said, taking notes on his phone as the other man spoke.

"Did he have any relatives?" Nemara asked.

"Just his sister. There was a rumor that she . . . well, I shouldn't say that."

Gil moved a step closer. "Please," he said. "It's all confidential unless we have to use the information to solve the murder."

He looked from one to the other and shrugged. "A lot of people spoke of it in whispers. There was a rumor that Marley's sister had something going with Dirk Handley. He was married, of course, and that was grounds for gossip in this little community. Things like that are frowned upon, even though no one could prove whether their romance was before or after he married. She died of a heart attack soon after the rumors started, though." He shook his head. "I had to perform the autopsy on her because it was a sudden death. Hardest thing I ever did. She was sweet, like Marley. Funny thing, too, nobody even knew she had heart trouble."

Gil was typing like mad. It was a gold mine of information. "Did you find evidence of a heart attack?" he asked.

The surgeon frowned. "You're thinking like an investigator." He smiled. "Yes, I found blockages in all the arteries leading to her heart. They were severe enough to warrant open heart surgery, but she never went to a heart specialist as far as I know. People have these blockages and are unaware until symptoms present. They're usually found in an echocardiogram, or CT scan with contrast, or failing that, a heart catheterization."

"It was a natural death?"

He nodded. "Yes." He sighed. "I was sweet on her, but she didn't feel anything like that for me. I'm not sure she even had feelings for Handley, either," he added. "Despite the gossip, she wasn't the sort of woman to involve herself with a married man. She went to the same church as her brother, and she taught a Sunday school class as well." He smiled sadly. "She was a good woman."

"Nice to know," Gil said. "Thanks very much for your time, and this information."

"You're welcome. I hope you can find whoever did this," he added with one last long look at the skeletal remains. "It's not right."

"I know exactly what you mean," Gil replied.

Samples of the tattered shirt the victim was wearing were taken, especially the part with the charring above the penetrated shoulder bone. There were some odd pieces of what looked like crochet thread on the back of the ripped trousers, and samples of those were taken as well.

There were leaves clinging to the fabric; one of those was removed and bagged because it would identify possibly the place where the victim died. Likewise, they took samples of bark that had worked its way between his leg bones.

The evidence was bagged and tagged and sent to the FBI lab from the sheriff's office. Meanwhile, Gil and Nemara made a list of people they needed to talk to about the late victim.

"He had so many friends," Jeff told them. "But most of all, Mayor Handley. They were good friends. Handley took it hard when they couldn't find the man. He even helped with the searches. His wife sat at home and drank martinis and watched television," he added with faint contempt. "She couldn't be bothered with such boring activities."

"She sounds like a bad woman," Nemara replied.

"She's worse than that." Jeff sighed. "Poor Mayor Handley. Rumors were that he was in love with some other woman, but we never found out who. He doesn't talk about the past. Not ever."

"I got a lot of information from the medical examiner," Gil told Jeff. "He knew both Douglas and his sister."

"Yes, he was sweet on Marley's sister, but she never dated anybody." He shook his head. "They said she fell in love with some man who didn't want her, so she just gave up on men." He shook his head. "She was a pretty woman. Much prettier than the mayor's wife," he added with a chuckle, "but don't quote me."

"I wouldn't," Gil agreed. "I hope the lab can find something that will help us solve the case. I don't want to end up like one of those poor detectives who had to hunt serial killers and died before the perp was ever found."

"You won't," Jeff assured him with a smile. "It's a small town. The list of possible perpetrators isn't going to be that long."

"Yes, but we can't rule out somebody who came here from out of town."

"That's not likely," Nemara said. "I mean, he was wearing socks, you know. He had to have taken his shoes off in somebody's house, in a place where he felt comfortable," she added.

Gil cocked his head. "That's not a bad guess."

She laughed softly. "Thanks."

"I feel bad for the mayor," Jeff remarked. "His wife is a very difficult woman."

"We make our own beds," Nemara said softly. "And then we have to lie in them."

"Very true." Gil sighed. "Well, we have a list. Let's go wear out some shoe leather."

Nemara nodded. "It's still the best way to investigate a murder," she said. "Despite all our electronic aids."

"I've found that to be true," Jeff told her. "Most people we want to interrogate won't even answer an email. But if we go talk to them, they'll usually tell us all they know. People skills are becoming a thing of the past, thanks to social media. It's not a good thing."

"Tell me about it," Nemara said, shaking her head. "I deleted all my social media accounts. I stay home and play . . . well, I stay home." She hesitated to tell the men what she did with her leisure time. It was a little embarrassing for a woman her age.

"Me too," Gil said. "At the end of the day, I just want to go home and have a beer with Bert."

"Bert?" Nemara asked. "Oh, I remember, your dog."

"He's my pet—"

"Better get going," Jeff interrupted with a level stare at Gil that made the point. He'd better be quiet about his roommate if he was finding common points with their out-of-town visitor. Gil just chuckled.

"Yes, we should," Gil agreed.

He checked his reminder list. "I want to talk to Mayor Handley . . ."

"What a stroke of good luck," Jeff murmured, nodding toward the door.

Mayor Handley was just coming in. "I heard that you've already identified the body," he said abruptly. "Was it Marley Douglas?"

Gil took a breath. "Yes, sir, it was."

Handley cursed under his breath. His eyes were lackluster. "He was my best friend," he said. "We played chess every week at my house. I knew him all my life. We were in school together." He looked up. "It's a blow, let me tell you!"

"I'm sorry for your loss," Gil replied sincerely.

"Who did it?" Handley demanded. "Do you have a suspect yet?"

Gil took another breath so that he didn't say what he was really thinking.

Nemara beat him to it. "We don't. Not yet," she told the mayor. "Right now, we just have skeletal remains."

"Well, you have to find out who killed my best friend. You have to!" he told Gil.

"I'll do my very best," Gil promised him.

"Should I call in the media? They might help find something," Handley offered.

"It would probably be better if we don't," Gil replied carefully. "If they stir things up too much, they might frighten witnesses away, if there were any."

"Considering how poor Marley ended up, I doubt anybody saw what happened," Handley mused.

"We're just going out to ask some questions. Actually, Mayor Handley, I'd like to interview you, if you're willing. You knew the victim. You might know something that would help us solve the case; something you're not even aware of."

Handley was nodding, but his face was taut. "Yes, yes, I'll be glad to help, but I can't right now. We've got two people sick and out of work at the business, so I'm needed to help with sales. Give me a call next week, okay?" he added as he walked to the door. "And keep me posted! I want this murderer caught!" He closed the door firmly behind him.

"Well," Jeff exclaimed.

"For somebody who wants a crime solved, he wasn't very helpful," Nemara ventured.

"I noticed that," Gil said. "He was first on my list of interviews. We'll have to find some other people who knew the victim. I'm particularly interested in whether or not he had enemies."

"Go back and talk to Judge Garrett. She knows more about this town than anybody alive," Jeff suggested.

Gil nodded. "I think that's a good idea. And I want to walk around the area near that water line," he said. "We might turn up something."

"After twelve years?" Jeff mused.

"Not trace evidence or anything." Gil frowned. "I just want to look at some leaves."

Jeff's eyebrows almost hit his hairline. "Leaves?"

"It sounds goofier than it is. I'll explain later," Gil promised. He turned to Nemara. "If you're ready, we can go."

"Oh, yes," she agreed.

They took the clean patrol car this time. Nemara noticed, but she didn't mention it. She was enjoying Gil's company and surprised at how much they had in common. It made her feel funny. Excited and safe, all at once. She'd never really experienced such emotions.

"You'll like Judge Garrett," he told her. "She's been probate judge as long as anyone can remember. Nobody runs against her at election time, which says a lot for the way she does her job."

"Indeed it does," she agreed. "She knew the victim?"

"Yes. She told me all I knew about him until the medical examiner added to it."

"You want to walk around the crime scene," she mused.

"It's a secondary crime scene, isn't it, and somewhere there's a primary one."

"Somewhere," he said. "And after twelve years, there likely won't be any evidence, even trace evidence."

"You want to see if the leaf we sent off matches anything at the secondary crime scene," she said.

He laughed, surprised. "You take a little getting used to," he commented.

"I do? Why?" she asked, and wide gray eyes held his for a few long seconds.

"You have the most incredible insight," he murmured. "You see things that other people miss, including me."

"It's a gift and a curse," she replied. "I blurt out things that I shouldn't, and people run the other way." She shrugged. "I figured that since I had this, well, gift of insight, I should get a job where I could put it to good use."

"Does it run in your family?"

"My dad had it, they say. I never knew him. He was killed overseas during an incursion of some sort. Top secret. Black Ops. Classified stuff. My mother remarried less than two weeks later," she added curtly.

"To someone you don't like," he guessed.

"Someone I didn't like," she agreed. She sighed. "There was a plane crash in Italy a few years ago. I imagine you read about it? She and her new husband were on board."

"I'm sorry," he said, and meant it. "Brothers? Sisters?"

She shook her head, paused and looked up at him. "All I have left is an aunt and an uncle. How about you?"

He shook his head. "My folks are long dead. I didn't have siblings."

She grimaced. "It's lonely at holidays," she said simply. He nodded.

"That's why I had Weatherby," she replied, and fought tears. She turned her head to avoid letting them show.

"It's why I have Bert," he told her.

She drew in a steadying breath. "Pets help so much."

"They do." He pulled the car onto the road where the body had been found and parked the vehicle near the water line.

As they got out, he threw up a hand and waved at Red, who was overseeing the repair of the line. It had been completed. Now they were filling in the hole with the backhoe.

Red came over. "Did you find out who it was?" he asked.

"Yes," Gil replied. "It was Marley Douglas."

"Oh, good Lord, I'd forgotten that he went missing." He grimaced. "I remember putting in this water line. We came to work in one of the worst storms we've ever had. It was pouring rain, but people thought it was dangerous to leave a hole that big open where people or even cars might fall into it. So we filled it with the backhoe. I never thought to look in it, except to check that the line wasn't leaking. I swear to God, I did not see a body in that hole!"

Gil laid a hand on his shoulder. The man was distraught. "It would probably have had a few shovelfuls of dirt over it, Red. Whoever killed him was anxious to get rid of the corpse. Given the weather, he probably thought nobody would notice Douglas in the hole, especially if he covered up the body."

"I still feel bad about it. Poor old Marley, I was in the Sunday school class he taught for adults," he added. "He was such a good man. I was in on all the searches. I hoped so hard that we'd find him, but we never did."

"Well, we did find him today, Red," he reminded the other man. "And he's at peace."

Red let out a breath. "I guess he is." He shook his head. "Life is hard."

"And gets harder every day," Gil agreed. "Do you know

anybody else local who knew him, besides the mayor and Judge Garrett?"

Red frowned and thought for a minute. "The owner of the florist shop, over there. He nodded across the narrow street to a small building with fairy lights around the eaves and the door.

"That's a big help. Thanks, Red."

"I hope you find the scalawag who killed him," Red said. He turned and went back to work.

"This case gets stranger and stranger," Nemara pointed out.

"Well, it's certainly not boring," he agreed. "Let's have a look around."

They wandered over near where the body was found. Gil noticed that Red's eyes followed them. The poor man liked the victim. He hoped they could find out who killed him.

Since it was autumn, colorful leaves were falling everywhere. Gil bent down on one knee and looked through a pile of them until he pulled out just one and stood up.

"This is the leaf," he murmured, showing it to Nemara. "Now, I need to identify the tree it comes from."

She pulled out her phone, opened an app, had Gil hold the leaf in his palm, and aimed the phone toward it. Seconds later, the leaf was identified and the source given.

"Amazing," he exclaimed.

She grinned. "Isn't it neat? I love to go walking. I find all sorts of unusual trees. I wanted to know what kind they were, so I got this app. I have one for rocks, too. You can point it at a rock, and it will tell you what sort of rock it is."

"Is it expensive?" he wondered.

She hesitated. It wouldn't do to open that can of worms. Especially not now. "Well, not very," she said, and told him what the subscriptions cost.

He shook his head. "Your job must pay a heck of a lot more than mine," he commented. "I have to budget like mad. I love my job, but it will never make me a millionaire." He chuckled.

She flushed. "The thing is to love the work you do, not do it just for money. At least, that's what I think."

He studied her for a long moment and smiled. "It's what I think, too."

She managed a shaky smile. He was really affecting her. He had a strong face, with soft almost black eyes and blond, blond hair. His hair was thick and straight. His nose had probably been straight, but it had a faintly noticeable dent.

"Are you looking at my nose?" he asked pleasantly.

She laughed. "Sorry. Yes, I am."

"I had to arrest a man in a bar, who turned out to be a patrolman from a neighboring county. He was harassing the female bartender and making threats. I tried to put the cuffs on him, and he clocked me in the nose."

"What did you do?"

"I hit him back, of course. We both ended up in the emergency room, and when his superior got the report, he was fired." His face tautened. "There aren't many people in law enforcement like that, but they make it difficult for the rest of us when they do such things in public." He shook his head. "I was glad that his superior had the guts to fire him. The guy was a tough customer. A lot of bosses are too afraid of repercussions to fire anybody."

"Yes. The loudest voice often makes policy," she replied. "That's how government works. You have a committee with several politicians on it, but there's always one who's belligerent and loud and people are too afraid of him, or her, not to agree with whatever bill is created. However insane it really is."

He chuckled. "You could be right," he conceded. "Well, let's go talk to Judge Garrett. Then we'll look for the big-tooth maple trees your app identified."

She smiled. "Works for me!"

CHAPTER 3

Judge Garrett was a gold mine of information on Benton and its surroundings and, especially, the people who lived there. She hadn't gone to school with Marley Douglas, but she had been friends with his sister and knew her well.

"Melly was a quiet girl," Judge Garrett told them as she perched on the side of the desk and faced the chairs where they were seated. "She had a sweet nature. I never knew her to speak ill of anyone."

"She never married, they say," Gil remarked.

"That's true." She sighed. "It was a sad thing. She was just crazy about Dirk Handley, and then he broke up with her for some reason and married that awful Riley girl, Nita." She shook her head. "I could have told him she was worthless, but he had to find it out for himself. She wanted what he had, and made it plain that she had no other use for him. No kids, especially. She wasn't risking her figure."

"That's so sad," Nemara said quietly. "Children are a gift."

"Are you married?" Judge Garrett asked with a smile.

Nemara shook her head. "But I love children. I used to work part-time for a daycare center. We had kids of all ages. It was such fun!"

Judge Garrett laughed. "I can only imagine. I never

married, either. I had my chances, but I liked being by myself. I still do," she added with a grin.

They laughed.

"Mr. Douglas's sister died of a heart attack, they said," Gil continued after a moment.

"Yes. She had blockages in all her arteries." She sighed. "I told her cooking with all that lard was going to do her in. I only use olive oil when I cook. Well, sometimes I have to add a little vegetable oil, when I need to have really high heat. But no fat, ever. It was that fat that caused the blockages. That, and her high cholesterol. She refused to take any medicine for it."

"Some people are stubborn," Gil remarked.

"And some people are stupid," she shot back.

"I have to agree," Gil said. "It's how we catch a lot of our criminals. Not that we have an abundance of them in Benton."

"I hope you can find whoever put poor Marley in that hole," she replied. "Why not just leave the body on the road so it could be found?"

"Beats me," Gil confessed.

"Somebody killed him, didn't they?" she asked, and looked pointedly at Nemara.

Gil hesitated. "Well, yes. The indications are that he was murdered."

"Then somebody in Benton is a killer, young man," she pointed out. "And for the good of this community, you have to find him."

"Or her," Gil returned. "We've had female killers as well as male ones."

She shook her head. "What a world we live in."

"I can't argue with that. It gets crazier every day." He looked at his notes. "Did Marley have any enemies that you know of?"

"No. Everybody loved Marley," Judge Garrett replied gently.

"Not everybody, Judge Garrett," he returned.

She sighed. "That's right. Yes, I guess that's right."

They stayed a few more minutes to see if there was anything more Judge Garrett could tell them, but there wasn't. They said their good-byes and went back out to the car. Gil drove them back to the water line. The men had finished filling in the deep hole and they were gone, leaving caution signs around the soft earth.

Gil and Nemara walked all around the area, looking at trees. Most of the leaves had turned, and many were falling, but some were still on the trees. Nemara had a picture on her phone of the maple tree they needed to find, but so far, no luck. Just quaking aspens and birch and fir trees.

"Let's go see the florist," Gil said suddenly, remembering that she might also have some information about the victim. Everyone said he had no enemies. But he had at least one. And Gil needed to find out who it was.

"Good idea," Nemara agreed.

Mrs. Teague ran the local florist shop and had for as long as anyone could remember. She was in her fifties, spry and full of fun, and smiling as she greeted them.

"Hello, Gil," she said. She'd known him since he was a young boy.

He chuckled. "Hi, Mrs. Teague. This is my colleague, Nemara." He nodded toward the other woman, who smiled. "We're investigating the murder of Marley Douglas."

"Marley . . . was murdered?" she exclaimed, catching her breath. "Oh, my goodness, when? And by whom?"

"Those are questions we hope to be able to answer soon," he said. "We don't know a lot just yet. So we're asking around to see what people remember about him. You must have known him."

"I certainly did," she replied. "I was in his Sunday school class, the one he taught for adults. Bible study." She drew in a long breath. "We had so many search parties out when he disappeared," she recalled. "He was loved in the community. A kind man, with a very big heart. Have you told the mayor yet?" she added, concerned. "They were best friends. Always together in the summer. They went camping and fishing." She shook her head. "It will just kill him!"

"He knows," Gil replied. "He was very upset."

She drew in a long breath and leaned back against her counter. "Marley's sister was really in love with Dirk Handley. I think he loved her just as much. They had some sort of disagreement, and things went downhill. He married that, that witch he lives with—Nita Riley—to show that he could live without Miss Douglas. What a sad, sad decision that was."

"Did Marley have enemies?"

She smiled sadly. "He was loved," she said simply. "He was the first on the scene if anyone needed help. He was a volunteer fireman. He was on the hospital board. He helped out in our soup kitchen. I don't think anyone ever said a harsh word to him. He was that sort of person."

Gil ground his teeth. This case got harder and harder.

"Do you know the native species of trees around town?" Nemara asked.

Mrs. Teague blinked, startled by the change of subject. "Well, yes. I mean, I love flowers and trees, and I've lived in Benton my whole life."

"Can you show her the leaf we found?" she asked Gil.

He pulled it out and displayed it on the counter.

"My app says it's a bigtooth maple," Nemara volunteered. "But we've looked all around, and we can't find a single one."

She chuckled. "You looked in the wrong places. The only bigtooth maples around Benton belong to the mayor. He has an open fireplace—huge thing built with river rocks—and he burns the trees for heat in the winter."

Nemara blinked. "I thought there were regulations against . . ." she began.

"Oh, the mayor's above such things," she said, not altogether teasing. "He does what he pleases. I believe Gil's had at least one run-in with him about a leaf fire that got out of control in his yard . . ."

Gil grimaced. "It was a hell of a run-in," he agreed. "I told him he had to be more careful, and he told me Jeff could find a deputy to replace me."

"What happened?" Nemara asked.

"Jeff happened." He chuckled. "He told Mayor Handley that if he fired me, the whole damned force would quit. He'd talked to the chief of police as well, and that gentleman said the police force would follow suit. The mayor was suitably shocked. And I kept my job."

"But he's still burning trash and letting fires get wild." Mrs. Teague sighed. "He and Marley had words about that pretty often. You see, Marley's home was only a stone's throw away, up behind the mayor's house. One of those wildfires caught some brush on fire in Marley's yard and threatened the house. Marley was even-tempered, but he could get mad, and he did."

This was interesting. Nemara listened intently.

"Very mad," Gil agreed. "But he was not a violent man. I've seen him lose his temper at people in county commission meetings that I had to attend for funding requests." He shook his head. "He never got physical, no matter how angry he got."

"Well, that's one suspect down," Nemara said sadly.

He smiled at her. "We'll find more."

"You'll really have to dig," Mrs. Teague told them. "But why would somebody kill Marley in the first place?"

"That," Gil replied, "is the main thing we have to solve. Thanks very much for your time, Mrs. Teague. If you remember anything else, will you call the office?" he asked. "If I'm not in, they can always track me down."

She laughed. "That's the beauty of small towns," she replied.

"And the curse," Gil teased. "Thanks again."

"So the mayor has the only trees that this leaf matches," Nemara recounted as they drove back toward the office. "But even if he and Mr. Douglas argued, the mayor doesn't get physical when he loses his temper." She frowned. "I really thought there might be something to that."

"So did I," Gil replied. "But it's early days yet. No investigation solves itself that quickly. I'm afraid this may take some time." He glanced at her. "How long will your boss let us keep you?"

"Probably until Christmas or New Year." She sighed, looking at the purse in her lap. "I didn't make many friends where I came from."

"Why not?"

She shrugged. "I don't mix well with other people. I'm opinionated and I open my mouth when I should keep it shut." She made a face. "One of my co-workers said that I was arrogant, because I corrected him on a point of anatomy when we were going over a case." She looked at

Gil with sad eyes. "Just because someone has a degree, it doesn't mean they really know the subject matter. A lot of people slide by with D's, and they get jobs where they need to be good in their fields. But they aren't. Because they partied instead of studied. And when I put my two cents' worth in, I get stomped flat because I'm upstaging people and hurting their feelings." She ground her teeth together and looked straight ahead. "I am so damned tired of biting my tongue because I might hurt somebody's feelings!"

"Oh, join the club," Gil replied. "I signed on as a deputy sheriff straight out of the military, but I'm more social worker and arbitrator than someone designated to keep the peace. I'm surprised that we're still allowed to carry guns on the job!"

She smiled shyly. "So am I."

He smiled back. "A Taser is just as deadly in the right circumstances," he added as they pulled up at the sheriff's department. "In fact, they had a fatality in the county next to us. One of their officers used a Taser on a man who was drunk and threatening his wife with a knife. He had an unknown heart condition and died on the spot. Sure, a bullet can kill you, but a Taser can, too."

"That ten-second rule about knives," she began. "Is it true?"

"What, that a man armed with a knife can get to you and kill you in ten seconds, before you can draw your service revolver? It's absolutely true. I saw it happen when I was in the military. We had a hard-nosed squad leader who thought it was a bunch of bunk. We were in a little village overseas, and the squad leader offended the tribal leader. The man pulled a knife and ran at him. Before the squad leader's gun cleared the holster, the knife was buried in his heart. He died instantly. None of us was fast enough to stop it."

"My gosh!" She stared at him. "What about the tribal leader who killed him?"

His face tautened. "He got away with it. Our commander said that we needed the man's cooperation. If we arrested him, we'd *offend*," he emphasized the word as he glanced at her, "his relatives, and we'd have an insurrection on our hands."

She shook her head. "No wonder you feel the way you do."

"We have to fit into the world as it changes around us, Jeff says," Gil told her as he parked the car. "Maybe he's right."

"It's not like we can go settle on some other planet, I guess," she said on a sigh.

He chuckled. "It's exactly like that."

Jeff looked up as they walked into the office. "Well?"

"He was a great man. Everybody liked him. He was first on the scene when any disaster happened. He didn't have an enemy in the world."

"Then why is he dead?" Jeff asked.

"If we can determine exactly how he died, and what instrument was used to cause his death, we might narrow down the list of suspects," Nemara said quietly. "He hit his head, but it wasn't as if he was struck with something. We know a weapon of some sort was thrust into his chest and it burned him, and there was a depression on the back of his skull that, to me at least, indicated he might have fallen backward onto a hard surface. It was sufficient to break the skull, and I would imagine the impact did severe damage to the brain. There were no surviving organs or soft tissues, so it will be difficult to reconstruct the exact cause of death."

"Suppose he wasn't completely dead when he was tossed into that ditch and covered up?" Gil pondered.

The others actually winced.

"I know," he apologized, "it's a gruesome thought. But how would an everyday person who wasn't a doctor know if the victim wasn't just in a coma?" He pursed his lips. "How would that affect somebody with a conscience?"

"We don't have a suspect," Nemara pointed out.

"He was loved by everyone," Jeff added. "No enemies. How about checking his bank statements? Maybe he'd paid out money to someone over a disagreement, or lost a lot at gambling . . . ?" He grimaced. "God, I'm sorry, Gil!" he said.

Gil had averted his eyes and swallowed, hard. But he just shrugged. "It was a long time ago." He turned back to Jeff. "I'm not that thin-skinned, Jeff," he said softly.

Jeff smiled. "No, you're not."

They both ignored Nemara, who was eyeing Gil with open curiosity.

"Where did he bank, I wonder?" Gil asked.

"Go see Tom Jones, over in Raven Springs," Jeff suggested. "He's head of the bank's security office, but he was FBI. He might have some insights, even if he doesn't know where Douglas banked."

"Tom Jones?" Nemara asked.

"Not the singer," Gil replied with twinkling black eyes. "And if you ask him about that, make sure you're wearing track shoes."

She burst out laughing. "Okay. That's a promise."

* * *

The bank in Raven Springs was brick and big for such a small town. Tom Jones was like the bank, big and sturdy. He had silver sprinkled in his thick, dark hair, and he had eyes that could pierce steel—at least, that was the impression Nemara got.

Behind his desk on a table were framed portraits of himself, a pretty blond woman, and two pretty kids.

He noticed Nemara's glance. "My wife and kids," he said, and smiled. "She's a nurse at the local hospital in Benton. I came here on a case and tried really hard to leave. We were at the airport. I started to walk away, and I couldn't. I just stood there. I turned around . . ." His face softened. "We were married very soon after that, and I gave up the FBI for small-town crime fighting because she refused to be married to a man with a target on his back."

"She's a nice woman," Gil commented.

"She's a nice woman if she likes you," Tom said, and chuckled. "What can I do for you?"

"We're investigating a murder," Gil said, sobering. "Red found skeletal remains in a hole he was digging to repair a pipeline. It turned out to be a missing local man, Marley Douglas."

"Not somebody I know," Tom replied, leaning back in his chair.

"He disappeared twelve years ago, before you came here," Gil told him. "They sent out search parties, but he was never found."

"Trace evidence? And if there were skeletal remains, you'll need a forensic anthropologist . . ."

Nemara raised her hand. "University of Tennessee at Knoxville," she told him. She smiled. "Dr. Bill Bass's stomping grounds."

"Yes, Dr. Bass," Tom said, and smiled. "He's a wonder.

One of our guys actually wrote him a fan letter. He wrote the book on stages of decomposition with his Body Farm."

"I've read about that," Gil said, impressed. "I often wished I could study there. But I was in the military, and then at the community college here. I envy you that education," he added with a smile at Nemara. "It must have been fascinating."

She beamed. "Most people find it gory, if they aren't physical anthropology students," she replied. "I've loved forensics since I used to watch *Quincy* on YouTube."

"*Quincy!* My God, that was decades ago!" Tom chuckled.

"You can find any older series on YouTube," she replied with a grin. "I always loved the opening scene, where Quincy jerked the sheet off a cadaver, and grown men went running out to throw up."

"I imagine grown women would do the same these days," Gil teased. "Some grown women," he amended.

She smiled shyly. "I did throw up on my first visit to the Body Farm," she confessed.

"Don't feel bad. So did my partner, and he'd been in law enforcement for five years," Tom said. "But living in a small town, he'd never seen a decomposed person. Lucky devil," he added, shaking his head. "I worked Chicago. You see lots of them when you work homicide there."

"Homicide?" Gil asked.

Tom nodded. "I was a patrolman, then a homicide detective, and after that I joined the FBI," he replied. "I guess I've spent my life in law enforcement, in one capacity or another. And I'm still doing it." He waved a hand around. "Except that I don't get shot at here. Yet."

They both laughed.

"What do you need?" Tom asked.

"I want to find out where Marley Douglas banked. We'll

go over the house where he lived. It's surely been sold by now, twelve years after his disappearance."

"Let me make a phone call," Tom said.

Nemara and Gil sat quietly while Tom spoke to somebody. It wasn't possible to follow the conversation until he mentioned Marley Douglas's name and asked a few more questions. He thanked the person on the other end of the line and hung up.

"He had an account at the Miner's Bank in Benton," he told them. "He and his sister had an income from their father, who was wealthy. They had stocks and bonds in a formidable portfolio with a local investment counselor, and a small fortune in CDs and a savings account in the bank."

"Who inherited?" Gil asked, hoping for a lead.

"Nobody," Tom said simply. "The accounts are still there, in limbo. Nobody asked to have Marley declared legally dead, and there were, apparently, no relatives surviving."

"There goes that possible lead," Gil said sadly.

"That somebody offed him for money?" Tom asked. He grinned. "Highly unlikely. If you can do it without getting in trouble, can you tell me what you found when you examined the remains?"

Gil nodded to Nemara. She drew a breath. "There was a small round penetrating wound through the chest into the shoulder, and it left charred flesh and fabric. The back of the skull was slightly indented, and cracks radiated out from the impacted area. If I were making an assumption, he was attacked with an extremely hot round metal object and fell backward onto a hard surface, which was the cause of his death."

"Where did you send the evidence?" Tom asked. "State crime lab?"

"Oh, no," Nemara said. "Not that we're not the best around here," she added quickly. "But the FBI lab is superior to most crime labs. We sent what we had to them."

Tom smiled. "Smart move. I've seen those guys finger murderers from a grain of pollen, and that's a story and a half."

"Yes, it is," she agreed. "I tried to get on there, but they weren't hiring," she added. "It's an amazing place!"

"Truly," Tom agreed.

"What will they do about Douglas's estate?" Gil asked.

"The judge will appoint someone to administrate it," he said. "If there's a living relative in the world, they'll track them down. Imagine that," he mused with a chuckle. "Out of the blue, they'll be able to buy a Rolls or a yacht or a home in Venice. Go figure. My wife and I budget like mad and count every penny."

"But you wouldn't change a thing about your life," Nemara commented with a grin.

Tom chuckled. "You're perceptive. No, I wouldn't. I'm the luckiest man alive."

They returned to the office. By now, it was late afternoon and getting dark.

"You need to go back to your motel, and I need to go home," Gil said wearily. "I imagine Bert's getting hungry."

"Yes, you have to feed your pet," she agreed. She grimaced. "I wish I had to feed mine," she murmured.

"I really am sorry."

She managed a smile. "Me too."

He opened the door and escorted her to her SUV. It was a kind touch because it was almost dark. "How about breakfast?" he asked. "I can cook. I'll come get you and take you by my place before we come to work."

Her heart jumped. She hesitated.

"Of course, if you'd rather not," he began quickly, worried that he'd been too forward.

"You . . . you really want to have breakfast with me?" she asked, stunned and showing it.

His eyebrows arched. "Why is that surprising?"

"Well, nobody ever wanted to take me out to a meal or a walk or even . . ." She cleared her throat. "Yes. I'd like that very much."

He smiled. "I'd like for you to meet Bert."

She beamed. "I would love that!"

He sighed and grimaced. "I truly hope that's how it turns out," he said, half under his breath. "I'll see you in the morning. About seven thirty?"

"That's fine. I'm always up early," she said.

He watched her drive away and then wondered if he'd lost his mind. She'd probably scream and run out the front door and avoid him like the plague for the rest of the time she was in Benton.

He went into the sheriff's office to find Jeff on the phone with somebody who was obviously giving him a hard time.

Jeff was nodding and speaking, mostly one-word answers, and finally he hung up.

"Damn, I know how a sheep feels when it's been shorn," Jeff said, wiping his forehead.

"Who was that?" Gil asked.

"The mayor. He wants to know who killed his friend. He's raging about how slow we're moving."

Gil blinked. "It's been two days," he said. "And we're tracking a phantom killer who didn't leave a trail to follow! We don't even have results from the crime lab. That takes time!"

"It's just Handley being Handley," Jeff told him. "The mayor has an attitude problem. If I was married to his wife, I'd have one, too," he pointed out.

"Tomorrow I'm going over to speak to him. We found a leaf on the body," Gil mentioned. "It was from a bigtooth maple. The only ones around here are in the mayor's yard. He burns them in his fireplace for heat."

"Yes, I know. The man's fascinated with fire. Loves to make big bonfires when he burns leaves in autumn, and usually sets fire to somebody else's yard because he's careless."

Gil nodded. "The florist said that Marley Douglas had words with Handley about that. A fire got away and almost burned his house down." He frowned. "That's something else I want to see: Douglas's house."

"I doubt you'll find anything there of value to the case," Jeff said.

"Probably not, but I'll get an idea of what sort of person he was by looking at the things he treasured. If I'm really lucky, he might have left something in writing about an argument, a disagreement, anything untoward."

"Get a search warrant first," Jeff told him. "The house has been locked up all these years. There's a neighbor, Miss Helens, who keeps the key and tends to the house. She and Melly Douglas, Marley's sister, were friends. Miss Helens has been the caretaker for twelve years. It will be easier if you show her a search warrant." He rolled his eyes. "Talk about people with attitude problems!"

"Another one, huh?" Gil sighed. "Okay. I'll ask the judge for one."

"Just a tip, do it for Handley, too."

Gil scowled. "But I was just going to talk to him," he said. "And I have no idea what I'd be looking for even if I got one. I'd have to spell it out on the warrant."

"I know. I was kidding." Jeff chuckled. "Handley, well, he's a pain. But he did get us a new fire engine and a couple of new patrol cars by yelling at the county commission about the contract we have to give aid to the city. He said our old patrol cars were a shame and a disgrace, and if the commissioners didn't replace them, he was going to call in a news crew. Scared them spineless."

"No doubt. We have a hard-hitting news station just down the road. Even Denver envies them."

"You going home now?"

"Thought I might." He paused. "I'm going to cook breakfast for Nemara in the morning."

"At your house?" Jeff asked. "I thought you liked her."

"Well, I do. But it's just as well to find out how she reacts to Bert early on, you know?"

"She'll react, all right," Jeff said. "I expect she'll run out the door screaming and get a speeding ticket on her way back to Denver."

"She lost a pet that she loved," Gil said. "Maybe she'll be less, well, spooked, by Bert."

"How many women have left your house screaming and never dated you again . . . ?" Jeff asked with raised eyebrows and twinkling eyes.

Gil glared at him. "He's a nice pet. He's never bitten anyone, not even me."

"It's not how he acts, Gil, it's what he is." He pursed his lips. "Maybe if you had somebody sew him a body suit with arms and legs out of that fake fur, you could pass him off as a thin teddy bear," he suggested.

Gil shook his head and sighed. "Not nice. Bert's sweet."

"I hear dinosaurs were, too, back in the day . . ."

"Going home now," Gil told his boss with a chuckle, and went out the door.

* * *

On the way to his house back in the woods, Gil thought about the long day and all that he and Nemara had turned up.

But they still had a dead man, apparently murdered, and not even one suspect just yet. Worse, the mayor was impatient to find justice for his deceased friend, and he was very obviously going to be a pain in the neck while Gil tried to sift out a murderer.

He was grateful that he had Nemara for backup. From the abrasive she-cat she'd seemed at first, she'd turned into someone he really wanted to get to know.

First, however, there was Bert. It would all depend on how she reacted to him.

Well, life went on. If she ran out the door, maybe they could still work together on the murder as partners. It was just that he was thinking along the lines of something more than a partner. He was thinking about it seriously.

CHAPTER 4

Nemara was all thumbs. It was so nice that somebody wanted her around, even just for breakfast. She couldn't remember the last time she'd kept company with an attractive man. In college, her devotion to her studies had attracted like-minded friends, but only friends.

She laughed as she remembered her class trip to the famous Body Farm at the University of Tennessee's Forensic Anthropology Center, started by Dr. Bill Bass. It had been the experience of a lifetime. It did rather set the forensic people apart from the rest of the student body, except for those studying in the medical field. They were as fascinated with the processes of death as Nemara and her classmates. Oftentimes they gathered in the canteen for quiet discussions in a corner because, of course, it wasn't a subject for the weak stomached.

She struggled with her wild hair and finally gave up and brushed its mad curls into a mass and secured them with a circular comb. She looked in the mirror and was surprised at the difference it made in her appearance. She didn't look too bad at all. Encouraged, she pulled out her small makeup kit and added just a little of a neutral lipstick and some powder. She'd never win a beauty contest,

Nemara decided as she slid on her big-rimmed glasses, but this would do.

She frowned at her reflection. Her choice of frames wasn't a good one. She was going to go back to the optometrist when she got home and get some small gold wire frames. They'd stand out less than this black plastic horror she was wearing. The frames made her look severe.

Well, that was what she'd wanted when she was sent here, reluctant and resentful that her colleagues were trying to get rid of her. She had been something of a pain, defensive because someone knew who her family was and had mentioned it in a slighting fashion. Thanks to social media, you could find out anything about anybody, and Nemara was no exception.

Usually that knowledge sent people racing to her, sensing favors if they played up to her. Not the crew at the crime lab. They were job oriented. But Nemara might get them some extra funding, some better equipment.

When she pointed out that she had no influence in that quarter, they ignored her. Her response was to be as abrasive as possible, and she was good at being abrasive. Hence the push to send her out to the boondocks in exile on a cold case.

But now that she was here, she was actually enjoying herself. Nemara had met people, been accepted by them. Gil seemed to like her. After all, he was making breakfast for her!

She tried to curb her enthusiasm. He was a virile, very handsome man. She was less than beautiful. She liked a type of pet that would probably send him running. There were so many reasons that she shouldn't let herself dwell on him.

Yet, he was sexy and exciting, and she loved being with him. They had so many things in common. She'd never expected to find anyone who not only liked her quirks but also shared them. It was a revelation.

She must go slowly, Nemara warned herself. She mustn't lose her heart. Men didn't want her, not for keeps. That was a lesson the forensic archaeologist learned before. She didn't want to repeat it. No, better to sit in her shell and grow old, rather than be rejected again, ever. Much better.

Gil was at her hotel door at exactly seven thirty.

She grinned at him as they left. She was wearing a magenta skirt and jacket with high heels and a burgundy Berber coat that fell to her ankles. He noticed her hair. It looked different, but nice.

"Where did you learn to cook?" she asked as they went toward his patrol car.

"Well, I did some cooking in the military," he said, and chuckled. "But it wasn't the same fare we eat here."

"Oh. Bugs and such," she teased.

He nodded as he opened the passenger door for her. "Bugs and such. But I learned to cook at home, long before I joined the military, out of necessity."

She wanted to follow up on that odd statement, but she didn't. It was too soon to try and pry into his life. "It's nice of you to offer to feed me," she said. "Especially when I was such a pain when I first got here."

"You were grieving," he said gently. "If I'd known that, I'd have been less abrasive to you."

"Oh, I deserved it," she said honestly. "I went out of my way to be rude. I was hurting so much, I just wanted to think about anything else . . ." She stopped suddenly because she had a pincushion in her throat and tears threatened. She looked out the window instead and took a steadying breath. "This is really pretty country," she said after a few seconds.

"Thanks," he replied. He could feel her pain. He knew how he'd feel if he lost Bert. "We think it's the best place on earth."

"I love the mountains," she said softly. "That's why I wanted to work in Denver. I'd always lived where it was flat. Well, most cities are flat, aren't they?"

"Yes, if we exclude San Francisco . . ."

She burst out laughing. "Caught me," she said.

He chuckled. "What city do you come from?

"I'm from Kentucky, originally," she replied. "Up around Lexington, where all the horse farms are."

"Is that grass really blue, or is that an urban legend?" he teased.

She laughed. "It really is blue," she replied. "I'm going on memory, of course. We left Lexington when I was about six. I grew up in Maryland."

"From landlocked to ocean?" he teased.

She nodded. "I learned to love the ocean," she said. "We lived inland, but it wasn't far to drive, to go fishing or even just play in the surf." She glanced at him. "Are you from Colorado?"

He sighed. "I'm from Benton, actually," he replied. "I've lived here all my life, except for military service."

"What branch?" she asked.

"Army," he said, smiling. "My whole family from way back has been Army."

"And mine's been Navy," she said. "Even my mother."

"And you said your parents are no longer alive I recall."

She drew in a long breath. "No. I have family, and they've taken good care of me. But nothing makes up for the loss of a parent."

"I know what you mean," he agreed. "Like I told you, I don't have any family left at all. I miss my mother every day. She's been gone for fourteen years."

She noticed that he didn't mention his father. There was probably a good reason for that. She didn't want to pry.

"I've noticed that about you," he said abruptly as he paused for a traffic light and glanced at her.

"Noticed what?" she asked, surprised.

"You don't ask questions. You just let people talk if they want to, but you don't push." He shrugged. "I like that."

She felt warm inside, as if she were cocooned. "I was taught not to push . . . when I was very small. People didn't like it when I piped in and started asking embarrassing questions." She laughed. "My parents were very strict." She didn't mention why.

"My mother was a pussycat," he recalled, moving forward as the light changed. "I could get her to agree to anything. My father . . ." He stopped abruptly, and his face hardened.

She was looking ahead. "It's snowing!" she exclaimed, watching the first huge flakes hit the windshield.

He laughed, surprised. "Listen, it's Colorado. Snow this time of the year isn't exactly unexpected."

"Oh, I know, but I'm just a kid about it, after all these years. I love it!"

"You wouldn't if you had to cover wrecks," he pointed out.

She wrinkled her nose. "I don't have to, so I can like it if I want to."

He smiled. She really was like a kid, in many ways. He liked the vulnerability in her that came out occasionally. She seemed like a different person after just a few days in Benton.

"You didn't really want to come here, did you?" he asked, turning down a long dirt road.

"Well, no. But it wasn't because of the case," she added. "You see, they wanted to get me out of the office. I'm not like the rest of them. I love my job, but I sort of have some baggage that I drag around with me. They knew about it."

"Baggage? Now I'm intrigued."

She glanced at him. He gave her a wicked grin, and she relaxed and started laughing, too.

"Not that sort," she muttered with twinkling eyes.

"Darn. Go ahead. Shatter my dreams." He turned into a driveway. "And we're here."

She caught her breath. It was a log cabin, a beautiful log cabin set against the backdrop of the mountains in a nest of lodge pole pines. "Oh, it's just . . . perfect," she blurted out. "Like one of those Christmas cards people used to send before the electronic ones became popular!"

She couldn't have said anything that would have pleased him more. Not that he brought many women home, because of Bert, but one visiting attorney had remarked that he must think of himself as a hermit, because no normal man would live in such a dump. The comment had hurt his feelings, but he hid his reaction.

"It's been called worse things," he said involuntarily.

She glanced at him, and all at once she could see a city woman making fun of it, making fun of him. "It must have hurt," she blurted out.

His eyebrows almost met his hairline.

She grimaced. "Sorry. Sorry! I try so hard to keep things to myself—"

"Yes, it did hurt," he interrupted. "How in the world did you figure it out?"

She drew in a breath. "I don't know. My dad used to call it an uncanny insight into people. My mother, who was a Stuart before she married him, said that our ancestry included folk who had the 'second sight.' In other words, that psychic stuff we're not supposed to discuss in modern society." She shook her head. "It was one reason my colleagues were keen to get me out of the office in Denver," she confessed. "There was a death in the family of one of my co-workers, and I presented condolences before he broke the news. I found reasons to get out of the office after that. A lot of them."

She didn't add that even her connections didn't help after people realized that she saw more than they wanted her to.

"We have old Mrs. Jones, who can talk off warts and talk out fire. And there's Harry Bates, who can dowse for water and find it even when licensed drilling companies can't," he informed her. "Nobody thinks anything about it. We have lots of people like that, out here in the country. You'd fit right in."

She studied his handsome, strong face. "I've never fit in, anywhere, in my whole life," she confessed quietly.

He felt a pang of conscience about the rudeness he'd shown her at first. She was very vulnerable, at a level he hadn't guessed she had.

He averted his eyes. "Breakfast," he said, turning and grinning at her.

She laughed. "Oh, yes. Breakfast. I usually just have coffee, so this is a treat."

He went around to help her out of the car. She stumbled on a rock, and he caught her. Even through two layers of coats, it was electrifying. She didn't look up, but her breath stuck in her throat and her heart started doing a dance.

He was feeling something comparable. Unexpected. His big hands tightened on her arms. "You okay?" he asked softly, his breath stirring the hair at her temples.

"Yes." She cleared her throat. "Yes. Sorry. I'm clumsy from time to time."

He let her go with faint reluctance. "Well, I have to agree. There was the time I slipped on the ice and slid under my patrol car, just as I was about to write out a citation for speeding in unsafe conditions."

"You didn't!" she exclaimed, her eyes gleeful.

He laughed. Nemara didn't look condescending or haughty. It was as if she was sharing a secret joke with him about a delightful subject. Gil felt his heart lift.

"I did," he said, and walked beside her to the front door. "Jeff laughed about it for weeks."

"I'll bet he did things just like that," she said.

"He did! He tripped over a limb, rolled down the hill, and fell into the river when he was trying to help a stranded motorist change a tire. He said he'd never been so humiliated in his life. The stranded motorist thought he was an idiot and told the story accordingly."

"Poor man," she said. "That wasn't nice."

"Not nice at all." He unlocked his log cabin door and pushed it open, letting her go in first. Silently, he prayed that Bert hadn't managed to undo the catches on his cage in his absence.

"Oh, this is nice," she exclaimed as her eyes drifted from comfortable stuffed furniture to woven rugs and pottery. "Very nice! It's so cozy!"

He thought about that. "Well, I guess it is," he said, never having given it much thought.

"The chairs are so comfortable looking. I hate sticky furniture," she said. "You know," she added when he looked puzzled, "straight chairs with no cushions."

"I hate those, too," he agreed. He shrugged out of his jacket. "Make yourself at home. I'll go deal with food."

"Can I help?" she offered.

"No need. Find something you like on TV," he added.

She made a face. She never watched television. She

gamed on an Xbox and watched movies on it as well, but she was no fan of regular programming.

Still, the news might be interesting, she supposed.

She turned it on, and her eyes fell on something familiar. An Xbox, and not the one she had, but the very newest one, the S. There was a PlayStation there as well, a piece of equipment she'd been pondering buying because of the games you couldn't play on anything else. She'd have to ask him about that later.

She sat down in a stuffed chair that was very comfortable and turned on the local news. Most of it was about a snowstorm that was going to bring at least two or three inches of snow to the local area around Benton.

She sighed as she listened halfheartedly to it. Suddenly she was aware of a presence. Not human, but . . . familiar.

She turned her head and there, peering around the legs of a side table, were a pair of red eyes.

Her breath caught. Its body was white with a brilliant yellow pattern. It was . . . beautiful!

"Oh, you gorgeous baby," she whispered, lowered a hand, palm up. "Come on. Come see me," she coaxed.

There was a slow, undulating movement toward her. She smiled and slid her hand under the long, elegant head and down under the soft belly, gently lifting. "Come on. Gosh, you're huge! Way bigger than my Weatherby! Want to watch TV with me?" she asked.

Apparently, it was a familiar invitation. The beautiful animal slid up into her lap and curled its huge length so that its head was propped in her hand and the rest of him placidly curved around her body in the chair.

She listened to the news halfheartedly, her fingers smoothing over the beautiful head resting on her other hand and forearm.

"I forgot to ask if you wanted bacon or . . ." Gil stopped

dead in the doorway, his eyes popping as he took in the scene.

There she sat with Bert in her lap, not screaming, not trying to claw her way out. Just sitting, with Bert's head in her hand, smiling.

"Bacon or . . . ?" she prompted.

"You like snakes," he blurted out.

"Oh, yes," she replied. "Weatherby was a tree boa. Nowhere as beautiful as this big baby," she said, nodding toward her companion. "But he was a lot of company and I loved him very much. This is Bert?" she added.

He nodded, still shell-shocked.

"He's an albino python, isn't he?" she asked. "I've seen them in pet shops, and I wanted one very badly, but I didn't think Weatherby would adjust to another reptile. He was very possessive." She laughed. "In fact, he kept me single. Men would find out about him and shudder." She shook her head. "Honestly. Weatherby never ate anybody!"

"I can think of at least one or two people I might have invited Bert to eat," he said, moving into the living room. He shook his head. "I brought a colleague home once, and she left skid marks getting out of the driveway."

"Poor Bert," she murmured, petting him. "I imagine it hurt his feelings something terrible!"

He drew in a breath. "You like snakes." He laughed. "Son of a gun."

She grinned. "You never said what Bert was. I thought maybe he was a dog."

"I'm allergic," he confessed.

"Me too! It's why I had Weatherby. No fur," she added.

He shook his head, still grinning from ear to ear. "I just can't get over it," he murmured.

She made a face. "Were you cooking something?"

He sniffed. "Oh, gosh . . . !" He ran into the kitchen.

Pans rattled. Muffled cursing. Not too much later he came back in. "Bacon's off the menu. Sorry," he said. "Do you like sausage?"

"I love it!"

"Whew," he teased.

She grinned. Bert was moving a little, into a more comfortable position. She shifted, too.

"He's heavy," he pointed out. "He weighs over a hundred pounds."

"I don't weigh much more than that," she said. She was smoothing her hand over Bert's head while he stared at the television. "Do you think snakes understand language?"

"Well, he's very restless during nature specials," he said. "And once, he tried to get to a rat on a program I was watching."

She laughed. "We should do a paper on snakes' comprehension of spoken language."

"You get started on that right away. I'll finish making breakfast," he said.

She was still laughing when he went back into the kitchen. Bert stayed coiled up in the easy chair while his human and the soft, warm companion had breakfast. The television was on, but neither of the humans could tell if Bert was watching it or not.

"He's just so beautiful," Nemara remarked as they ate scrambled eggs and sausage and toast.

"I thought I'd never seen such a pretty creature. He was the only snake they had in the pet store that used to be in town. Nobody liked snakes, and the owner was about to trade him for some fish when I said I wanted him. I'd never had a pet snake, but I figured I could learn how to take care of one."

"You do a great job," she said. "He's very healthy, you can tell."

"He's company," he told her. "I'm by myself a lot." He shrugged. "I come home and tell him about my day."

"I used to do that with Weatherby." She stopped, swallowed hard, and drank a sip of coffee to stifle the tears.

"I watched this thing on YouTube," he said abruptly. "It was on near-death experiences. Every one of the people said that while they were technically dead, all their pets came running to meet them."

She brightened. "Really?"

He nodded. "Really." He smiled. "Life is short, you know. Eternity is forever. It's kind of nice, thinking that all our loved ones and even our pets are there waiting for us to come over. I'm not in any rush to do it," he added. "But it's comforting."

She smiled. "Thanks."

He shrugged. "I've never lost a pet. I wasn't allowed to have one when I was a kid. But I've lost people," he said. "People I loved, people I served with overseas." He stared at her evenly. "It always hurts."

She nodded. "I guess that's what makes us human."

He smiled. "Absolutely."

She finished her breakfast and her coffee. "You're a good cook," she said.

"Do you cook?" he wondered.

Nemara made a face. "I cook dorky things."

"Excuse me?"

"Not entrées so much," she confessed. "I can make my own bread, and I can make exotic rich French pastries. But I can't even manage a macaroni and cheese casserole. Like I said. I cook dorky things."

"I love fresh bread," he said. "I can't even make a biscuit."

"Lots of people can't make biscuits," she said. "My aunt is sixty, and she was in her forties before she could make a biscuit. Know how she finally learned to do it? She threw away the recipes and just guessed at the ingredients. First time, she made the best biscuits I've ever eaten." She laughed. "So I guess it's not always a matter of how you measure. Now, bread? You'd better measure those ingredients!"

"I'd love to watch you make bread sometime," he said. "After we break this case," he added.

She nodded. "I'd be delighted," she said, then smiled shyly.

"What do we know so far?" Gil asked as he poured second cups of coffee.

"We have a guy who died twelve years ago who was found in a hole with a water line. There were leaves in the hole that are only found at one person's home in the vicinity. The victim was wearing nothing except socks, which indicated that he was someplace with his shoes off when he was killed."

Gil frowned. "Interesting. I wonder if anyone ever found a pair of shoes in an odd place?"

"We could ask around. Assuming that someone didn't kill him and take his shoes off before tossing him in the hole."

He shrugged. "Assuming that. The victim and the mayor were best friends."

Nemara continued. "They went fishing together." She frowned. "The victim had a sister. There was a rumor that the mayor had been sweet on another woman before he married his wife." She looked at him. "I wonder if we spoke to the mayor's wife and just let her ramble—would she tell us anything new?"

He pursed his lips. "Tricky, talking to politicians about murder. Especially about someone they knew."

"Yes, they can be problematic. The mayor might think we were accusing him."

"I'll see if Jeff can talk him into letting us speak to his wife. She might remember something the mayor didn't that would help us break the case," he suggested.

She nodded. "Politics. Boy, do I know how that works," she murmured without thinking.

"I guess you've had your own struggle with political cases?" he asked.

"What?" She cleared her throat. "Oh. Yes. Well, yes." She had, but not in the way he was thinking.

"So. Shall we go talk to Jeff?" he asked.

She grinned. "Good idea. I want to say good-bye to Bert first, though."

He laughed. "Be my guest."

"I still can't believe how beautiful Bert is," she sighed as they drove back to the motel. "I've never seen an albino that close up before."

"He's gorgeous, isn't he?" he asked, delighted that she shared his enthusiasm for his pet. "I wish a few other people had your perspective on that," he added with a sigh. "Jeff won't come near my place."

"Snakes are misunderstood," she said. "And a lot of that is Hollywood's fault. They always show them as evil, running around biting people for no good reason."

"I have to confess that I'm not fond of rattlesnakes," he pointed out.

"Oh, me neither," she agreed. "Well, I guess some snakes deserve their reputations. But pythons and boas are sweet. I like cobras and anacondas, too," she confessed.

He laughed. "Me too. Especially cobras. They fascinate me."

"There was this video where a cobra came up to a guy

who was holding a bottle of water, and the guy gave him a drink."

"I saw that!"

"In India they have a festival where they go into the wild and get cobras out of their holes, put them around their necks, take them to temple, and feed them milk. Then they take them back where they found them. These are wild cobras, not tame ones, but hardly anyone ever gets bitten," she added. "Our anthropology professor showed a film of it. I've been fascinated with them ever since."

"We had a pet shop in a neighboring town. It wasn't there for long. Owner caught a little timber rattler and put it in one of those plastic cages and kept it on the counter by the cash register." He stopped at a traffic light. "So this guy comes in, sees the little snake, and starts tapping the cage, shaking it, upsetting the snake. It strikes at the man over and over. The owner, who was helping a customer, sees it and makes the man leave the shop. A few weeks later, that same guy comes back into the shop. The minute the little snake sees him, it starts striking at the man through the plastic."

Her lips parted on the breath she'd been holding. "They remember," she said.

He nodded. "And that's the most terrifying thing I think I've ever learned about snakes. Imagine that you do something mean to one in the wild and then go back to that area a few months later." He shivered dramatically. "What an eye-opener!"

She laughed. "I guess we don't know everything about creatures we share the planet with."

"Absolutely we don't." He shook his head as he started forward again. "I'd never heard such a thing in my life. It really did change the way I thought about wildlife."

"I wonder if Bert remembers things?"

"He remembers people who bring him presents."

"How so?"

"This guy from Denver came to visit, an auditor, and he liked snakes. So he stayed with Bert and me for a couple of days. When he was ready to leave, he bought Bert a freeze-dried animal and gave it to him. Bert was so happy! So last year, the guy came back. He didn't stay with me, he was just stopping by, but the minute he walked in the door, Bert actually climbed him!"

She laughed out loud. "Oh my goodness!"

"He's still telling that story, I hear. It has a happy ending, though. I drove over to Raven Springs where we still have a pet shop and bought Bert a freeze-dried animal. If a snake could smile, he did!"

Nemara arrived at the sheriff's office about the same time as Gil, and they both went inside. Jeff was having a difficult conversation with the mayor.

"But I don't know where they are . . ." Jeff spotted them coming in the door and visibly relaxed. "They're right here, Mr. Mayor," he said with evident relief.

Mayor Handley turned to face them. "So, what have you turned up?" he demanded. "Do you have a suspect yet?"

"Not yet," Gil said. "It's a twelve-year-old case, sir. It will take a little time . . ."

"I want this case solved! I loved Marley," he said, and seemed to choke up. "We went fishing together every single summer. He was at my house, or I was at his, all the time. He was my best friend!"

Nemara moved forward and stood looking up at the redheaded mayor. Oddly, she felt no sympathy at all for him. She frowned as she studied him.

"What?" Handley demanded belligerently.

Her eyes narrowed. "You argued," she said softly.

He drew in an audible breath. He started to stammer out something and couldn't. He just stared at her blankly for a minute. Then he turned away. "No damned progress yet, I see. I'll check back later. You solve this case!" he almost shouted at Jeff, and he was gone.

Jeff stared at Nemara with wide eyes. So did Gil.

She looked back at them with a feeling of deep sorrow. "They argued," she said simply. "They argued."

CHAPTER 5

"How do you know that?" Jeff asked after a minute.

"I'm not sure," she said simply. "I just . . . feel things."

"She's uncanny," Gil said, but he smiled. "She likes Bert."

"She likes . . . Bert?" Jeff exclaimed.

"He's beautiful," she told Jeff.

Gil pointed to Nemara. "See? Not every woman is intimidated by a sweet little snake."

"Gil," Jeff said, "the sweet little snake weighs a hundred pounds, and if he got really hungry, you'd be the first person on the menu."

"It would take an anaconda to eat Gil," Nemara said with a grin.

"Thanks," he said. "I think."

"What about the argument?" Jeff prodded.

"I don't know," she said. "I just felt that they'd argued. We need to talk to the mayor's wife, but we don't want him to think that we suspect him of doing something terrible to his best friend. Could you get her to talk to us?"

He made a face. "Nita Handley is the nearest human thing we have to a spitting cobra," he muttered. "Nobody can talk to her. She's a walking shredding machine."

"Right up your alley," Gil told Nemara with a smile. "If anybody could get her to talk, you could. You have that amazing insight into people."

She blushed. "Thanks."

Jeff noticed with concealed amusement the way Gil and Nemara watched each other. If ever two people were compatible, these two were.

"So. Suppose you happen by her house?" Gil asked her.

"It's not exactly on the beaten path," Jeff reminded them.

"Neither am I," Nemara mused. "I could get lost."

Gil chuckled. "Yes, you could."

So she did. Or so it seemed. She parked below the house and looked around helplessly, finally seeming to notice the house above.

She'd already ascertained that the mayor was in conference in city hall with the city manager and the city attorney. It was a good time to speak to the mayor's wife.

Nemara knocked on the front door.

There were curses, and finally a thin woman with dyed black hair and an attitude opened the door. Her eyes were blood red, and she was smoking a cigarette.

"What do you want?" she demanded.

Nemara just stared at her. She frowned. "You hate alcohol. Why are you drinking?" she asked softly.

Incredibly, the woman burst into tears. Nemara went inside and put her arms around her. She rocked the smaller woman in her arms gently.

"There, there," she said. "It's all right."

"No. It's not. It will never be!" the older woman sobbed.

She pulled back and seemed to draw herself together. "Who are you?" she asked.

Nemara smiled. "I'm Nemara. I was over here with one of the sheriff's deputies the other day looking at skeletal remains. I came back to examine the site again but I'm . . ." She turned around. "I'm just lost. There are no road signs here, and I'm not even sure which direction Benton is in." She made a face as she turned back to the mayor's wife. "I have an honor's degree in anthropology. I graduated summa cum laude. I should be able to find a town the size of Benton," she exclaimed.

The mayor's wife laughed. "I have an honor's degree in English from Vanderbilt," she replied. "And when my family first moved here, I couldn't find Benton, either. Do you drink coffee? I think I might like to sober up just for a few minutes. I don't get many visitors," she added after a minute, almost shyly.

Nemara sat with the mayor's wife over cups of strong black coffee at the table with its beautiful white lace table-cloth.

"This is lovely," Nemara commented.

"My mother-in-law crocheted it for me many years ago," she replied, touching the acrylic overlay that protected it from stains. "I'd hoped I might have a daughter to leave it to, but my husband didn't want children."

That was news. Nemara had heard that it was Nita Handley who didn't want children. "He didn't?" she said.

There was a pause. "He was in love with somebody else. They argued and he married me to get even with her, only to find out that someone else had lied to him about what she supposedly said." She drank coffee. "So then she said she wouldn't have anything to do with him if he divorced me, because it would be like she'd broken up our marriage. He was stuck with me." She laughed. "It's not really funny. But it is."

"I'm sorry," Nemara said softly.

Nita looked at her through watery blue eyes. "You aren't like anyone I've ever met," she said abruptly. "You know things, don't you? I mean, you know things that people don't even tell you about."

Nemara hesitated, then she nodded. "It's something of a curse," she replied.

"I would call it a blessing."

"No, you wouldn't, if you had to live with it," Nemara replied quietly. "I knew when and how my father was going to die."

Nita drew in her breath sharply. "Did you tell him?"

"I tried to. He laughed."

"I begin to see what you mean." She sipped coffee. "Have you always had this ability?"

"Yes. Since I was very small. My grandmother tried to explain that it was a blessing in disguise, that one day I'd be happy about it." She sipped coffee and sighed. "I'm still waiting to be happy about it," she added wryly.

Nita looked into her coffee cup. "You know something about me, don't you? Rather, about my husband and me. A secret. A bad secret."

Nemara studied her. "Yes. But I don't tell things that I . . . learn. It's not my place."

Nita scowled. "Not even bad things?"

"Not even bad things," Nemara replied. "If I found something out in a normal way, yes. But this is . . ." She shrugged. "Well, it's not a normal way. And I don't, I don't . . ." She sighed. "I can't find the words."

"You don't tell."

Nemara smiled. "I don't tell."

Nita grimaced. "My husband wouldn't understand. He'd think I told you."

"He won't know."

Nita hesitated. Then she nodded. "What an odd thing to happen. I mean, your showing up here looking for directions and knowing . . . THAT . . . about what happened here, and being so compassionate. I don't talk to people. I don't talk to anybody!"

"You should get out," she replied.

"Out of my marriage . . ."

"No! Out of this house," Nemara said. "You should join a club, go to meetings, get involved in politics, plant flowers and join a garden club. That sort of getting out. Too much time alone is a very bad thing."

Nita laughed. She was amazed at how long it had been since she'd laughed. "I used to," she said. "But I was afraid—"

"That you'd let something slip," Nemara finished for her. She smiled at the other woman's surprise. "Very soon that won't matter anymore. Did you know that intent is everything in law?"

Nita was listening carefully. "Intent?"

"Yes."

"You mean, if you plan something, if you intend harm," she stammered.

"Exactly."

"Oh."

Nemara smiled. "You're in a bad place in your mind. But only in your mind. It's sunny outside. Go and look at the snow."

Nita laughed. "You make scary things seem so very simple."

"They are."

Nita sighed. "Well, I feel worlds better."

"I'm glad. Live your life."

Nita shook her head. "I haven't, yet."

"This is a very good time to start." She studied the older woman. "Less hair dye, less makeup, less alcohol. Buy new clothes. Go to a different hair salon. Smile more."

Nita laughed. "Well, I will!"

"Good. Now, how do I get to Benton?" Nemara asked in all innocence.

She was back at the sheriff's office in less than ten minutes.

"What did you find out?" Gil asked, because Jeff had already gone out on an accident call.

"Things I can't tell you yet," she said. She was very serious as she looked up at him. "I'm not supposed to know."

He blinked. "Excuse me?"

"It's complicated," she said after a minute. "I mean, I think I know what happened, or sort of know, but it isn't something I can share. I don't tell what I find out . . . in unusual ways. I don't have solid evidence."

"Oh. I see," he replied. He smiled gently. "It's that ability that we don't talk about out loud."

She nodded, smiling back.

He sighed. "Well, what can you tell me?"

"That there was an accident. Something happened that wasn't intended. Now everybody's terrified of discovery and prison terms. That sort of thing."

His black eyes widened. "You're amazing," he said, and he wasn't kidding.

She laughed. "Thanks. But it wasn't an ability I learned or anything. I was born with it."

"Anybody else in your family equally blessed?"

She sighed. "My aunt. She gets a lot of odd looks from colleagues because she's pretty good at knowing the truth, even when they try to hide things from her. And my uncle," she added. "He has an uncanny knack for seeing hidden things that benefit all the wrong people."

"And that's clear as mud," he teased.

She flushed and laughed softly. "Sorry. It's too soon."

His eyebrows arched.

"Too soon to be spilling all my secrets," she added.

"Okay. But I'll be waiting for revelations," he pointed out.

She was looking past him, out the window. "It's just so pretty," she said absently as snow came down in huge flakes, building on the sidewalks and roofs and, especially, the street. They had snow in Maryland, of course, but out West there was lots more of it. She loved snow.

The phone rang. Jane answered it and glanced at Gil.

"Don't tell me," he said with a sigh. "There's a wreck."

Jane laughed. "Yes. Sorry. The sheriff's radio went out, and that's a first, so Jeff just called it in. Corner of the Sutton Highway and Lone Pine Road."

Gil glanced at Nemara and grimaced. "Sorry. I have to go."

"Wear a raincoat," she said softly.

He grinned at her. "I have one in the car. You drive slowly," he added, tapping her on the nose.

"I'll be fine," she said. "I had to learn to drive in frozen stuff when I moved to Colorado."

"Okay."

She watched him go with a sigh.

Jane saw that and grimaced, but Nemara didn't notice. Still smiling, she went out the front door.

It was a slippery mess already. Nemara got back to her motel in one piece, but Benton was in mountainous territory and some of the streets were big hills. When she got in the door, she let out a long sigh. It had been a harrowing trip, even for somebody used to winter driving.

She'd barely plopped down in a comfortable chair when her cell phone rang. She checked the number and smiled to herself.

"Aunt Vera," she said. "How are you?"

"Fighting my way through another partisan bill that nobody wants, not even the party that endorsed it," she said gruffly. "What's this I hear about you investigating a murder in Benton?"

"How did you hear that?" Nemara asked.

"Your uncle Roger. Don't forget what he does for a living," Vera added.

Nemara laughed. "Nobody ever forgets what he does for a living," she teased.

"So, what's the story?"

"There isn't much of one," Nemara said, sliding out of her shoes, which had gotten soaked as she walked back and forth to her car in the snow. Her hose were almost dripping. "This case is going to be rather quickly solved."

"You don't sound happy about it," Vera returned.

"Well . . . there's this gorgeous deputy. And he loves snakes."

"My goodness!"

"He has a pet albino python. It sat in my lap and watched TV with me while the deputy cooked breakfast for us."

There was a long silence.

"He came and got me at my motel and took me to his house for breakfast," she explained.

"Oh." Vera cleared her throat. "I'm sorry, sweetheart. I don't move with the times."

"Neither do I," she assured her aunt. "But he is very gorgeous and so is his pet."

Vera laughed dryly. "That's a first. A man who doesn't run when he sees a snake."

"I thought so, too. He's been very kind to me. Losing Weatherby was tough."

"I know it was. I'm sorry I couldn't come to Denver and be with you. But . . . well, we're up to our ears in legislative bills," Vera began.

"I know that. It's okay."

"And your uncle has a minor hiccup in his department. You might have noticed if you watch the national news. He's being french-fried in Congress at the moment. Both sides want him cooked."

"Uncle Roger will have them for breakfast if they're not careful." Nemara laughed. "Don't they know what he used to do for a living?"

"The newer members don't. They'll learn very quickly if they prod his temper."

"Yes, they will."

"I just called to make sure you were all right," Vera said. "Often, murders leave people who should have been prosecuted free on the streets to stalk anyone trying to solve the case."

"Yes, I know of a couple of those," Nemara agreed. "But this doesn't involve a cold-blooded person."

"Even a warm-blooded person, if cornered, can be dangerous," she said.

"Like that nutty guy who insisted you were concealing an alien spaceship in your building?" she teased.

"It's okay, we got help for him," Vera returned. "In fact, it turns out that he has a degree in theoretical physics. He went a bit overboard when he lost his wife. He's all better now, and Roger got him a job at Area 51."

"Ooooh, where they're hiding the spaceships!" Nemara said with mock enthusiasm.

"Don't even joke about that," came the gruff reply.

A voice spoke nearby, and Vera groaned. "All right, I'm on my way," Vera told the newcomer. "Sweetheart, I have to go, they're reconvening. You stay out of the line of fire! And if you need help, I'm right here and so is Roger."

"I know that," Nemara said affectionately. "I don't know what I would have done without you and Uncle Roger when . . ." Her voice trailed off.

"Family takes care of family." Vera's voice was unusually soft. "I'll talk to you soon."

"Good luck with the wars," Nemara teased.

"Right now, the noble opposition is the Barbary pirates and I'm the British Navy," came the reply. "Bye, sweetheart."

Nemara chuckled. Her relatives were nothing if not amusing.

A little later, her phone rang again.

"What about supper?" Gil asked when she picked up.

"Gosh, I'm so busy," she said with mock exhaustion. "I mean, Hollywood stars keep pestering me for dates, and all!"

"Chuck them all. Want to make some bread? I've got yeast and plain flour."

"Wow! Yes, I do," she said. "How do I get back to your house?"

"That reminds me, how did the lost tourist act work out?"

"Very well. I'll tell you all about it over supper."

"Great! I'll come get you as soon as my shift ends. About . . . thirty minutes from now."

"Sounds fine. I'll be ready!"

She put on jeans and a sweatshirt, boots and her raincoat. She was waiting when Gil knocked on the door.

"Now, that's the way to dress for the weather," he teased, helping her to the patrol car.

"Thanks," she said as she moved aside a sheaf of reports so she could sit down.

He started driving, turned a corner and barely avoided a car coming right at him. The driver managed to get it back into his own lane and gave Gil an apologetic wave.

"People move here from back East and go nuts when it snows," Gil told her. "That was old man MacElroy. He bought a little ranch out here and opened a furniture shop to help keep it going. If you ever see a little gray car weaving all over the highway in the snow, that's him," he added on a chuckle. "Amazing that he's never had an accident, and he's been here two years."

"People are incredible." She laughed.

He pulled up at his front door and helped her into the house. The living room was warm, and Bert was draped over the sofa.

"Hi, big guy," Nemara greeted, smoothing over his head with her fingertips.

Gil repeated the gesture. The huge reptile gave them a bright-eyed look and then sprawled back on the sofa.

"I fed him last night," Gil said. "He's in his post-meal ignore-the-humans phase right now."

Nemara grinned. "Just like Weatherby." She sighed. "I should hear back from the vet soon about a cause of death.

It won't bring him back, but I'd just like to know if it was something I did or didn't do . . ."

He pulled her into his arms and rocked her. "Animals die," he said against her hair. "Sometimes we never find out why. But I'd never believe it was neglect, or anything lacking on your part. Not the way you love animals."

She smiled, her cheek against his clean uniform shirt. She drew in a contented breath. "Thanks," she said.

"You can share Bert while you're here," he said softly. "He likes you."

"I like him, too."

"I did notice," he teased.

She drew back reluctantly and looked up at him with all her vulnerabilities showing. He held her eyes until she felt the look to the bottom of her feet. Incredible sensations went swirling along her body. She'd never had such stirrings before. It was the feeling of belonging. True belonging.

Gil cleared his throat. "Well. Bread," he said after a minute.

"Bread," she agreed, breathless.

She followed him into the kitchen, still tingling all over from the look and hug they'd shared. On the counter, he already had flour and yeast and oil waiting, in addition to a big bowl, measuring spoons, measuring cups for both dry and wet ingredients, and pans.

"Well," she exclaimed.

He laughed. "I hope that's all you'll need."

She nodded. "Except for milk."

"Coming right up."

She put her coat in the living room and rolled up her sleeves. She loved cooking. It relaxed her.

"What did you find out at the mayor's house? I mean, the part you can tell me," Gil added as they worked together at supper.

"His wife isn't the horror people make her out to be," she replied. "She's become a recluse because she's afraid she'll let something slip."

He stopped carving ham from a foil-wrapped pan and looked at her.

"And apparently her husband is belligerent for the same reason."

"This sounds bad," he said.

She warmed milk in the microwave and then added it to her yeast and sugar and oil in the big bowl. "Yes, it does. But it isn't. I mean, it isn't what it seems."

"You have to tell us what you know," he persisted.

"I can't," she told him quietly. "I have to persuade them to tell you."

"How in the world do you expect to do that?" he asked.

"I'm not sure right now," she confessed. "But there's a way, and I'll find it. We aren't looking for a serial killer or a vicious murderer," she added gently.

He frowned. "An accident, maybe?"

She sighed. "I'd love to be able to say. But I really can't."

"Care to tell me why?"

She covered the bowl to let the ingredients rest for scant minutes and turned to him. "It's hard to explain. You see, this is knowledge that isn't gained in any conventional way. It isn't even admissible in court. So it doesn't seem right to blurt it out when it would sound accusatory and might result in an arrest that wasn't warranted."

Gil stared at her, a little taken aback.

She sighed. "Please trust me until I can talk to them tomorrow."

"Tomorrow."

She nodded. She wiggled her eyebrows. "This recipe makes really good bread," she said, indicating the bowl.

"When it is fresh out of the oven, crispy crust, fresh butter. Can't you almost smell it?" she persisted.

"Go ahead, hit me in my weakest spot," he muttered comically.

She grinned.

"Okay. I won't grill you until tomorrow morning."

"Fair enough!"

The bread was delicious. Gil had carved slices of lovely ham and made a potato casserole to go with it, while Nemara improved a can of bland peas to accompany it.

"I didn't make a dessert," he apologized as they were helping themselves to second cups of coffee.

"I'm not keen on sweets," she replied.

"Neither am I," he said with a chuckle. "I like salty things."

"Me too."

"So it's just as well that we didn't waste time on dessert. Anyway," he added, "I'd take bread over cake any day, especially fresh, homemade bread."

She beamed. "Nice of you to have real butter to go on it, though," she said.

He chuckled again. "Just doing my part." He finished the last of his slice of bread with a sigh. "That was delicious."

"So was the ham," she replied. "I never get a ham done properly. Either it's not cooked enough, or it's too well done."

"It took me a while to get it right," he said. "And I burned up several hams in the process."

"Could you always cook?" she asked.

He toyed with his coffee cup. "I learned when I was

about thirteen. My dad drank. He drank all the time. He was violent." He grimaced. "He hit my mother, and when I was little, I couldn't protect her. But I grew taller and heavier than him, and after I confronted him one time, he never touched her again. He died of a heart attack before I finished high school. I didn't even grieve for him, but my mother did."

"That surprised you," she surmised from his expression.

He nodded. His eyes were blank, staring straight ahead. "She said that he was a different man when they first married. That he was good and kind and protective. But alcohol got a hold on him, and he couldn't break it."

"That happens."

"It happens a lot," he replied. "She mourned him. One day, I came home from work—I'd just started with the sheriff's department, fresh out of the military, and I found her." His face tightened.

She reached out and smoothed her hand over his.

He stared at it for a minute before he linked it with his fingers. He drew in a breath. "She left a note. She said she couldn't live without him, so she was going to look for him on the other side." He was quiet for a minute. "The medical examiner said she'd taken antinausea medication first, then she'd opened the arteries under her arms. There was so much blood . . . !" He swallowed. "He said she probably didn't feel much of anything; it would have been pretty quick. She was white as a sheet. Her eyes were wide open. She was just sitting there, like she used to when I'd put food on the table."

"She didn't cook?" she asked gently, squeezing his hand.

"No. In one of his drunken escapades, my father broke a whiskey bottle and slashed her hands with it. The surgeon put the tendons back together the best he could, but my

mother couldn't really use her hands for much after that."
He looked up. "She was an artist," he added gently, indicating a beautiful still life painting on the wall.

Nemara caught her breath. "It's gallery quality," she said unexpectedly.

"Yes. She exhibited her work. She could have sold them; she had the talent. But before she had the chance to build up a clientele, he destroyed her hands."

"I'm so sorry," she said, still staring at the painting. "She had such a gift!"

"She was philosophical about it," he replied. "She said that God made choices for us and that we just had to go forward any way we could."

"It's not a bad philosophy," she murmured.

"No. I guess not."

She studied him, still aware of the way he was holding her hand. It felt very nice. "You had a hard childhood," she said, as if she could see the terror of a young boy watching his mother being beaten by a drink-crazed man.

He nodded. He turned her hand over and studied it. "And what about you?" he asked.

She blinked. "Me?"

"You never speak of your parents. Just of an aunt and uncle."

She sighed. "I guess it's easier not to speak of it," she said after a minute. "My mother was a clerk, and my dad taught mathematics at university," she said.

"And . . . ?"

She just stared at him. "That's almost all I know about them," she said hesitantly. "My aunt and uncle weren't really forthcoming about their backgrounds. My father was well known in his field, but I don't understand exactly how."

He was frowning. It sounded odd.

She saw his confusion. "Like I said before, I think he was in Black Ops. I was four when Dad died, then my mom and stepdad died a few years ago in the plane crash," she said, clarifying it for him. "I don't really remember Dad. We have photos, I mean, but that's not like personal experience. I spent a lot of time with Aunt Vera and Uncle Roger, anyway. They were already like parents. After I lost my own, they became my parents. I lived with them until I graduated from college. They were very good to me."

"What do they do for a living?" he asked, just making conversation.

She was staring at the clock. "Goodness, is that the time? I need to go to bed."

He laughed. "I didn't realize it was so late," he replied. "I'll drive you back to your motel."

"Thanks." She went to get her coat and say good night to Bert.

"He's so beautiful!" She sighed as they went out the door, and she had one last glimpse of Bert looking over the back of the sofa at them.

"You should get one," he said. "Surely there's a pet shop in Denver that has baby albinos."

"There probably is," she replied, depressed and not sure why. "I'll have to go shopping!"

He was feeling the same depression, and he wasn't any wiser about it than she was.

"In the morning," he said, "you have to clear up some of the mysteries for me. Okay?"

She smiled up at him. Snow was still falling softly. "Okay. I had a good time. Thanks. I don't mix well with people. It was fun, working together in the kitchen."

"For me, too. I enjoyed it." He smiled, but it was a social

smile. He felt a chill, a foreshadowing. He wanted to kiss her. He wanted to run. She was getting too close, too soon. He felt something like panic, but he fought it down.

He helped her into the passenger seat and went around to get under the wheel. "Snowing again," he remarked as he pulled out into the highway. He sighed. "I'll bet you money that I won't sleep much tonight, and Jeff probably won't, either. We always get one or two wrecks out on the highway."

"And I'll bet you wish that people who don't know how to drive in snow would stay off the roads," she remarked.

He chuckled. "Something like that. We usually end up doing a tag team event with the local police. There's plenty of carnage to go around," he added heavily.

"It's like that in Denver," she replied.

He let her out of the car at the motel and walked her to her door. "Well, thanks again for the bread," he said.

"Thanks for the ham," she replied. "Good night."

He averted his eyes. "Good night. I'll see you at the office in the morning."

"Sure thing." She forced a smile.

He nodded and turned back to his patrol car. He didn't waste time leaving.

Nemara stood looking after him and feeling empty. He'd acted as if he couldn't wait to get away from her. She wondered what she'd said or done to make him feel that way.

She sighed and unlocked her door. It was the way her life usually went, she told herself. Men would talk to her and then just take off, for no reason she could understand. It wasn't unusual that Gil had backed away. He'd seemed so interested in her at first. Now he acted as if she had a contagious disease. Maybe she shouldn't have asked about his childhood. He was a very private sort of person.

Well, she told herself sadly, she'd have to return to Denver when they cracked the case anyway, so there was no reason to try to build a relationship with a man she'd likely never see again. But it hurt. She'd really hoped for something . . . more.

CHAPTER 6

Gil had a troubled night. He liked Nemara, a lot, but he had reservations about her. She was a colleague, after all, not a romantic interest. She seemed to respond to him, too. But he wasn't sure that he was ready for anything permanent.

He recalled his own upbringing, how devastating it had been, how unsettled and miserable he'd been. It wasn't much of a recommendation for marriage. He'd told her about his tragic childhood, something he'd never shared with anyone except Jeff. It troubled him that he'd shared something so private with a woman who was, basically, a total stranger. It embarrassed him. He couldn't understand why he'd been so forthcoming.

He remembered that aching hunger to kiss her. That was when he'd wanted to run. It would have been a step forward, into the unknown, into an uncertain future. He'd been alone most of his adult life. He was used to it. Except for Bert, he'd never had much company. Now, here was a woman who seemed to fit right into his life. Part of him was intrigued by her. Another part had very cold feet.

Well, he reasoned, it was better to put it behind him and go on. After all, he'd known the woman only a few days. He probably wouldn't remember her name a week after she left. He thought about that, about Nemara going back to Denver. It left him feeling cold and hollow inside. He shut that thought down at once.

He went into the office by himself the next morning, not offering to pick up Nemara on the way in. Jeff noticed that.

"Is Nemara coming?" he asked deliberately.

"I'm sure she is," Gil said with just the right amount of professional interest.

Jeff raised an eyebrow. "I thought you took her home to supper last night?"

Gil was wide-eyed. "How did you know that?"

"Harris was driving by on patrol. He spotted the two of you going into your house," Jeff confessed.

"Oh. Well, yes. She made bread. Homemade bread. She really can cook. And Bert likes her."

Jeff was watching him closely.

"I'm not in the mood to settle down," Gil said quickly. "I'm happy with my life as it is."

Gil didn't notice Jane brighten at the statement as she put a report on Jeff's desk for a signature. But Jeff noticed. Neither of his companions saw him grimace.

Jane smiled at Gil. "You know, there's a party coming up over at Miss Jeffries's house, Gil, to benefit our animal shelter," she said. "Wouldn't you like to go with me? I mean, if you're not going with anybody else?"

He cleared his throat. Here was his opportunity to show Nemara that they were just colleagues, that he wasn't thinking about a serious relationship. He smiled at Jane. "Sure."

Her eyes widened. Everybody knew how standoffish Gil was about women. She beamed up at him, delighted with his instant acceptance. "Okay, then! It's Friday night, starting at six. You know where I live, with my sister?"

"I know. I'll pick you up about five thirty, that okay?"

"That's just fine. I bought a new dress, just to wear for it!"

He smiled. "Great."

Neither of them saw Nemara come quietly into the office. Jeff saw her, but it was too late to cover for his friend. He saw the hurt on her face, quickly concealed, and was sorry for her. She wouldn't understand why Gil had agreed to go to a party with Jane, but Jeff did. Gil was feeling an attraction he didn't want, and he was going to fight it to the bitter end. It must be a very deep one. He was like a fish on a hook, looking for a quick escape. Poor Jane. She'd think she made a conquest, but it wasn't that at all. She was refuge for a fleeing escaped hostage.

"Oh, hi," Jane said to Nemara, and fought down a faint feeling of guilt when she saw the quickly erased pain on the other woman's face. "I'll just get back to work."

Gil turned, and the look on his face was almost comical as he realized that Nemara had heard everything he'd said to Jane. It wasn't something he should feel guilty about, he told himself. Certainly not. He was a free man. He could date anyone he pleased.

Nemara didn't meet his eyes. She just smiled. "Are we ready to go and speak with the mayor?" she asked Gil.

"I'm ready when you are," Gil agreed, his voice a little curt.

They walked out together, but she went to get into her own vehicle instead of riding with Gil. He felt as if a knife had pierced his side. She didn't fuss, she didn't glare at him, she didn't make sarcastic remarks. She simply accepted that he was going on with his life in Benton, that she had no part in. Apparently, Jane did. Lucky Jane.

* * *

She drove ahead of him to the mayor's house, not even sliding in the deep snow. She seemed very adept at driving in less than ideal conditions.

Gil parked behind her at the mayor's residence.

"Is he home?" he asked as he joined her on the sidewalk.

"Yes," she said. "I phoned before I got to the office and asked if he'd meet us here."

"Was he angry?"

"Not that I noticed," she said, and went to the door.

"Nemara. About the party," he began.

She didn't even look his way. She rang the doorbell.

Mayor Handley opened the door. He might not have sounded angry earlier, but he was obviously loaded for bear now. He glared at both his visitors and stood aside without even bothering with the courtesy of asking them to come in.

"I understand that you've been pestering my wife," Handley rounded on Nemara as he closed the door behind them with a snap. "I sent her to bed!"

Nemara stared at him, seeing guilt and fear and belligerence all combined.

"Your wife is very protective of you," she said gently.

He glared harder. "I won't talk to you," he said shortly. "Not to either of you. And if you try to come here and question either of us again, I'll have your job . . . !"

"No," Nemara interrupted quietly, "you won't."

"I know people in Denver . . . !"

She took a breath. "My aunt Vera is the senior U.S. Senator from Colorado," she told him. Even as he paled, she added, "and her husband, my uncle Roger, is Deputy Director of the CIA." She smiled. "Would you like to make any further threats, or would you like to sit down and listen to me?" She pulled out her cell phone. "Or shall I make a phone call . . . ?" She looked at him enquiringly.

Gil, standing beside her, was shocked to the back teeth. He hadn't dreamed that she had such connections. And she hadn't bragged, or belittled the meal he'd cooked, when she probably grew up eating at five-star restaurants.

Mayor Handley sat down heavily in his easy chair. He hadn't said a word.

Nemara sat down on the sofa across from him. "You argued," she said, continuing a remark she'd made once before to him. "He'd taken off his shoes. It was raining and his shoes were drying by the fireplace," she added, her eyes faintly narrowed. "You argued about some piece of legislation that you wanted passed and he didn't. You'd both had something to drink, not much, but enough to make tempers flare. He got in your face and you grabbed the hot fire poker. You pushed him with it, a little too hard. He went backward. His head hit there," she said, looking toward the fireplace, where it was raised on huge river rocks. "I noticed when I examined the skull that it would have been almost certainly fatal, and instant."

He looked down. All at once, the fight seemed to drain out of him. He looked twice his age.

"He was my best friend," he said huskily. "I'd have done anything for him. A stupid, stupid argument. I'd had too much to drink; I never meant to hurt him!"

"And then you realized what you'd done, and you panicked," she guessed.

He swiped at his eyes. "Yes," he said without lifting his gaze. "My wife said I should call the police, that nobody would blame me. But I was running for the mayor's office, a shoo-in to win, everybody said. All that power, and if people knew what I'd done, even though it was an accident . . . I could have kissed my political career good-bye, or so I thought." He looked up. He was paler than usual, and his face was taut with pain. "I didn't realize what it would be like, to have to live with it."

"People never do," she replied quietly.

He took a deep breath. "So I remembered that they'd just put in the water line and that they were waiting for the rain to stop, to fill in the hole. I didn't think they'd waste time digging around, they'd just cover up the pipes. I wrapped him in some plastic and put him in the hole, covered him with just enough dirt that he wouldn't be seen, and they'd just think the dirt fell in the hole from the rain. I went home and took a shower. They came with a backhoe and filled in the water line. Twelve long years, living with that nightmare," he added on a groan. "I couldn't forgive myself. My poor wife . . . !"

A door opened. Mrs. Handley came out, her eyes red from crying, maybe from a little too much alcohol as well. "I told you we should have called the police," she reminded her husband.

He looked up at her and grimaced. "You were right. I should have listened. I'm so . . . sorry!" His voice broke.

His wife went to him and hugged him close, rocking him in her arms. "It will be all right," she choked. "I saw what happened. I'll testify that it was an accident. We'll get the best lawyer . . . !"

"Intent is everything in law," Nemara said quietly. "It will be all right. There may be charges, but a good attorney can defend you. They'll take all the facts into account."

"Do you want to arrest me?" Handley asked Gil.

"Not right now," Gil said. "You can come in and give us a statement in the morning. We'll go from there. Okay?"

Handley nodded. He managed a smile. "Thank you."

"I told you that you should have talked to her," Mrs. Handley was telling her husband. She smiled at Nemara. "Thank you. You were right. I'm going to live my life."

Nemara smiled. "It's going to be okay. Honest."

Nemara paused by Gil's car. "I don't think your district attorney will want to prosecute, unless he's a die-hard by-the-book attorney."

"He's not," Gil said. "It will probably be pleaded down to something like concealing a body, which is a misdemeanor. Especially given Mayor Handley's sterling reputation here." He cocked his head. "You never mentioned your relatives' occupations."

She laughed. "No. I try not to. It's rather intimidating for people." She shrugged. "To me, they're just Aunt Vera and Uncle Roger. They're my family."

He drew in a breath. "Listen . . ."

Her polite social smile was plastered on her face, like a shield. "I'll stop by your office. I'd like to tell the sheriff what I discussed with Mrs. Handley yesterday."

"Okay."

Nemara went into Jeff's office, and they had a long talk about the mayor and the accidental death.

"He can afford a good attorney," Jeff told her. "And he's got a lot of friends here. He's never been in trouble in his whole life. I don't expect he'll do time."

"Neither do I," she said. "He and his wife seem like nice people."

"They are, though some don't like Nita much. So," he added, "I guess that wraps up your case."

She smiled. "I guess it does. I'm going to go home and shop for an albino python like Gil's. Bert is unique."

"You people and your weird pets," Jeff said, shaking his head. "I'll take a nice dog anytime."

"Snakes don't bark," she pointed out as they went to the office door.

"Yes, well, they do bite occasionally," he retorted.

She chuckled. "Which we could also say for dogs." She shook hands. "It's been a pleasure."

"Same here." He hesitated. "About Gil," he began.

She held up her hand, palm out. "That ship has sailed. I'm not sure I'm really suited to work in Denver. I may look for a place in Maryland, near the farm my aunt and uncle bought. They have a house in Denver, too, but they mostly work in D.C."

"Oh? What do they do?" he asked as he opened the door.

"Interesting things," she said, and smiled. "Nice to have met you, Sheriff. You too, Gil," she said to the man waiting by the counter, without moving a step closer. The smile she gave him was plastic. It was the stuff of cocktail parties and formal dinners.

"You're leaving now?" Gil asked, startled.

"Yes. I have things to do," she said. "Good-bye."

And she was out the door and gone.

Just like that.

Gil was distracted for the rest of the day. He'd halfway planned to stop by the motel and maybe ask for Nemara's address, for her phone number, for some way to keep in touch. He was pretty sure that he'd forget her name in a few weeks. But it never hurt to leave a door open somewhere.

So when he finally got off duty and went to the motel, it was to discover that she'd been gone for several hours.

He went home, stunned by the suddenness of her departure, shell-shocked by his own inexplicable behavior. They'd had so many things in common, more than he'd ever found with anyone else in his whole life. So why had he closed that door between them so quickly?

He sat down on the sofa where Bert was sprawled.

The big snake looked at him and put its head back onto the sofa.

"You liked her, too, didn't you, Bert?" he asked.

Gil sighed as he looked around him at a house that felt suddenly empty and cold. "Maybe a few logs on the fireplace," he murmured to himself as he got up and went to build a fire. "That might warm things up."

He wished he could convince himself that anything short of Nemara was ever going to warm this place again.

Nemara went back to work at the crime lab. There was a new case, just skeletal remains but in much better condition than the late Benton, Colorado, victim. She threw herself into her work without pausing to consider that move back to Maryland.

She called Aunt Vera that night and told her about the case she'd just finished.

"What about the young man who likes snakes?" Vera asked.

"Oh, he's got a girl already," Nemara said with forced

lightness. "She works in the sheriff's office with him. But he was nice company."

"I see." And Vera did see. She knew her niece very well, so she changed the subject, hoping to ease the pain she could almost feel in the younger woman's voice.

"I thought I might move to Maryland," Nemara said after a minute. "I'm not really happy all alone in Denver."

"I'll be home for a few weeks when we recess for the holidays," Vera replied. "You might wait until spring for that move. They're building some nice apartments near the farm."

"That sounds lovely," Nemara lied. Her mind was on Gil, far away in Benton.

"Put the tree up yet?" Vera teased.

"Aunt Vera," she exclaimed. "It's not even Halloween yet!"

"Never stopped you before," came the amused reply.

"Well." She sighed. "I think I'll put out the lighted pumpkins for the time being. When are you coming home?"

"I'll text you when I know," Vera said. "If those scalawags try to run that bill around me just one more time . . . !"

"They're terrified of you," Nemara teased. "Of course they're looking for ways around you."

Vera chuckled. "Maybe they are. I might not be in time for Halloween, but I'll manage Thanksgiving. Order something nice."

"I'll have it catered," Nemara replied.

"That sounds lovely. Well, back to work. Stay dry and warm."

"You too." She hung up and went back to her desk.

"Funding?" her colleague, the one who'd waved her off to Benton with glee, asked, wide-eyed.

"You can't ask her when she's being hounded by the other

party over a bill she doesn't want passed," she explained.
"Wait until she comes home for Thanksgiving. I'll even
invite you over so that you can talk to her yourself."

"You'd do that?" he asked excitedly.

"I'd do that."

He sighed loudly. "Thanks! Thanks a million!"

"I work here, too," she reminded him. "A little extra funding never hurts. Especially for things like carbon dating,
tree-ring dating, maybe a portable X-ray machine . . . ?"
She was giving him an amused glance.

He rolled his eyes.

She grinned. "Okay. Maybe funding for a couple of
extra techs, how about that?"

"Now you're talking," he agreed at once. He grinned
back. "And maybe a portable X-ray machine . . ."

She just laughed.

It had been several weeks, and Gil hadn't forgotten
her name. He'd tried to. But then he'd remember finding
her with Bert in her lap, watching television. He'd remember the scent and taste of homemade bread. He'd recall
that uncanny insight she had, that ability to draw out the
most painful memories and make them bearable.

He'd gone to the party with Jane, as he'd promised to,
but his heart wasn't in it. Jane knew, too. She'd hoped for
a shot at Gil, who was much sought after around Benton,
but it was quickly obvious that his mind was elsewhere,
and it wasn't on work. She recalled the look on Nemara's
face when she'd overheard him accept the invitation to the
party with Jane. She felt guilty.

Gil didn't notice her preoccupation. He was deep in
memories of the woman he'd turned away from. He wished

he could go back and make different decisions. But he hadn't heard a word from Nemara, not even some curiosity about what had happened to the mayor.

"Your mind isn't on dancing, Gil," Jane remarked as they sipped punch by the snacks tray.

He sighed. "Sorry," he said, forcing a smile.

"She has a phone, you know," Jane added. "You might call her."

"If she recognized the number, she'd probably hang up and block me," he said sadly.

"I'm really sorry," Jane said. "I feel responsible. If I hadn't stuck my nose in," she began.

"She has powerful relatives," he broke in. "Her aunt's Colorado's senior senator and her uncle's the Deputy Director of the CIA."

Jane was surprised and it showed. "Really? Wow. But, Gil, you don't have a choice about who your family is," she pointed out. "She never tossed their names around or traded on them."

"No, I guess not. She probably wouldn't have said anything about them if the mayor hadn't threatened her job."

Jane laughed softly. "I'll bet he wished he could take that back," she said.

"He did." His black eyes sparkled. He shook his head. "I don't know how she knows the stuff she does. But she's got this incredible empathy with people."

"And she likes snakes," Jane added, because Jeff had mentioned that.

He nodded. "And she likes snakes."

He almost added, "I wish she liked me, too." But he didn't. He'd burned his bridges there. Burned them to the ground.

* * *

Thanksgiving was fast approaching. The office was beginning to glisten with holly and fir branches, candles and wreathes, and a huge artificial Christmas tree.

Gil stared at it halfheartedly.

"You haven't taken a day off this year," Jeff said, coming up to stand beside his investigator with his coffee cup in one hand. "Why don't you go to Denver and tell our anthropologist how her case came out?"

Gil's heart jumped. "I could just call her." He grimaced. "If I had her number."

"She works for the state crime lab in Denver," Jeff pointed out. "Do you know how to use your phone for Google information?"

Gil let out a rough sigh. "Look, it's been weeks . . . !"

"And you've moped around here like a lost soul," Jeff pointed out. "How many women do you know who like snakes and can make homemade bread?"

"Well, actually, just one."

"So?"

"Her aunt's a senator and her uncle is at the CIA," Gil said doggedly.

"You wouldn't be talking to either one of them. Just to her."

Gil wavered.

Jeff clapped him on the shoulder. "Think about it." He didn't say another word. He went back into his office.

Nemara bought new clothes. She had her wild hair tamed and styled. She bought glasses with small gold wire frames. She learned to use makeup. She bought jewelry.

None of it cheered her up, even if it did make her feel better about herself. One of the guys in her office had even asked her out. But she refused, very nicely, noting that she was getting over a broken heart at the moment. It was close enough to the truth.

She was decorating the Christmas tree when the buzzer sounded. She went to the door and there was Aunt Vera, tall and thin and dear.

Nemara hugged her and hugged her. "Where's Uncle Roger?" she asked as she ushered her aunt into the sprawling apartment.

"Trying to learn invisibility. He's being grilled by a committee." She rolled her eyes. "Still. You'd think they'd run out of questions!"

"Unlikely. He belongs to the wrong party." Nemara chuckled.

"So do I, when it comes to that." She shook her head. "You look nice," she said.

Nemara sighed. "I must. One of the techs asked me out."

"And you said no."

Nemara shrugged. "No sense spending an evening with somebody I'm not interested in."

"Good point. Why don't you call that snake lover in Benton and invite him up to see your new"—she swallowed hard glancing toward the big aquarium in the living room—"pet."

"Livingston is a very nice snake," Nemara protested.

"He's very large," her relative pointed out. She eyed the younger woman. "He could probably ingest you if he got hungry enough."

"Not until he gains another forty pounds, honest."

"I'll take your word for it. You just make sure those latches are in place," Vera added with a shiver.

"He's like a lizard, but he doesn't have legs."

"That won't help. And you'll never get your uncle in this apartment if he realizes Weatherby has a successor."

"Imagine that! A former CIA operative, now deputy

director of the agency, intimidated by a little white and yellow snake." She clicked her tongue. "Imagine the gossip!"

"You tell anybody, and I'll have a few public things to say about your little spider phobia," Vera threatened.

She laughed. "All right, I give up. But he's really a very nice snake."

"There's no such thing."

"Is Uncle Roger coming for Thanksgiving?"

"If they haven't cooked him too thoroughly, yes," Vera said. "Pity his boss is in the hospital getting over that nasty virus. The committee couldn't get to him, so they zeroed in on poor Roger instead. But you'll have to come to us for dinner. You won't get him near your friend in the aquarium."

"Fair enough. I'll have a nice sandwich for lunch and come to your place for the catered supper."

"Make sure Livingston knows that you're not lunch," she advised.

"He'd never eat me. He'd break out in hives!"

Vera gave a jovial laugh.

The day before Thanksgiving, one of the lab techs paused beside Nemara's desk. "We had this weird phone call," he said.

She looked up over her notes on a new case. "We did?"

He scowled. "Yes. Guy sounded absolutely drunk. He wanted to know if we'd had a lady working here who liked snakes!"

She laughed. He made it sound sinful. "What did you tell him?"

"That we did. Then he asked if she still worked here."

Nemara had a sudden thought. "Was it long distance?"

He shook his head. "Don't think so. Sounded local."

"Oh." Well, that ruled out Gil. And why would he call here looking for her when he couldn't wait to see her leave town? she wondered sadly.

"He said he was asking for a friend who needed advice about getting a snake of his own," he added with rolled eyes.

"What did you tell him?"

"That a pet shop would be a better bet than calling the state crime lab for advice about pets."

She sighed. "You've got a point." Her mind was back on the case she was working on. "Was that all he wanted?"

"I guess. Larry talked to him. He said the guy really sounded odd."

"Odd, how?"

"Well, not his voice, just the background. He said it sounded like a train station or a bus station or something."

"We've got those," she agreed.

"It's the time of year," he commented. "People get weird."

She laughed. "I noticed."

Nemara went back to her desk and put the odd phone call out of her mind. It had been an exciting few weeks. One of her assignments was to be lifted down onto a cliff by helicopter to investigate a crime scene on a ledge where the narrow walkway had fallen, or been helped to fall, down into the canyon below. It was, she told them, definitely a murder. There was an ax buried in the poor victim's skull. But it was a cold case, and she thanked her lucky stars that it was just skeletal remains. She was grateful that she rarely had to deal with victims who had fleshy parts remaining.

She was putting the finishing touches on the Christmas tree when her doorbell rang. She was irritated at the interruption. Her aunt, who was coming to pick her up for

Thanksgiving supper, wasn't due for another two hours, and she still had to get dressed. The very last thing she was in the mood for was a salesman or a talkative lady like the nice elderly soul down the hall. But she plastered a smile on her face and opened the door.

A tall blond man in uniform was standing there with a battered, gaily wrapped box in his hands and an uncomfortable smile on his face. His black eyes were riveted to her face.

"You look different," Gil said hesitantly. "Nice! Just . . . different."

Her heart was going like a steam engine. She could feel her pulse shaking her. "Thanks," she managed. She couldn't look away. It seemed like years since she'd seen him. She fought tears.

"Can I come in?" he asked after a few seconds.

"Oh! Yes, of course . . ."

He came in and she closed the door. She turned around and she was in his arms, being kissed half to death.

CHAPTER 7

Nemara was first shocked, and then completely overwhelmed. It was like having all her dreams come true at once. She reached up and linked her arms around his neck while he kissed her until both had to stop for breath.

"Bert is so lonely," he managed as he picked her up and headed toward the living room.

"Bert has you," she began, caught up in delicious madness.

"He needs a woman's . . . hello." He hesitated near the aquarium. "Wow!"

"Livingston," she said. She smiled shyly. "Only he's a she. I didn't know until I took him to the vet for a checkup when I bought him. I'm superstitious. I didn't want to change the name."

"She'll like Bert," he said, turning his attention to her. "And he'll like her."

She blinked as he carried her to the sofa and placed her on it, following her down without even stopping to take off his coat. "Are you bringing him to visit, then?" she stammered.

His mouth ground down into hers, and she stopped talking and thinking and just gave in to the delicious feel of his body moving on hers, his hands exploring her under her blouse, while her pulse and her breath became quickly audible. Along with the moans.

Which was probably why neither of them heard first the doorbell, then knocking, then a key inserted and a door opening.

A keenly interested elderly face peered over the back of the sofa.

"Okay, now I understand why you weren't expecting me this early," Aunt Vera murmured while they fought to return to some sort of decency with red faces and a lot of throat-clearing.

Aunt Vera was delighted. "You'd be the young man with the other snake, I gather?" she asked Gil, who nodded self-consciously.

"Don't look so shocked. I'm a senator. Nothing embarrasses me. At least, not since a couple of members of my husband's staff were caught in the Oval Office in, shall we say, less than publicly viewable circumstances?" And she grinned.

Gil lost his uneasiness and laughed, too.

Aunt Vera hugged him. "I'm very happy to meet you. Talk to me while my niece gets dressed and you can come over for Thanksgiving dinner, too."

"But I'm not dressed . . ."

"Young man," Vera said gently. "You're dressed in the uniform of your occupation, which is a noble one, if I might say. My husband started life as a deputy sheriff right here in Colorado," she added surprisingly, "I have the highest regard for law enforcement. My own father was police chief in the small Colorado town where I was born. So you have no need to apologize for your clothing. Okay?"

He grinned. "Okay."

Nemara, who was still catching her breath, just beamed.

* * *

They had supper with Aunt Vera and tall, silver-haired Uncle Roger, who traded stories of arrests he'd made with Gil. Some were uproarious.

"I hope we'll see you again," Vera said to Gil, standing with Roger's arm around her as they parted with the couple at the door of Nemara's apartment after they'd driven the younger couple home.

"I have no plans to let her escape again," Gil mused, with a soft, hungry look in his eyes as he smiled down at Nemara.

"Good man." Roger nodded. "Never let a great catch get away. That's exactly how I am when trout fishing season comes."

Vera punched him. "Stop that. Our niece is not a trout."

He made a face at her and then grinned.

"We'll see you again, soon," Vera said after she'd hugged them and Roger had shaken hands with Gil.

She turned as they started to leave. "However, next time I'll hire a brass band to play something noisy before I use my passkey to Nemara's apartment," she added, and wiggled her eyebrows before she walked out, hand in hand, with her husband.

Gil and Nemara could hardly stop laughing.

Inside, they took off their coats and hung them up. Gil retrieved the package he'd left on her coffee table earlier. He sat down beside her on the sofa.

"I bought these two weeks ago," he confessed. "But I had to work up enough nerve to come to Denver." One side of his sensuous mouth pulled down. "Listen, I'm just a lawman. I make a good salary, but . . ."

She put her hand over his mouth. "But nothing. What's in the box?"

He kissed her gently. "Open it."

It was about the size of a ream of paper. She tore off the wrapping and opened the box. Inside was another, smaller, gift-wrapped box. She looked at him, but he only smiled.

There were two more boxes. But in the last one, the smallest, was a jeweler's box, made of polished wood.

She caught her breath. Then she opened it, and tears stung her eyes. She looked at Gil with her whole heart in them.

He shrugged. "It's probably the wrong size, but I remembered that you have small hands, and it can be resized. They can be . . . resized. If you . . . I mean . . ."

She reached up and kissed him while tears rolled down her face. It was all her most secret dreams coming true at once.

Because there, inside the box, was a set of rings. A small, but perfect, diamond in a yellow gold setting, like the cross she wore and never took off or the small gold stud earrings she favored. It was proof of how observant he was. And something more . . . that he loved her. Because no man bought a wedding set unless he meant business.

Three days later, they were married, in church, in Denver, with Aunt Vera and Uncle Roger and half a dozen crime lab employees for witnesses.

Nemara wore a white suit and a perky hat with a lace veil that covered her face. Gil, resplendent in his dark blue suit and paisley tie, lifted it to kiss her.

"Mrs. Gil Barnes," he whispered softly, and love beamed from him.

She smiled under his lips. "Mr. Gil Barnes," she whispered back.

And they were married.

* * *

"I'm sorry," she moaned as they spent their first night together. "About the light, I mean . . ."

"I didn't want it on, either," he confessed. They were in a damp, spent tangle after an hour of energetic celebration of their new married state.

She was still trembling from an excess of passion and abstinence, all mingling in a crescendo of pleasure that had them both moaning.

"If they gave awards for men, I'd buy you one," she murmured as she slid her bare leg against his.

He chuckled. "For what?"

"Well, I'd never . . . you know, and I was a little scared . . ."

He kissed her tenderly. "I hesitate to mention that I read several books before I came up here."

She let out a breath of laughter. "Really?"

"Oh, yes. It's amazing what you can find if you look. My goodness, I had feverish dreams for two weeks before I ran out of excuses and bought a bus ticket here."

She cuddled close to him. "I had feverish dreams, and I didn't read the books."

His big hand smoothed down her bare back. "I'm still having them, I might add," he murmured as he bent to her mouth. "Once is never enough. Didn't they make a movie with a title like that?" he asked as he slid down over her and teased her long legs apart.

"They probably did," she said breathlessly.

He moved against her. "It never is enough," he agreed.

"Oh, definitely! Yes . . . do . . . that!" she gasped as he touched her in a new and even more exciting way.

"The lights are on now," he pointed out.

"I don't care!"

He moved again. She felt him there, right there, becoming part of her. It was fascinating. Frightening, because the pleasure came so quickly this time. She dug her nails into his back and moaned piteously.

"Like this?" he whispered, and moved quickly, impaling her.

"Oh . . . yes!"

And then she didn't say anything else, at least, anything intelligible, for a long time.

They shared a cold drink while they recovered.

"I never thought it would feel so good," she confessed.

He laughed. "That's it, pump up my ego."

She looked up at him with loving eyes. "You're amazing," she told him. "And I love you madly."

The smile left his face. He just looked at her with soft, hungry black eyes. "I love you, too, Nemara," he said gently. "I've never been more lonely in my life than I was when I let you go. I got cold feet," he added with a grimace.

"So did I, so don't feel bad. After all, it worked out very well, don't you think?"

"Well, except that you're used to a champagne lifestyle and I'm on a beer diet," he sighed.

"I'll be living in Benton," she pointed out, "on call for the crime lab. My uncle worked it out. And they're rich, not me," she told him.

"You make it sound so simple."

"It is simple," she said. "We love each other. We'll go live in Benton and our snakes can live together, too. Maybe we'll have baby snakes and baby people eventually."

He pursed his lips. "Will we, now?"

"I can almost guarantee it."

He chuckled. "I don't have a single complaint about that!"

So they lived in Benton and had baby snakes and baby people.

And lived very happily ever after.

RESCUE: RANCHER STYLE

REBECCA ZANETTI

CHAPTER 1

Scarlet and golden leaves lit the trees on both sides of the country road as Tara Webber drove her convertible, singing "American Girl" at the top of her lungs. It had finally stopped raining, and the sun shone down at a perfect temperature for late September.

She had just reached the second chorus of the song when a massive ball of fur jumped across the quiet road. Shrieking, she hit her brakes and spun out, careening off the pavement and sliding into a thick meadow bogged down with mud and weeds. Only locals knew this swampy spot existed. Tourists often pulled off voluntarily here and then got stuck. She came to a stop and tried to collect herself.

Her head rang and she took several deep breaths, prying her fingers off the steering wheel. She was okay. Everything was okay.

A quick glance to the other side of the road confirmed that a huge wolf had leaped in front of her car. He sat looking at her, his head cocked. His eyes were deep gold and his fur a myriad of colors from red to white to black.

Tara shoved open her door and looked down at the muddy mess all around her car. This was a disaster. She knew she shouldn't have worn heels to church today, but they had looked so cute with her yellow dress that she couldn't help herself. "Darn it, Harley," she yelled. "When are you going to stop causing accidents in this town?"

The wolf snorted, turned, and ran between the colorful trees, soon disappearing from view.

She sighed. Now what? She reached into her massive purse and dug around for her cell phone, pulling it out. Nope, no service. That just figured.

She turned to look in the back seat to make sure the two casserole dishes were still intact and covered. They were. She was taking them out to Henry Jones, who had lost his nephew a couple months before and hadn't been to church in a while. He didn't seem to cook much, so she delivered meals to him at least once a week. He lived quite a distance from town on his ranch, and she should have known to bring a pair of boots with her just in case. But she'd been late that morning, as usual, so she'd hurried to church and then figured she'd visit Henry. Now she was stuck in the mud with no phone service while wearing heels.

She kept her door open and looked around for a rock or something to step on. Both sides of the dirt road were filled, right now, with swampy grass, muddy from recent continuous rain. While the trees seemed to enjoy the dampness with their sparkling leaves just starting to fall, the wet grass was an absolute disaster. There were no rocks anywhere near her.

The rumble of a truck down the way caught her attention, and she sat back in the car, wincing. There were only two ranches this far out, and one was owned by Henry Jones. Hopefully Henry had headed to town earlier and was now going home. She cranked her neck to peer around the bend but could only hear a diesel engine. Finally, the truck rounded the turn and her heart sank. It was not Henry Jones. "Oh, man." She was not ready for this.

The truck pulled to a stop in the middle of the road right where Harley had been. The driver's door opened. Greg Simpson stepped out, all six feet four of him. She'd seen him in the back of the church earlier, and she'd smiled a greeting as usual, but other than that, she hadn't gone near her ex.

He'd worn his black boots, dark jeans, and a white button-down shirt to church, and he looked every inch the long and lean cowboy he'd become. Yet the edge was still there in his movements and in his eyes when he flicked them her direction. His time as a soldier had marked him hard, and she was positive she didn't know half of it.

He tipped his Stetson back and walked closer to the edge of the field. "You okay?" His voice was a low rumble that licked across the distance between them.

"I'm fine," she called out, looking around at the muddy swamp.

His grin was a quick flash of teeth and then it was gone. Even so, she blinked. When was the last time she'd seen him smile?

He'd been home for three months to take over the ranch after his brother had died, and she'd seen him around town only a few times. Not once had he smiled. Though she couldn't blame him. Life couldn't be easy at the farm raising three teenagers who'd lost their mother a decade ago and their father this year.

"I'm kind of stuck," she called out.

"I can see that, darlin'." Greg looked down at the mud and then shrugged his shoulders, heading straight for her.

"Wait." She held up both hands. "No, no, no. I—"

He reached her before she could finish the sentence. "You what?"

She had no clue what she was going to say. Instead, she tipped her head back, looking way up into his chiseled face. He'd been handsome in high school, and the years had honed his good looks into raw, animalistic sexiness. There was no other way to describe Greg Simpson.

He reached down and plucked her out of the car as if she weighed absolutely nothing. "Let's get you to the road, and then I'll pull the car out."

She bit back a yelp and settled against his hard chest, trying not to touch him in too many places. His arms were iron bars around her and his torso a solid rock wall of muscle. Considering she had a boyfriend, she shouldn't be noticing how nice he smelled. His scent had always been a combination of the forest and something spicy and masculine.

If he noticed her discomfort, he didn't say anything. Instead, he turned and easily walked back to his truck, opening the passenger side door and placing her on the seat. "This won't take me long," he said.

"I think . . ." She stopped talking. What did she think? She didn't think she could pull the car out herself, and she had no cell service to call anybody. Greg was just being neighborly; there was no doubt he would've helped anybody in this situation. Why did she always feel so awkward around him? Oh, yeah, because he was her first love. She had fallen head over heels for him her junior year of high school, while she'd lived in Casper and he'd lived in Redemption.

She was a cheerleader and he was a football star, and they met up often. He proposed the day after graduation, and she'd been thrilled, eagerly saying yes. Then he'd gone off to the Marines and trained, not coming back for a year.

He'd been a different man then, bruised and battered and with a look in his eyes she couldn't decipher.

Greg tossed his hat across her to land in the seat, showing his military buzz-cut dark hair. "Are you okay? You didn't hit anything when you spun out, did you?"

"No," she said, lost in memories of the time he'd come home.

He'd ended things then, saying he probably was never coming back. She'd been devastated, but she'd started college, where she'd met Brian. Theirs had been a whirlwind romance. Sometimes she wondered whether she'd thrown herself into that relationship so quickly in an effort to banish the ache that Greg had left in her heart.

Yet when Greg had called her, saying he'd made a mistake, she'd been more than ready to break up with Brian. Until Brian told her about the cancer, which he wanted to keep secret so as not to worry his grandfather, who'd been his only relative. Then she just couldn't leave him; instead, she'd married him. She'd loved him, but not with the soul-deep fire she'd had with Greg.

Greg leaned in closer to draw her back to the present. "Are you sure you're okay? Your eyes look off."

"I'm fine," she said. "Just a little shaken up. That stupid wolf ran across the road, and I swerved to avoid hitting him." Even so, she remained lost in that moment with Greg when he'd returned and she'd rejected him.

He'd been furious and had incorrectly assumed that she wanted a cushy life with Brian and his large bank account instead of roughing it with a soldier.

The ass.

Now she jerked herself back to the present. "That darn wolf is a menace."

Greg shook his head. "That beast has caused more accidents than alcohol in this town lately."

"I know," she said, trying really hard not to notice how well he filled out that white button-down shirt. It was a physical impossibility *not* to notice him. She looked in the back seat. "Where are the kids?" All three had been with him at church.

He lifted a shoulder with a tough-guy shrug. "The boys went to a friend's house to watch football film taken by Jack's mom, and Hannah's working at the coffee shop on Sunday afternoons to make a little extra money. So it's just me."

Just Greg Simpson.

"Okay." Tara took a deep breath. For years, she'd tried *not* to think about him. He'd been back in town for nearly three months since his brother had died from a bizarre staph infection after being cut with barbed wire, and she'd avoided him as much as she could. Of course, now she was dating Joe. So it really didn't matter. Did it? "What can I do to help?"

Greg rocked back on those size fourteen boots. "About the car? Nothing." His gaze flicked away and then back, and he shoved his hands in his jeans. "However, I was going to drop by and talk to you later this week anyway. I need a favor."

She stiffened. Obviously, he didn't *want* to ask for a favor. "What can I do to help?"

He looked as if the words were caught in his throat. "How do you feel about coming to court with me on Tuesday? I need a character witness. Somebody who knows both me and the kids. My lawyer says that as a teacher who's taught two of the kids, you'd have sway with the judge."

So his lawyer actually wanted the favor. The entire town was abuzz with news about the custody hearing. His brother's widow, his niece and nephews' stepmom, was suing for the kids and part of the ranch, even though she'd been in their lives for only a couple of years, if that. Sharon had been a mean girl in high school who'd returned to town and somehow charmed Chris Simpson into a marriage that was on the rocks the day it started. "I'd do anything to help those kids," Tara said. This was for them, not for Greg.

"You have a speck of mud on you." He reached out and gently wiped dust off her chin. The pads of his fingers were rough, and the caress sent jolts of electricity through her entire body to land in her abdomen. The slight touch was gone quickly. "Thanks, Tara. You always were a fighter."

CHAPTER 2

Greg looked at the smoldering mess. He tossed the burned remains of chicken casserole in the sink and scratched his head. Wincing, he opened the windows above the sink and tried to fan smoke out of the kitchen. At least the alarm wasn't going off this time.

Lucas, his oldest nephew, sauntered through the door to the garage, where he'd probably been parking his Jeep. He was tall and lanky like his father had been with the same black hair and deep brown eyes. "So, popcorn for dinner again." His hair was wet from a shower he must have taken after football practice.

"No," Greg snapped. "We are *not* having popcorn again."

Jordy appeared behind his brother, his face set in a perpetual scowl. He was built more like Greg, tall and wide with a muscular frame. His hair was a mite lighter than his brother's and his eyes more of a tawny brown, like Greg's. "Why don't we just have Hannah cook dinner? She knows how and she's good at it."

Greg stared down at his youngest nephew. "We're not asking Hannah to cook just because she's the only girl among us. We all should take turns cooking." Why did he have to explain that for the fiftieth time? He'd been clear. They weren't going to take advantage of Hannah just because she could bake decent cookies.

Jordy threw up his hands, showing fresh bruises on his knuckles. "But she likes to cook, man."

"It still isn't fair," Greg returned. How had he gone from battling insurgents to dealing with three teenagers? More important, why was he better at fighting with knives and guns than he was at handling three hurt, lost kids? He'd never had a lot of patience, and he wasn't sure he had much of a heart, but he was doing his best.

Lucas, who was usually the most easygoing of the group, scowled. "I've about had it with this. Why can't we just, I don't know, have somebody come cook for us?"

Greg slowly turned his head and met the kid's eyes, waiting until Lucas swallowed. "If you've got a cache of gold somewhere I don't know about, then by all means pony up," he murmured, keeping his voice light.

Lucas's smile was unwilling, but it was there, nevertheless. The kid had a great sense of humor, and that was the best way to get to him.

Greg hadn't figured out how to get to the other two yet, but he would. At the moment, they were all on edge because of the hearing Tuesday. Sharon Simpson was doing everything within her power to get her hands on half of the ranch so she could sell it to some developer who wanted to create luxury condominiums in the middle of a Wyoming mountain range. Greg owned the other half of the property, so that wasn't going to happen. More important, the woman had signed a prenup.

Greg took a deep breath and opened the freezer. "Frozen pizza?" he asked.

Lucas groaned and Jordy sighed. "Whatever," they said in unison.

Fair enough. Sounded like a yes to him. Greg took the

box out of the freezer and set it on the counter. "Hey, wait a minute. I thought you were supposed to pick up your sister."

Lucas shuffled his feet. "She wasn't there. I swung by the coffee shop and Cami said that Hannah had left with a couple of friends to go grab dinner."

Greg calmly reached for his phone and texted Hannah to find out where she was. She knew to check in with him before she went anywhere. The freshman was pushing boundaries as fast as she could, and he was barely keeping up.

Lucas reached for an apple on the counter and took a big bite. "Bet you're missing those days when you could just stab anybody you didn't like."

The kid had absolutely no idea. "I didn't just stab people," Greg muttered, taking the pizza out of the box. "You all know to check in with me, right?" Twin eye rolls met his statement. He also remembered when younger soldiers were afraid of him. Not these kids—not one of them was afraid of anything. He could remember feeling invincible at their age, but now he knew better.

He glanced at his phone. Hannah had not returned his text. He was actually going to have to ground her. Did he even know how to ground a teenager? What did he take away? Her phone? No, because he needed to know where she was. He could take away TV, but she didn't seem to really care about TV. He was in so far over his head, it wasn't funny. He'd give her five more minutes to text him and then he was going after her.

He slapped the pizza on a round tin and shoved it in the oven. "Jordy, what happened to your knuckles?" he asked without turning around.

Silence met his question. He turned to see both boys just staring at him. He knew Lucas wouldn't give up his brother, and that was something he appreciated. "I ain't going to ask you again."

"Sure you are," Jordy said reasonably. "If not, what are you going to do?"

Irritation clawed down Greg's back. Not because the kid had challenged him, which he understood, but because he didn't have an answer. These kids had lost so much. He was fighting himself when he took anything away from them. In fact, if he had more money, he'd give them everything they wanted. But he had to start thinking like a parent and not a favorite uncle.

So he cleared his throat. "Well, I guess there are two things I would do. The first is I would tell your football coach that you are unavailable for your game next Thursday evening." He waited until Jordy's eyes widened before continuing. "The second thing I would do is start playing nonstop nineties music around this house. Doesn't even matter what time. It'd be all Nirvana, Destiny's Child, and the Foo Fighters."

A very unwilling smile briefly lifted Jordy's lips. "Whatever. I have to write a paper on photosynthesis for some dumb reason." He stomped out of the room, his ears turning red.

"Nicely played," Lucas said, dropping his backpack by the table.

"Thanks." Greg eyed him. "What happened to your brother's knuckles?"

Lucas looked from the empty living room to the kitchen. "He hit a wall a few times."

Greg checked on the pizza. "I know he hit a wall. I've punched a wall or two in my time, Lucas. *Why* did he punch the wall?"

"Don't you think you should ask him that?"

"I just did."

Lucas shuffled his feet. "That's true. All right. Don't say anything, but I guess he and the JV coach got in an argument."

Greg frowned. "About what?"

"No clue. He wouldn't tell me."

That wouldn't do. "I'll talk to him."

"I've got it," Lucas said. "You have enough going on."

Greg cocked his head. "That's okay. I'll figure it out." Relief filled the kid's eyes, and Greg took the punch to the gut. He had no idea what he was doing with these kids. "How was practice for you?" Sometimes he forgot to pay attention to this older kid who seemed to be trying to hold everything together with both hands.

"It was good." Red crept up Lucas's neck to his face. "I mean, I thought it was good. I'm going to start as quarterback next week against Titan."

Greg's chest puffed out. "Yeah, you are. Not bad for a junior. You're just like your dad." Just then his phone rang and he picked it up. "Simpson."

"Hey, Greg, it's Austin McDay."

Everything inside Greg went cold. "Sheriff, what's going on?"

The sheriff cleared his throat. "We had a little bit of a problem out here at our property. Your niece and a couple of boys apparently decided to get drunk behind a shop."

Getting drunk? "I'll be right there." He looked at his nephew. "Finish making dinner." Then he jogged out to his truck, his mind spinning. Hannah was way too young to be trespassing and drinking beer.

The drive took too long, and he still didn't have any idea how to deal with his niece by the time he arrived.

He pulled his truck into the main parking area of the Cattle Club, intrigued once again by the layout of the complex where the town sheriff lived. A sprawling clubhouse loomed in front of him, while sturdy metal shops flanked him on both sides. He was well aware that the Cattle Club men had all sorts of toys, ranging from snowmobiles to utility terrain vehicles to motorcycles, so the shops were no doubt necessary. However, the former soldier in him could see the advantage to the layout. It had been designed specifically as a fortress, in case one was necessary.

He tipped his Stetson back and jumped out of his vehicle. Maybe it hadn't been a good idea to let the kids work out here during the summer. He needed to start thinking like a parent instead of an uncle.

Austin McDay strode out of the clubhouse, wearing dark jeans, a black shirt, and a badge at his waist. His gun was strapped to his thigh. The man was at least six feet five and packed hard. He had a look in his eye that Greg recognized well. Whatever Austin had seen in his life thus far hadn't been pretty.

"Sheriff," he said.

Austin sighed. "I don't know if I'm going to get used to people calling me that."

Greg nodded. "I get it." Their former sheriff had moved to the capital to begin a campaign for the governorship, and the town had voted in Austin almost immediately.

Greg couldn't help but wonder if the Cattle Club men were just trying to keep a handle on things in town. They'd apparently showed up within the last year, purchased about three hundred thousand acres of ranch land, and seemed to be settling in nicely. He wished he could trust them. "Tell me what happened."

Austin ran a broad hand through his thick hair. "I don't know where they got the beer, because they won't tell me. But for some reason they decided to come out here to drink it." He grimaced.

"Kids are idiots," Greg agreed.

Austin shrugged. "I don't know if it was some sort of dare, or if they were looking for the wolf who hangs out around here, or if they thought they could get more booze from the bar."

"My guess is that's it," Greg said. "You don't lock the door. Do you?"

"Sometimes," Austin said. "Most people know not to come out here unless they're invited."

"Kids are stupid," Greg repeated. "We were, too, at one time."

Austin grinned. "Okay. I get it."

"What's your plan, Sheriff?"

"Considering that this is my first minor-in-possession situation, as well as trespassing, I figured we'd scare the hell out of them and let them go. I know your girl is on the volleyball team, and I don't want to hurt her chances of playing. While I don't think the other two are involved in school activities, I don't see any reason to mess them up because of one mistake. But the warning's going to be strong, and they're not going to get a second chance."

"That's fair."

Austin nodded. "Not for nothing, but if she were my kid, I'd keep her away from Roland Kingsley. I know trouble when I see it."

"She was with Roland Kingsley?" Greg asked, his temper stirring. "Isn't that kid a senior?"

"Yeah," Austin said.

All right. Greg had to figure out a way to handle this. He had all three kids in counseling right now, but it didn't seem to be helping. "Let me talk to her." He walked into the main clubhouse to find the three teens sitting on one of the leather couches. Hannah's hair was back in a ponytail, her eyes wide, and she was pale. She had her mom's blue eyes and sandy blond hair, and she looked young and defenseless sitting there. Next to her sat two boys who looked much older, one sneering, one looking upset.

"Let's go, Hannah," he said.

She immediately stood.

"The sheriff isn't going to draw up charges this time. But next time you won't be so lucky," Greg said.

The Kingsley kid rolled his eyes. He was tall and blond with scruff on his chin and very blue eyes.

The other kid didn't move.

"Who are you?" Greg asked.

"Johnny Larrabee," the kid said, his voice shaking. He was tall and lanky with longish brown hair and light brown eyes. His clothes were clean but well worn.

The shaky voice was the appropriate reaction. "What year are you?"

"I'm a freshman, like Hannah."

"Okay, great." Greg gave both boys the same look he would've given a young cadet who'd screwed up. "Stay away from Hannah. Your friendship with her just ended. Tell me you get me."

Johnny swallowed audibly and turned even paler. "I got you."

Even the Kingsley kid drew back. "Yeah, whatever, man. Good enough." He looked at his knees.

"Let's go, Hannah," Greg said. The kid had been through a lot, and he wasn't going to give her a hard time. He should probably buy a parenting book or two, because so far, he wasn't getting any of this right.

CHAPTER 3

Tara sat back in the booth at Sandra's Diner and meticulously organized her brightly colored file folders. Anticipation filled her at thinking about the newest project for her advanced art class. The town of Redemption had a pretty small junior/senior high school. Grades seven through twelve were held in the same building. She mainly taught art, but she also taught creative writing and would end up with kids from all different grades in that class. It was one of her favorite classes.

Sandra bustled by and put more water glasses on the table. "We're packed in here. I may have to seat somebody with you." Her strawberry-blond hair was escaping her ponytail, and a flush brightened her pale skin. "Is Joe coming in?"

"No." Tara and Joe Kingsley had started dating a few months ago, but he was busy at the car dealership and she with school. They were supposed to see a movie together the night before, but he'd begged off, saying he had a lot of work to do. It should probably concern her that she hadn't minded missing the date, but she'd worry about that later.

Sandra stacked the menus. "All right. Be prepared for companions."

"No problem." Redemption was a small town, and most folks were friends. Tara turned back to her lesson plans.

Clothing rustled and a powerful body walked by her, moving into her view. She knew who it was before looking up at his rugged face. The man had presence. "Hi," she said.

"Hi," Greg said, motioning for the three kids to follow him. "What are you doing?" He looked down at the colorful file folders, and a smile tickled his lips.

"Getting ready for a new project," she said, unable to contain her excitement. She looked over at the kids and smiled. "Hey, guys." She'd had Lucas in her class the year before. He was smart and conscientious, although he goofed off a little bit, which she'd found more endearing than annoying. Jordy had attended her creative writing class last year. The kid was incredibly talented. She hoped to see him in the more advanced class either this year or the next.

"Hi, kids," she said.

They all nodded. She hadn't had Hannah in a class yet but probably would next year.

Greg looked around the diner. "We just came in to grab something to eat and discuss the hearing tomorrow." The entire place was full of families preparing for school the next day after having gone school shopping.

She scooted over. "Join me. There's nowhere else to sit."

The kids sat across from her and Greg slid in next to her, taking more than his fair share of the booth. With his wide shoulders, he didn't have much of a choice. For a second, she was transported back more than a decade ago, when he would've naturally rested his arm over her shoulders. She'd forgotten how safe he'd always made her feel.

Greg nudged menus toward the kids. "At least it won't be burned."

Lucas grinned, Jordy snorted, and Hannah continued looking at the table.

"Did you guys get your school shopping done?" Tara asked. Their school had a policy of waiting a few weeks after school was underway before requesting that parents purchase supplies. That gave the teachers and administrators time to see what they really needed for the year.

Again—Lucas nodded, Jordy shrugged, and Hannah looked down at the table.

Greg sighed. "We tried, but the store was out of Kleenex as well as the required notebook paper listed on the supply sheet, so we may have to go into the city tomorrow. As for clothes, I think we got what we needed."

Tara looked at the girl, wondering how she'd fared, shopping with the three men. For shopping, they'd all worn jeans and old T-shirts. Greg's held a Marines logo. She took a sip of her water. "Hannah, what about you? Did you find anything good?"

Hannah shrugged and looked down at her napkin.

That probably meant no.

While Greg and the boys both had brown eyes and dark hair, Hannah had sandy blond hair with her mama's blue eyes. Tara had known Hannah's mother back in high school. Well, Tara had been in junior high, but she remembered Laura Simpson, who'd been kind to everyone.

A blare of motorcycle pipes roared down the street outside, and the boys instantly perked up.

"Oh, man, Sheriff McDay has a new bike," Jordy said, sliding out of the booth. "Can we go look?"

Lucas was on his heels and even Greg was trying to look through the window.

Tara laughed. "Why don't all three of you go look while Hannah and I hang here for a few minutes?"

Greg's gaze caught hers, missing nothing. "Yeah, that sounds good," he said, a hint of gratefulness in his tone. The boys ran out the door with Greg not far behind them.

Tara leaned back. "What's going on, Hannah?" She'd heard about the fiasco the day before when Hannah and her friends had been caught drinking out at Sheriff McDay's clubhouse.

Hannah reached for a napkin and started tearing it apart. "Nothing."

Tara's heart hurt for the girl who had lost so much in such a young life. She remembered what it was like to grow up without a mother. Hers had died of leukemia when she was only ten. "Are you missing the Klosky twins?" If she recalled, Hannah and the two girls had been close, and the twins had moved to Helena recently.

"Yeah," Hannah muttered. "Their dad had to take that job, and they miss it here. I miss them. Volleyball isn't nearly as much fun."

Tara sipped her water. "I'm sorry about that. Can I do anything to cheer you up?"

"Like what?" Hannah snapped.

Tara would start with something easy. "I don't know. Why don't you show me the clothes you bought for school?"

"It's just a couple of T-shirts and some jeans," Hannah said.

"No dresses?"

"Like I'm going to buy dresses with those guys?"

Tara grinned. "That's a good point."

The girl winced and then shifted her weight, her hand going to her stomach.

"Are you all right?"

Hannah's chin firmed. "I'm fine."

"Do you have a stomachache from the alcohol yesterday?" It would be late to have a stomachache at this point. But she had to make sure Hannah didn't need medical help.

"No, I'm fine. I only had one beer," Hannah said. "It didn't even taste good." Then she frowned. "How do you know about that?"

Tara took another drink. "Honey, you live in Redemption, Wyoming. Everybody knows everything."

"Oh." Hannah hunched down, staring at the napkin bits.

She had to cheer the girl up. "But there's one good thing about that."

"What's that?"

"We all grew up here, too. So you need to know that even the grown-ups giving you a hard time were kids once a million years ago. Kids who goofed up like all people do. Even me."

Hannah finally looked at her, her eyes bluer than a summer sky. "Oh yeah, what did you do?"

Tara grinned. "I accidentally drove my dad's car into Motley's Pond."

Hannah's jaw dropped. "You did?"

"Yeah. I was trying to put a different song on the radio, and I stopped paying attention. Then I don't know what happened, but I ended up in the lake. My dad was so mad." It had been Greg who dove in to get her safely out of the vehicle. Even then, he'd been saving people.

Hannah finally smiled. "I can't even imagine driving Greg's truck into the lake."

Tara winced. "Nah, I would recommend against it."

Hannah reached for one of the glasses of water on the table and took a sip, almost hiding a grimace before pressing her hand to her side again.

Tara cocked her head. "Hannah, what's wrong?"

Hannah flushed again and kept her eye on the glass. She took a deep breath. "I mean . . . Well, it's, I, um, started . . ."

Realization smacked Tara hard. "Oh, sweetheart, did you start your period?"

Hannah sighed. "Yes." She cast a look out the window where her brothers and uncle were fawning over what looked like a regular old motorcycle.

"Oh." Sympathy swept through Tara. "You didn't want to tell your uncle?"

Hannah hunched her shoulders. "No."

"Good point. All right. So this is what we're going to do." Tara gathered her belongings and shoved them in her oversized laptop bag, tossed it over her shoulder, and then pulled her huge purse onto her elbow. "Let's go. You're in the sisterhood now." She waited for Hannah to get up and grab her bags.

"Where are we going?"

"This way." Tara put her arm around the girl and walked her from the diner, turning right once they were outside. She motioned to Greg that they'd be back, and he nodded. "So obviously we need to talk here," she said as they walked two blocks to the Outback pharmacy.

Hannah faltered. "I already know what it's all about."

"I know, but you don't *really* know what it's all about," Tara said, walking into the feminine product aisle. "All right. You want these and these and probably during the summer you are going to want these, so we'll get them now." She took out different boxes. "I really like these because they're easy to dispose of. And they don't ruin your underwear."

"Ugh," Hannah groaned.

Tara walked to the other aisle and grabbed a heating pad and then moved to yet another aisle to scoop acetaminophen and ibuprofen into the small basket. "All right. And we need . . . Oh, there it is. This way." She slipped her arm through Hannah's and all but dragged her to the candy aisle. "Pick out three of your favorite chocolates."

Hannah chuckled. "Really?"

"Oh yeah, girlfriend. Get the chocolate."

Hannah picked out three and now her smile was coming more easily.

"There you go," Tara said, going up to the counter.

Hannah stumbled. "Oh, I don't have any . . ."

"No, this is on me. It's the sisterhood," Tara said. She smiled at Mrs. Brinkley, who had to be about eighty-five, if she was a day. "Hey, Mrs. Brinkley, we've got a new member of the sisterhood."

Mrs. Brinkley squinted through her bottle-thick eyeglasses. "Oh, welcome to the sisterhood, sweetheart. These are good ones. They don't rip your undergarments apart."

Tara ran back to the makeup aisle and grabbed colored lip gloss as well as mascara. Hannah was probably a little too young for heavy makeup, but a couple of things wouldn't hurt. "If you feel crappy, sometimes it's nice to add a little color to your face. If you look better, sometimes you feel better." She returned to the counter and dug out her credit card to pay. She looked over at her young charge. "When was the last time you had your hair cut?"

Hannah shrugged. "I don't know. Uncle Greg offered to cut it the other day, but I just couldn't."

Tara gasped, letting her eyes fill with horror until Hannah laughed. "Oh, you will not." She reached for her phone and sent off a quick text. "We're going to go see Louise at her salon, and she's going to give you a nice cut to make you feel better. She'll also welcome you to the sisterhood."

Hannah impulsively leaped forward and pulled Tara in for a big hug. "Thank you."

CHAPTER 4

Greg watched the taillights of Lucas's Jeep disappear down the road before turning back to the diner, where Tara was once again in her booth looking over her materials for the next day. He owed her, whether he liked it or not. The bell jingled when he opened the door and walked inside, but nobody looked up. Everybody was used to that jingle. He slid into the booth across from her. "I'm not sure exactly what happened today, but Hannah looks happier than she has in the three months I've been here."

Tara looked up and her eyes focused. "Oh yeah, she was having a rough one. She started her period and then needed a haircut."

Greg blinked. "Um, well . . ."

"Exactly," Tara said. "You can't *um well* when it comes to this kind of thing. It's normal. It's natural. She needs to know that you're cool."

"I am cool," Greg said. Well, he was cooler with a gun and a knife in his hand a million miles away, but he was doing his best here. "So you . . . took care of things?"

Her eyebrows rose and amusement danced across her face. "Yes, Greg," she said slowly, as if speaking to somebody with a head injury. "We bought sanitary pads, ibuprofen, and candy before getting a good haircut."

"Thank you," he said, relief bursting through him. He hadn't really thought about everything this guardianship would entail, but the kids didn't have anybody else and he was going to make it work. "What do I do now?"

"Nothing about this. You're doing a good job."

He almost kept himself from chuckling. "I'm doing a horrible job. I have one kid who's type A and stressed out, I have another one who's punching walls, and I have a third who's a . . . girl."

Tara's pretty brown eyes softened. "They needed you and you're here. That's what matters." She cleared her throat. "Although you can't let the drinking go with Hannah. Kids need boundaries."

Irritation clawed through him. He didn't like indecision or not knowing what to do. "I can't ground her."

"You can and you should."

"Thanks, but I've got this."

Heat flared in her eyes, but she didn't argue any further. "You also might want to think about inviting the Klosky twins back to stay with Hannah during a long weekend or something. She misses them."

"I'll look at the calendar." He studied Tara's oval-shaped face. It had been well over ten years since they dated, and she was even prettier than she'd been back then. Her hair was a sandy blond and her eyes a stunning clear bronze. "I never really had a chance to talk to you," he said. "But I'm real sorry about Brian. He was a good guy."

"Thank you," she said softly. "He was a good guy. I'm sorry about him, too."

Greg needed to ignore his physical reaction to this woman. Just being near her shot his entire body into over-drive with the need to kiss her. To touch her. "I'm surprised you're working, considering Brian's fortune." While it had hurt that she'd rejected him for Brian, he could understand.

Money did make life easier, and Brian's family had a nice trust fund from years gone by.

Her chin lifted. "You're a moron."

He blinked. With his size and training, not to mention the look in his eye, most people didn't call him names. "You're a brat." The words emerged before he could stop them.

She snorted. Yeah, he remembered that about her. She had a good sense of humor. Curiosity smacked him. He hadn't heard of her dating anybody since. It'd been five years. "Are you seeing anybody?" Not that it mattered to him because he had three teenagers to raise and didn't have time for any woman, much less this one.

"Yeah. Joe Kingsley and I have been dating for a couple of months."

Kingsley had always seemed like a weasel to Greg, but he'd been out of town for a long time. "How's he related to Roland Kingsley?"

"Joe is Roland's uncle. Why?"

"No reason." So the entire family were weasels. Good to know. "Anyway, I'm sorry about Brian."

"Thanks." She tugged a ponytail holder out of her mammoth bag and piled her thick hair up on her head. Several tendrils instantly escaped. She cleared her throat. "About this hearing tomorrow. I'm having somebody sub for me in the morning and then I'll head to work after that. I figured I'll just talk about the kids and how well adjusted they've become with you. And I guess I should talk about school and what good students they are."

"Yes," Greg said. "I'm sure the attorney has questions for you. I just need a character witness. I can't let those kids go."

"I understand," Tara said.

Greg shrugged. "The problem is we have Judge Maloney as our lay magistrate, and he has to be about three thousand years old by now. The man never liked me. I'm worried that Sharon will charm him and he'll do something stupid."

Tara winced. "Yeah, last I heard he wasn't firing on all cylinders, but your brother's will . . . I mean, he gave you custody and also put his half of the ranch in trust. Right?"

"Yeah," Greg said. The will had been concrete and would hold up, as would the prenup. "The problem is if Sharon is awarded the ranch or custody by crazy Maloney, it'll take a while to appeal, and she could do a lot of damage in that time. We are just finishing a contract for the sale of a number of steers, and we need that money for the winter. The contract has an expiration date, and if the ranch gets caught up in litigation, I'm screwed." While he wanted to preserve the ranch, it was more important to keep those kids safe. "So I need to win at the hearing."

"I understand," Tara said. She reached out and patted his hand, sending a jolt of fire up his arm to his chest. Her hand was small and delicate against his. "It'll be okay, Greg."

He hoped so.

The bell jingled behind him, and she looked up, withdrawing her hand. He knew without looking who'd walked in. "Your boyfriend, I take it?"

Tara looked up and heat slowly crept into her face. She wasn't doing anything wrong by sitting with Greg, but still, she felt guilty. It was probably because she'd noticed his hard body more than once. "Hi, Joe," she said.

"Hey," he said, looking down at them both. "I hope I'm not interrupting."

"No, not at all," Greg said, sliding his bulk from the booth. "I was just thanking Tara for her help at the hearing tomorrow."

Joe tugged on his tie. His sandy blond hair was ruffled,

and his blue eyes looked mellow. "No problem. Though, I have to tell you, Sharon was in the shop earlier looking at a new car, and she really does care about those kids. Everyone knows you're headed back to the military as soon as you can, and it'd probably be nice for your brother's kids to have stability at the ranch, even after you leave."

Greg's expression didn't change, and yet tension emanated from him. Tara shifted uneasily in the booth. Both men were tall, but Greg had honed bulk that Joe did not. Joe was long and lean, and he looked professional in his tan Dockers, button-down shirt, and tie.

In his T-shirt and faded jeans, Greg looked more like a muscled panther whose aggression was barely caged. There was no way he would stay in Redemption, so Joe had a point. Greg looked at her. "Tara, I'll see you tomorrow."

Joe shifted his weight. "I don't mean to interfere, but—"

"Then don't," Greg said. "Mind your own business." His phone rang and he instantly pressed it to his ear. "Simpson." His gaze cleared. "Hi, Master Sergeant. Give me a sec so I can get clear to talk." With a curt nod at her, he turned and strode out of the restaurant. The tension slowly dissipated.

Master Sergeant? Oh, there was no doubt Greg was leaving town the second the youngest Simpson graduated in three years. He must've taken an extended leave from the military.

Joe slid across the booth and shook his head. "That guy will never be civilized. I have no idea what he's doing here, trying to raise three kids."

"He's doing his best, Joe," Tara said. "He and his brother were close. He knows those kids, and he is worried about them. Not for nothing, but I wouldn't trust Sharon Simpson as far as I could throw her. She made Chris Simpson miserable." The whole town had watched the fiasco. Poor

Chris had been completely taken in by that witch, until she'd showed her true colors. There was no doubt they would've gotten divorced soon.

Joe shrugged. "No, she didn't. She just had a different image of ranch life than the reality turned out to be. That could have happened to anybody."

"It happened to a woman who took on a family. There are three kids that were affected there." Sharon had always been selfish, even back in high school.

Joe reached over and took Tara's hand. "Let's not fight about this. It's none of our business."

A pang hit her in the heart. It really wasn't any of their business. A million years ago, her only business was Greg Simpson. She'd been so caught up in him and in their romance, she'd even considered postponing college to wait for him and create a home. Maybe he'd done her a favor by dumping her, because she loved teaching, and she couldn't imagine her life without it.

Joe ran his finger across her knuckles. "Are you finally going to come home with me tonight?"

She shifted uneasily in the booth. "No, not tonight."

He sighed heavily. "Come on, Tara. We've been dating for two months."

They'd kind of been dating, going to movies a few times, some lunches, some dinners, but she wasn't ready to trust him to that degree, so she wasn't going home with him. "I don't think so, Joe."

He released her hand and sat back. "I don't understand what your deal is."

"There's no deal," she said. "I'm just not ready to go home with you. I think it's pretty simple." Every time he'd tried to pressure her, it only made her dig her heels in more. She'd been intimate with one man her entire life, and she'd been married to him. She wasn't ready to trust another man to that degree, especially one who had stood her up more than a couple of times. Of course, he'd been working, so she couldn't complain. There were times she got caught up in her work and canceled plans as well.

Sandra bopped by the table. "Oh, hey, Joe. You want something to eat?"

His smile was charming. "Hi, Sandra. I need to finish up some work on my house tonight." He lived in a two-story at the edge of town, and he was remodeling it. "But thanks." He winked at her and slid from the booth. "Tara, I'll catch you later." With that, he turned and walked out of the diner.

Sandra looked around her busy diner and then quickly ducked onto Joe's seat. "Man, my feet are killing me today. I think I need new tennis shoes."

Tara watched Joe disappear down the street.

Sandra followed her gaze. "Was it just me, or was there some tension there?"

Tara took a sip from her water glass. "There's tension. He wants me to go home with him, and I don't know. I'm just not . . ."

Sandra reached out and grabbed her hand. "Don't push yourself for any man. Frankly, I'm not sure about that one."

Tara's eyebrows rose. "Why not?"

Sandra very rarely weighed in on anybody's personal matters. "Oh, I don't know. I've just seen him here having lunch and dinners with different women, and . . . I mean, I don't want to interfere."

"No, you're not. You're a good friend." Sandra had become one of Tara's best friends. "I wish Ella was still here."

"Me too," Sandra said. Ella had married their former sheriff and headed off to the campaign trail for governorship. She'd been a good friend to bounce ideas off. Sandra smoothed out a napkin in front of her. "What's the deal with Greg Simpson and you? I swear, the other kind of tension in this booth made me blush."

Tara rolled her eyes. "Nothing. We dated in high school, got engaged, he joined the military, decided I couldn't handle it, and dumped me. I met Brian and fell in love and moved on. Then Greg came back, all apologetic, and I said no. He accused me of wanting Brian's money. That was the end of it."

Sandra's mouth gaped open. "Okay. That's a lot. We've never talked about Greg Simpson, because I didn't know about the two of you since I didn't grow up here like the rest of you. But there's definitely something still between you."

Tara shook her head. "Nope, nothing. Absolutely nothing." Even though she said the words, her stomach cramped. "He's here until the kids are grown and off to college, and then he's gone. He's going back to the military, and he is never going to settle down."

Sandra's eyebrow lifted. "Are you sure about that?"

"Oh yeah. He was just talking to somebody from his unit," Tara said. "That man's a caged tiger, and he's going to be out of here the second he can. I am not dumb enough to think otherwise."

Sandra nodded. "I did see him earlier having lunch with his attorney and Sammy Jones. There was paperwork spread all over the table."

Tara sighed. "Sammy owns the ranch adjacent to Greg's. Maybe Greg was making plans to lease his land to Sammy once the kids are off to school?" The entire idea saddened her.

"Maybe." Sandra frowned. "What's this about a lot of money?"

Tara chuckled. "There was a trust fund, but we used

every bit of it, and more, for Brian's medical treatments." In the end, the cancer had still won.

"I'm sorry about Brian," Sandra said. "I wish I could've met the guy."

"Me too," Tara said softly. "You would've liked each other."

Somebody called for Sandra, and she sighed. "I need to deliver more food. Let's get a Mahjong game put together later this week. Hallie Logan is back in town, and I thought we could teach her the game now that Ella's off in the big city."

"Sounds perfect," Tara said. Hallie had married one of the Cattle Club men and seemed like a sweetheart.

Tara should probably call Joe later to see if he wanted to meet up for lunch after the court hearing tomorrow. Was she being unfair to him? She didn't think so, but maybe she should make more of an effort to see him. She'd been very reluctant to date again after Brian's death, and only Joe's doggedness had gotten her out of her rut. Yeah, she'd call him tomorrow.

CHAPTER 5

Tara looked composed and lovely on the stand. Not for the first time, Greg had the urge to ruffle her a little. He still remembered what she looked like after being kissed. He shook himself out of it.

He had one job right now, and it was protecting the kids.

Court was held in the second story of the sheriff's brick building. To be more accurate, a conference room took up the entire second floor and was used as a courthouse periodically. For the occasion, folding chairs had been placed on two sides of an aisle, with twin tables up front facing a much larger table, where the judge sat next to a bailiff and a court reporter. Somebody had opened the windows, and a fresh fall breeze blew inside, scattering the dust.

Greg sat at his table at attention and tried not to fidget. After being trapped in a cave a zillion miles away, he didn't like being in enclosed spaces, even after all this time, and yet he didn't have a choice. The kids sat behind him, his lawyer next to him, while Sharon and her lawyer sat at the other table.

Her lawyer wore a fancy navy-blue suit, probably worth three Black Angus steers. His lawyer had come in from the field and still had mud on his cowboy boots.

During the morning the judge had read the will as well

as Sharon's petition. She'd already testified as to how much she loved the kids and wanted to be with them, and Greg had barely kept them from rolling their eyes the entire time.

He had also testified, making sure to reference his brother's will as well as the fact that he always came home for Christmas to see the kids. All three had testified as to what they wanted. It was pretty clear to Greg that he was going to win this thing.

Even so, he gave Tara an encouraging smile. As she finished her testimony, stepping down to walk over and sit by the kids, something inside him settled. He hadn't realized he'd been so on edge until he saw her today. For court, she had worn a pretty pink pencil skirt with a ruffly blouse and little kitten heels that made her legs look long and toned, although she barely reached his chin.

Lucas nudged his shoulder, and Greg leaned over. "What's up, bud?"

"Are we going to win today?" Lucas asked.

"Yeah," Greg said. "Even if we don't, we'll appeal the decision to the circuit court. Judge Maloney is just a lay magistrate." Relief filled the kid's eyes. Greg nodded. "We've got this." Then he turned back around.

Judge Maloney was ancient with weathered, droopy skin, more lines on his face than graph paper, and thick silver hair. He was hunched over, and his gnarled hand shook as he read the legal papers. He cleared his throat. "The court needs a five-minute recess." He smacked the gavel down and then stood, his bones creaking as he did.

"Man, I never want to get old," Jordy muttered from behind Greg.

Sharon stood and stretched her legs, eyeing him. Then she walked toward him. For the hearing, she had worn a tight black skirt with a velvety red sweater that had puffed sleeves. Her heels were at least four inches high. "Greg, can we talk?" she asked, her eyes wide.

Greg stilled. Maybe she wanted to settle this thing? He wasn't going to give her a dime, but it wouldn't hurt to talk to her. "Sure." He stood.

She stepped back as he towered over her. Her shoulder-length hair was platinum blond, and her eyes a guileless blue. Thick mascara caked her lashes, and her scent was of fake roses. Probably something expensive. "Outside?" she asked.

"Sure," he said. "After you." He winked at the nervous looking kids and then let her precede him, following her out of the room and down the stairs to the sunny fall day outside. Main Street was fairly quiet, as most people had taken their kids to school and then gone back to work by now.

She reached in her designer handbag and drew out a vaping pen. "Do you mind?"

"Couldn't care less," he said, scanning the street out of habit.

"Good. I thought maybe we could settle this matter. You know how much I care about the kids."

Uh-huh. Right, she cared about the kids. She'd married their father and then disappeared to Cheyenne to go shopping for months on end. What had his brother been thinking? "I talked to Chris, Sharon. I know things weren't good between you." She hadn't realized ranch life wasn't glamorous, and it didn't pay as much as people thought. It was hard work from dawn to dusk. "So stop trying to trick me. What do you want?"

She fluttered her eyelashes and slid her red-painted nails up his arm. "I thought maybe you and I could talk about this."

"What do you want?" he asked levelly.

She took a big drag from her vape pen. "Fine. I'll settle for a million dollars and drop the case."

He couldn't help himself. He threw back his head and laughed. "Yeah, sure. I've got it in my truck."

"Seriously, Greg. I know how much the ranch is worth. I just need a little something to start my life without my husband. You don't know how hard it's been."

"Right," he said. He'd known terrorists with more emotional depth.

She released his arm and pressed her hand to her hip, jutting out her chest. "Maybe we could reach another agreement."

He dropped all civility and let her see the real him. The one honed on battlefields and in caves a world away from small-town Redemption, Wyoming. She took a step back. "Now you're getting it," he said softly, turning and striding back into the building.

He walked by the boys and patted Hannah on the shoulder before retaking his seat by his lawyer.

"Well?" Mark asked. Mark Grayson was an old country lawyer who spent more time ranching than he did in his law office, but he was sharp.

"Don't ask," Greg muttered.

"That's what I figured."

Sharon clip-clopped back to her seat, and then the judge returned with the bailiff and court reporter.

"Your Honor?" Sharon's lawyer said, standing. The guy had to be about fifty and was packed tight.

"Yeah?" the judge asked.

"I need to call a rebuttal witness to Ms. Webber's testimony."

Greg stiffened, looking over his shoulder at Tara. She blinked and then shook her head as if she had no idea.

"All right," the judge said. "Who are you calling?"

"I'd like to re-call Sharon Simpson," the lawyer said.

Mark objected. "You already called your client."

"Yes," the lawyer said, "but now she needs to rebut some of the evidence portrayed by your witness."

"I'll allow it," the judge said. "But let's speed this along. I've got to get to lunch."

Sharon wrung her hands together as she moved toward the front. The old guy probably didn't see how calculating her eyes were. Then she retook the chair next to him.

"You're still under oath," the judge muttered.

"Yes, Your Honor," she said, crossing her legs and smiling. The judge smiled back, his old jowls moving.

Her lawyer cleared his throat. "Ms. Simpson, as you know, Tara Webber just testified as to how well the three children are doing under Mr. Simpson's care. Did you hear and take note of that?"

"Absolutely," Sharon said. "I love those children, and I just want to help them. Of course I'd take notice. For the record, I think Tara really hates me, which is why she's not telling you the truth, Judge."

The judge stiffened. "Excuse me?"

Sharon's lawyer cleared his throat. "Sharon, please tell the judge what you mean."

"Well, Judge," Sharon said. "I don't know if you've heard about this because you've been out of town, but Hannah was caught drinking, and—"

"Objection!" Mark said, standing.

She stopped speaking and gasped.

The judge sat back. "What's your objection, Counselor?"

Mark seemed to think things through and then paused. "Hold a sec, Judge. Let me talk to my client." For court, he'd worn a button-down shirt, well-worn cowboy boots, and Levi's. He sat and leaned over. "It's hearsay and lack of foundation, but objecting might not make sense. If we fight this, they'll make the sheriff come in and testify, and we'll end up in the same place with the testimony being allowed, because from Austin it wouldn't be hearsay because he was there. I suggest we let it go. What do you say?"

"Fine. Get it over with," Greg said.

Mark stood back up. "Your Honor, we'll stipulate that the young Simpson girl was caught drinking one beer the other day, with a couple of her friends, like we all did in our youth. There's no need to go through testimony."

Sharon cleared her throat. "Also, I've heard that Jordy's having problems at school and has been punching walls."

The judge scratched his head. "Well, that ain't good."

Greg's heart started to sink.

Mark cleared his throat. "We'll stipulate that Jordy has had some problems in football and has punched a wall or two. Judge, I've punched walls. Haven't you?"

The judge reared up. "I most certainly have not."

Just great. Greg remained immobile.

Sharon cleared her throat, looking vulnerable but with a hard glint in her eye.

Her lawyer nodded. "Mrs. Simpson, you mentioned that Tara Webber hates you, which could be why she's testifying against you. Would you go into detail for the judge?"

Sharon looked down and her shoulders trembled.

Greg barely kept from groaning. She wasn't a bad actress, but she wasn't great, either.

Her voice shook. "I've been so sad and lonely, Judge. When Joe Kingsley started paying me attention, I wasn't thinking clearly. We've been having an affair." She clapped her hands over her mouth. "I'm so embarrassed and sorry."

Greg glanced over his shoulder to see all of the color leech from Tara's face. He was going to knock Joe Kingsley's teeth down his throat for hurting her.

Sharon shrugged. "Joe was lonely, too. According to

him, Tara is a cold fish who's just leading him on. We were two lost people who found each other."

The judge reached over and patted her hand. "Don't blame yourself. I've lost a spouse and know how hard it can be."

Lucas sighed heavily behind Greg.

"This does put Mrs. Webber's testimony in a different light." The judge held up his hand as Mark began to rise. "I don't need to hear any more testimony. Even if Mrs. Webber didn't know about the affair, we all know she and Greg Simpson used to date, so she's probably biased anyway."

This courtroom was a sham and a disaster. Greg's jaw hardened until his teeth ached. He'd have to appeal the decision.

The judge shook his head, looking at Greg. "I'm sorry, but I have concerns about a soldier who has no experience raising children, or running a ranch, frankly, being in charge there."

Sharon preened, still on the witness stand.

"Wait a minute," Greg said, standing to his full height. "I grew up on a ranch. I know everything about it, from raising cattle to cutting hay, Judge. You know that."

"You've been away a long time," the judge said, squinting at him across the short distance.

Greg's temper was fraying, so his voice quieted. "You never forget how to ranch. As for the kids, they're mine. They're not going anywhere."

His lawyer groaned next to him.

"Yeah!" Lucas said from behind him.

The judge shook his head. "I don't think you have the right temperament to raise these kids, especially a girl. It'd be one thing if you were married or something, but—"

"Wait!" Hannah said from behind him. She ran around to stand next to Greg.

He gently drew her between him and the lawyer, keeping her covered. He didn't like having her stand closer to the window than he was. It was a bad habit, but one he'd probably never beat. "What's going on?"

Hannah leaned forward. "Judge, you don't understand. He's going to get married."

"He is?" the judge asked.

Greg looked down at her but otherwise didn't move. Where was this kid going with that bizarre statement?

She nodded. "Yeah, you don't understand. They've been keeping it a secret because they didn't want it to look bad with the hearing and all. But I don't think they should keep it a secret from you, Judge. Tara and Greg are totally engaged and planning to get married, and then we're all going to live together."

Greg stiffened. Tara gasped from behind him, but hopefully only he heard.

The judge's face cleared. "Well, that's something." He leaned over. "Tara, you'd be great for these kids. I always hoped you'd find somebody after you lost Brian, and apparently Joe Kingsley is an ass. This is a really good thing. I'm so glad."

Tara stood. "Oh, but, Judge—"

The judge smiled. Yes. Much better. Isn't it nice when life works out? Greg definitely needs a woman's touch in this situation, and you could use a strong man. It has been so difficult seeing you lonely. All right, why don't we do this now?"

"What?" Hannah sputtered.

"Yeah," the judge said. "If you tie the knot now, then we don't have to continue this hearing. Tell you what— Bernice, call the clerk. Get him to sign the documents. I could do this as a lay magistrate, you know? Oh! I've always wanted to officiate at a wedding. I'll issue a temporary order in this case and confirm it in two months if everything is going all right with you two and your charges."

Greg held up one hand. "Whoa, whoa, whoa. Wait a minute, Your Honor."

"No," the judge said. "Let's get this over with."

Holy crap. Greg turned and looked over his shoulder at Tara. "We need a minute, Judge."

CHAPTER 6

"Are you kidding me? Are you really kidding me?" Tara threw her hands up. "This is crazy."

Greg edged closer to the street to keep his body between her and any possible danger. "I know. I just needed a minute to think," he said, appreciating her high color. He'd forgotten how dark her eyes turned when she was irritated. He suddenly remembered trying to identify all the different shades of brown in those stunning irises.

They stood outside the sheriff's office, right where he'd spoken with Sharon earlier.

Mark ambled outside, his Western shirt stretched tight across his torso. He had a rancher's body, skinny legs, barrel chest, and a belly from drinking beer. "This is unexpected," he said, brushing a hand through his silver-gray hair.

"Funny," Greg snapped at his attorney. "What do we do now?"

Mark scratched the white stubble on his chin. "If we go in and say that Hannah's lying, the judge will be angry and say she's out of control, and he'll probably rule in favor of Sharon."

"I can't believe this," Tara said. "Chris and Sharon had a prenup, right? The ranch can't go to her."

"Yeah," Mark said. "They had a prenup, but she's not challenging the prenup from a financial standpoint. She's challenging Greg for custody of the kids. There are no other relatives, and she's saying that he's not fit."

Greg crossed his arms. "Where the kids go, half of the ranch goes. So if she gets the kids, she gets the ranch." He was the guy called in to solve problems in a way others couldn't, but his skills weren't helping here. "She can't win this, can she?"

"No," Mark said. "Ultimately, she can't win this. If the judge rules against us, I'll appeal immediately, but I don't know what happens in the meantime. It's possible the judge could order Sharon back into the house and you out, and then who knows what she'll do with the ranch. I could try to get an expedited hearing, but it still might be a week or two." He winced. "Or months."

"I have a deadline with the PollyDorm corporation for those steers," Greg muttered. "The ranch needs that money to get through the winter. Can I delay this long enough to fulfill my end of the contract?"

Mark shook his head. "No. If the judge decides today, all ranch operations will be frozen as we appeal. You'll lose the contract."

Greg's stomach clenched. "I'm not leaving those kids with Sharon for weeks to months, and I can't risk losing the ranch. It's their heritage."

Mark ground a fist into his forehead and shut his eyes as if in pain. "All right, well, I guess you two could get married."

Tara gasped and stepped away, putting her flush against the brick wall.

Amusement struck Greg. "I'll try not to take that personally."

Her smile looked unwilling. "Seriously?"

Mark shuffled his feet. "Think about it, Tara. You're not

dating anybody now, and this'll show Joe. I mean, the guy cheated on you."

"Hey," Greg said. "Knock it off."

Mark shrugged. "It's true. Marrying you will shove it in Joe's face, and that idiot deserves it."

Tara looked away.

Mark continued. "Greg, you're not dating anybody. What if you got married just for a short time?"

Tara paled. "I am not getting married and then getting divorced. It's not something I want to do."

"Agreed," Greg said, his body flaring to life at the idea of marrying Tara. After breaking things off with her when they'd been so young, he'd realized his mistake but had been too late to repair their relationship when he'd finally gotten back home. She'd been engaged to Brian, so he'd moved on. Many a time through the years, when he'd been in dangerous situations, he'd thought of her. He'd missed her, even though she'd cut out his heart.

The moment he'd come back to town, he'd felt her nearness. Somehow. Everywhere he walked, he remembered her. Now, the idea of actually having her with him out at the ranch made the blood rise to his head and ring in his ears. Only problem was, he didn't have anything to offer a woman right now.

His body didn't care.

Mark cleared his throat. "Just hold a second. You could still get married. You may choose not to consummate the marriage, and we could file for an annulment in two months."

"Two months?" She still avoided Greg's gaze.

He fought himself to keep from taking her chin and forcing her to meet his eyes. He needed to see what she was feeling, and her eyes always gave her emotions away.

Mark nodded. "Yeah, then it's not a divorce. It's just a

legal annulment and the marriage goes away." He looked up at Greg. "Either way, you're going to win this. The question is, do you want to do it today, or do you want to do it in a couple weeks to months? I can't guarantee you when I can get another hearing in the city."

"I could take the kids away from the ranch if she gets it," Greg muttered. "Temporarily."

Mark shook his head. "No. If the judge rules temporary custody to her, you can't take them."

He'd do it anyway.

Mark caught his gaze and frowned. "Don't ruin everything now." He patted Tara on the arm. "You two talk and then tell me what you decide. It's only for two months." He walked back into the sheriff's building.

Tara looked up at Greg. She'd piled up her rich mass of hair with a clip, making her look unapproachable.

He reached out and snagged the clip, allowing her curls to tumble down around her slim shoulders. "Better," he murmured.

She swallowed and her eyes narrowed. "Knock it off." Her stern look was freaking adorable.

"Not sorry," he admitted. If he told her how kissable she looked, she'd probably deck him. "I know I'm not a good bet, but this would be temporary." He'd seen and done things for service and country that no doubt showed in his eyes, no matter how hard he tried to mask his experiences. That probably made him look much different from the boy she'd dated. He didn't even know the kid he'd once been.

She sighed. "I don't think helping Hannah with a lie is the right thing to do. What are we teaching her?"

Greg set his stance. "We're teaching her that we'll fight for her no matter what. She needs that." Deep in his gut, he knew all three of those kids needed it. "It's not fair, Tara. I know it isn't, but I have to ask if you'll do this." He should also ask himself if he was taking advantage of the situation. Just how badly did he want Tara Webber out at his ranch?

"I don't know."

"I can't pay you much," he said.

She took a step back. "Excuse me?"

He grimaced. "I didn't mean that how it sounded."

"Sure you did," she snapped. "I remember how angry you were about my marrying Brian for money."

He'd been hurt and angry, and he'd said unkind things. "I'm sorry about that. It's just, I knew you loved me, yet you still chose him. Money seemed to be the determining factor."

Her nostrils flared. "I chose him because he had cancer and was alone in the world. We used all the money he had to try and save his life."

Now Greg took a step back, his body jolting with shock. He should've known. The raw hurt he'd felt had stopped his brain from processing the clues. Of course, she'd had a better motive than money. Had he just protected himself all these years by purposely not seeing the truth? "Ah, damn, Tara. I'm sorry."

She crossed her arms. "Whatever."

He took a deep breath of the early fall, pine-scented air. Later on, he'd deal with this revelation and what a jerk he'd been. Right now, he had to protect the kids and the ranch. "I know I have no right to even think of asking you for help here, but it's for the kids." Maybe for him, too.

She stared at him for several long moments, and he let her.

He didn't move, he didn't try to cajole her, he didn't do anything but give her space.

"All right," she said. "But we're making it very clear to those kids why we're doing this."

He ignored the fiery bolt of possessiveness that ran through him. "Agreed."

This situation was absolutely insane. Tara sat out on the deck of the Simpson ranch, a glass of wine in front of her and a million sparkling stars above her. It was a cloudless night and the moon shone down, highlighting the entire ranch—all thirty thousand acres of it. She could make out part of the herd in the distance. The mountains rose around them, and she tried to let their peaceful, constant protection relax her.

Nope, not relaxed. A headache throbbed at the base of her skull from the knots in her shoulders.

Greg opened the sliding glass door and walked outside with the bottle and another glass before dropping into the chair across from her. "So," he said.

"Yeah, so," she said. She could not believe that she had just married Greg Simpson. "You know," she murmured, "when we were engaged a million years ago, this was not how I pictured our wedding."

"Me either." He took a sip of the wine.

Unwilling to help herself, she chuckled. "Greg, you know this is nuts, right?"

"Of course it's crazy." He sat back and the material of his T-shirt stretched tight across his muscled chest.

Her mouth watered, and she quickly looked away. How had she forgotten how sexy he was? The years had been both generous and rough on him. He'd been a good-looking kid, but now he had a fierce wildness that would intrigue any woman. She could own up to that. "I wish you'd let me clean the kitchen." It was a disaster, and cleaning relaxed her.

"No. You're not here to work." His voice was flat and his expression immovable.

She sighed. There was no doubt he'd return to the Marines the second Hannah graduated and headed off to college. Tara had to get a grip on herself. Hours after saying, "I do," her lips still tingled from the quick brush of lips he'd given her as a kiss to seal the deal.

Upon arriving at the ranch house, they'd had a family meeting at which Tara explained in great detail that what they were doing was wrong, but forgivable, because they were doing it for the right reasons. The kids hadn't really seemed to care. Lucas seemed amused by the situation, Jordy looked irritated, and Hannah appeared to be absolutely delighted. If Tara didn't know better, she'd think the girl was actually matchmaking.

Greg suddenly stiffened next to her. "Go inside, Tara."

She stilled. "What?"

Three men walked around the deck, and it took her a second to recognize them. One was Sheriff McDay and the other two were twins Zeke and Zachary Snowden, who were part of the mysterious Cattle Club men.

"Hello," she said.

Greg just studied them.

Austin smiled and walked up on the deck, his cowboy boots clunking loudly. "Howdy. We heard you two got married and wanted to come by and express our congratulations."

Greg still didn't move.

The twins followed the sheriff and drew back chairs. All three men dropped into their seats as if they'd been invited.

"What are you doing on my land?" Greg asked, his voice a low rumble.

Tara shivered.

Austin smiled. "You had a downed fence and some of

your heifers moved onto our property, so we brought them back. We're also here to congratulate you."

Greg slightly tilted his head in a way that appeared more threatening than curious. "I'd say the three of you are making the rounds to get the town comfortable with your presence. That's what I'd say."

Zachary smiled. Of the twins, he was the one who seemed the more congenial. "That's fair. We do want the town to be comfortable with us. We showed up out of the middle of nowhere, we bought a huge piece of property, or several rather. We're just trying to make a home here, Simpson. Part of that is helping to take care of our neighbors."

"Ah. Well, if you want to take care of things, Sheriff, then Judge Maloney needs to retire. He's a good man, but it's time," Greg drawled.

"I've heard that," Austin said with a hint of a smile. "We'll definitely have to look into it."

Tara studied the twins. They were both tall with black hair, dark eyes, and various scars. Zachary had one that went from his ear down his throat, while Zeke had two deep white scars across his right temple. Whoever had stabbed him had definitely tried to kill him. So far, Zeke hadn't said a word. She was uncertain she'd ever heard him speak. "Can I get you gentlemen anything to drink?" Manners mattered.

"Thanks, but we brought our own," the sheriff said, pulling a beer out of his pocket and twisting the cap off. He took a deep drink. The twins followed suit.

She couldn't help but smile. "How's Cami, Zachary?" Her voice was sugar sweet.

Zachary lost his smile for a brief moment, but then it returned, full of charm. "I assume Camila is well. We're just friends."

"Your loss," she drawled.

Only a short head nod from Zachary showed he'd even heard her.

Greg took a drink of his wine. "We appreciate you three dropping by, but my new bride and I have some plans to make."

At the word "bride," a jolt of electricity zipped through her body and landed low in her abdomen. Bride. She was actually married to Greg Simpson. For a moment, she couldn't think. She had spent plenty of time visiting the homestead through the years and joining different pot-lucks at the ranch house. It occurred to her then there was no spare bedroom.

Where exactly was she going to sleep?

CHAPTER 7

Greg strode into the house and tore off his shirt, which had been muddied when he'd mucked out one of the stables. After meeting with the Cattle Club guys, he'd needed a few moments with his paint, and the powerful horse had relaxed him, as usual.

The house was quiet with the kids in bed. Tara had fallen asleep on the sofa with a book over her chest, and he studied her for a moment. Her lips were slightly parted, and she breathed evenly. Her mass of curls tumbled around her face, and she looked young and defenseless in her worn T-shirt and yoga pants with fluffy bright blue socks on her small feet.

Not for the first time, he wondered where they'd be if he hadn't broken things off. She'd been more than willing to travel wherever he was stationed, if necessary, but there was no doubt she was a small-town girl. He should've known that she'd sacrifice herself for Brian.

She was so pretty his heart hurt. During the years apart, she'd filled out very nicely. Her skin was smooth and her features fragile. How was he going to let her go?

Not that he had a choice. She wasn't really his to keep. The woman was just doing him a favor, and he needed to remember that fact. No doubt she'd eventually marry some nice, mellow guy who wasn't plagued by nightmares and who didn't have a ranch to run and three lost teenagers to raise. She'd have her own kids.

The thought was like taking the blunt end of a knife to the chest. Something that had actually happened to him.

He moved to the master bedroom that had once belonged to his parents and chucked the shirt into the overflowing dirty clothes hamper. He took a quick shower before drawing on a pair of worn sweats. Finger-combing his wet hair, he walked back into the living room, where Tara had curled up on her side and the book had fallen to the floor. He gently lifted her off the sofa and returned to the master bedroom, where she jolted awake and slapped his chest.

"It's okay," he murmured. "I'm just putting you to bed."

She started to struggle, so he placed her on her feet.

"Wake up, Tara." He put command in his voice and held on to her arms until she'd gained her balance.

She blinked up at him as realization dawned in her pretty brown eyes. "Oh, I must have fallen asleep." She pushed her wild sandy blond hair over her shoulder. "Sorry about that."

"No problem." The bed was large and comfortable behind her, and he made himself look away from it. Just touching her for a moment and having her in his arms had shot intense hunger through him.

She looked around the room, appearing lost and pretty much adorable. "I was figuring I'd sleep on the sofa."

He may have been a soldier for a long time living in dirt and caves, but his mama had definitely taught him better than that. "No, you're taking the master bedroom. I've got the couch."

She looked up, her forehead wrinkling. "You don't fit on the couch, Greg. You're too tall."

He had slept in much worse places. "That's okay. I've got this. You're taking the bedroom." He wasn't going to let her win on this one.

She looked around again, and a light pink filtered up from her neck to cover her face. "I guess we could share?"

"Not a chance," he said.

She frowned and took a step back. "What do you mean 'not a chance'?" Was that hurt in her eyes?

"There is no way I could share that bed and not touch you."

"Oh." Awareness and fire finally lit her eyes. "That's just stupid. I mean, we're not teenagers anymore. Give me a break."

He moved then, almost without conscious thought. Fisting his hand in her T-shirt, he drew her forward and took her mouth in a kiss. The kind he wanted that went deep and hot and nearly consumed them both. With a soft murmur against his mouth, she kissed him back, opening for him. Fire flashed through him, hitting every zone on the way until the blood pounded in his ears.

Forcing himself to release her, he took a step away. "That's why."

He looked at her flushed face and saw both desire and confusion. Her lips were bright pink and slightly swollen from his kiss. "I'm willing to stay," he said. "But it wouldn't be on opposite sides of the bed."

The kiss wasn't fair and he knew it, but they were married. They'd said the vows, and right now, he couldn't find it in himself to care about why. Not with the sexiest woman he'd ever seen standing an inch from his bed. He'd just had a taste of her, and he wanted more. Now.

For the first time, her eyes narrowed. She frowned. "Did you engineer this?"

"No," he said honestly. However, he had taken full advantage of the situation the second Hannah had come up with the idea. Why he'd done so, he didn't even want to answer for himself. It wasn't fair to bring anybody into the shitstorm that his life had become. Even so, with Tara in front of him looking so delectable, he had to make the offer: "Do you want me to stay?"

Desire and need commingled in her eyes, but her delicate jaw firmed. "Absolutely not," she said.

A noise awoke Greg from an uncomfortable sleep on an uncomfortable sofa. He was on his feet immediately, going on instinct, heading for the closet near the front door. Reaching up with one hand, he tapped in the code to unlock the gun safe and pulled out his Glock. He had two shotguns in the kitchen, but he felt better with a Glock in his hand.

The moon shone bright through the open window blinds. As he tried to pinpoint the sound, Tara came to the doorway of the master bedroom and yawned, wiping her eyes. He gave her a hand signal to go back in and get down. She blinked several times and frowned, looking young and adorable.

"Get down," he said.

She just blinked. Another noise came from the other side of the house. Barefoot, still only wearing his sweats, he crossed over and went by the boys' rooms to reach Hannah's. At the door, he listened. There was whispering and giggling. It sounded like something hitting the ground outside. Oh, she was *not* sneaking out.

He immediately pivoted and jogged through the living

room, grabbed a flashlight from the kitchen, and ran out the back sliding glass door. There he moved silently across the deck and down to the grass.

Turning the corner of the house, keeping his gun level, he advanced quickly, and then turned, gun out, flashlight up. Three startled teens met his gaze. The Kingsley kid, the Larrabee kid, and Hannah all stared at him with wide eyes. The Larrabee kid dropped a six-pack of beer and put his hands up. Roland moved slightly behind Hannah.

"What are you doing?" she screamed.

He kept the gun up. "I heard a noise."

Movement rustled behind him, and Tara ran to his side. He didn't look away from the boys. "I told you to stay in your room," he said.

"Greg, put the gun down," she said, reaching for his wrist.

"Back away now," he ordered.

She gulped and stepped to the side.

Hannah moved toward him, obviously not caring about the gun. "Would you put that down? We weren't doing anything."

"Really? It's after midnight on a school night. Define *not anything*." He kept his gaze and his aim on the boys, noting how pale they were. "I could have shot you."

Hannah put her hands on her hips. "Well then, you're not a very good Marine, are you?"

Okay, it was a good point. He wouldn't have shot anybody. "Go inside, Hannah. You too, Tara," he said.

"No," Hannah said, stomping her foot. Tara reached for the girl, and Hannah shoved her. "I said no."

He turned his head then, only his head, and let her gaze meet his. "Get inside now."

Her lower lip trembled, but she threw her hair over her shoulder, lifted her chin, and stomped away.

Tara hovered next to him.

"You too," he said.

With one last look at the frightened boys, she turned and followed Hannah back around the house.

Greg stared at the boys. "At this point, you're trespassing and possibly kidnapping. Do you really want to take this further?"

Johnny Larrabee gulped and looked down at the mud, but Roland stared at him. Not moving, but not nearly as frightened as he should be.

"We were just going to go have some beer," Johnny said, his voice shaking.

Greg shook his head. "This is your last chance. I told you both to stay away from Hannah. I'll be calling your parents tomorrow. If I see you with her again, I will have you arrested and charged with trespassing and kidnapping."

Oh, he knew he couldn't make the kidnapping charge stick, and frankly, probably not the trespassing, either, considering Hannah had no doubt invited these kids.

He stared at the Kingsley boy. "You're a senior and she's a freshman. It's time for you to move on, Roland."

"Whatever. We'll leave her alone." Roland turned away. Obviously, this kid wasn't getting him.

Johnny reached down for the beer.

"No," Greg said. "Leave the beer."

"Okay." Johnny backed away. "Sorry about this. We were just trying to have some fun." Truth be told, he seemed like a decent kid.

"You're in with the wrong crowd, Larrabee. Wake up." Greg made a mental note to call Johnny's parents the next day. If he recalled, they were decent people who ran the farmer's market every weekend during the summer. The boys ran down the driveway, where they no doubt had stashed a car.

Greg lowered the gun and retraced his steps back into the house, where Tara waited on the sofa, still wearing the old T-shirt and yoga pants.

"Where's Hannah?" he asked.

"She went to bed," Tara said. "I don't think the gun was necessary."

Was that an irritated tone? "I used the gun because I didn't know who was out there," Greg said.

"And when you did realize it was just kids?" she asked.

"Go back to bed, Tara."

She stood and faced him, her hair a wild mess and her eyes glittering. "No, we need to talk about this."

"There's nothing to talk about. I handled it the way I wanted to."

She waved a hand in the air. "I'm fine with you going out with a gun and even scaring those kids. But what are you going to do about Hannah?"

That was a great question. "I'll talk to her tomorrow."

Tara shook her head. "Greg, I've worked with kids for years. You have to set some limits."

He was setting every limit he could with his family, and that included Tara. The second they'd arrived at the house, she'd tried to clean the kitchen. Then she'd tried to start laundry. He stopped her every time. She was doing him a big enough favor without having to lift a finger. "I told Hannah she couldn't see the Kingsley kid again."

"Did she listen?"

He shook his head.

"Then you need to do something."

He sighed. "I'm not going to punish a girl who just lost her father." Besides, he had no idea how to ground a girl, what to take away. "I can't take her phone away because I want her to keep it on so I can reach her."

"You need to do something, or she knows she can get away with anything. I like Hannah a lot, but kids need boundaries."

All right. He'd had enough. "Thank you, Tara. I appreciate your helping us and your being here, but you're not her guardian. I am. So go to bed." Even as he said the words, he knew he'd regret them.

CHAPTER 8

Tara worked late the next afternoon preparing her lesson plans for the next two weeks so she could head home early on certain days to avoid the fall storms. Home. After arguing about Hannah the night before, Tara had tried to clean the messy kitchen. Apparently, the boys had gotten up and had late-night snacks.

Greg wouldn't hear of it. In fact, he'd set down a decree that she was to do nothing, including cooking, while she lived at the ranch. She couldn't be home without cooking once in a while. Her back aching, she finished packing up for the day and walked out toward staff parking, catching sight of Hannah in the student lot with Roland Kingsley. Seriously? She marched over to them.

They stood next to an older beat-up Mustang, and Roland was carving his name in the driver's side door before adding Hannah's beneath it.

Tara settled her heavy laptop bag more securely over her shoulder. "Hannah, what are you doing?"

"Nothing," Hannah said. "Volleyball practice was over a half an hour ago."

Tara looked around at the nearly empty lot. "Where's your brother?"

Hannah shrugged. "He's finishing extra weight training

right now. I told him I was getting a ride with you, but now Roland is taking me home."

"I was fairly certain Greg laid it out for you last night," Tara said.

Hannah shrugged. "He's not going to do anything. I mean, last night the big, bad Marine showed up with a gun. Who cares? I could probably have *him* arrested."

Tara looked from one to the other. "You two aren't supposed to be anywhere near each other. You're too old for her, Roland."

Hannah pushed forward. "No, he's not. He's putting my name on his door. That means something."

Yeah, it meant that idiot was fine ruining his car. Tara shook her head. "Greg's not going to like this."

"You're going to tell him?" Hannah asked.

Tara faltered. She didn't want to be a tattletale, and she definitely wanted the girl's trust. But here Hannah was disobeying her uncle less than twelve hours after being caught sneaking out. "No, you're going to tell him."

"No, I'm not," Hannah said, smiling. "Even if I do, he won't do anything about it, and you know it."

Unfortunately, that did seem to be the truth. So Tara smiled. "I have good news for you. Mrs. Balderdodge needs help in the library dusting books right now, and I just volunteered you. Then you can catch a ride home with your brother. I mean, unless you want to discuss being late for your first period today."

She'd smoothed the way so Hannah wouldn't get in trouble earlier, and now she regretted it.

Hannah blew out air. "Whatever. Fine." She stomped back toward the school and jerked the door open, heading inside.

Roland stood and turned around. "You know, you don't need to be involved in any of this. I know it's a fake marriage.

I know you're not her stepmom or even a real aunt. So just back off." His fingers closed into fists.

The kid was about six inches taller and probably fifty pounds heavier than Tara. For the first time, she wondered if he was actually dangerous. So she stepped forward into his face. "That better not be a threat. Is it?"

He paused. "No. No threat." Then insolence once again covered his expression. "But it sure was nice talking to you, Mrs. Webber." He turned and crouched to finish vandalizing his vehicle.

She hurried toward the staff parking lot, shaking her head. She should tell Greg about this, but Hannah had a point. He might threaten Roland, but he wouldn't do anything to discipline Hannah. Tara hopped in her car and drove toward town, taking a right on Main Street after going under the arches that marked the entrance and then parking in front of Sandra's Diner.

It was almost dinnertime, so she dodged inside and found her friend Cami already sitting at a booth. "Hey, I didn't think you could make it," Tara said.

Cami sipped water. "Yeah. I needed a break and Mrs. Thomas came into the bank. So I told her she had to work for a while. She didn't like it."

Tara laughed. "Doesn't Mrs. Thomas own the bank?"

Cami flushed and smiled. "Yeah, she does. But you know, every once in a while she should come to work. Especially now that Ella is gone."

"I agree," Tara said. She studied her friend, who had long black hair and soft brown eyes. "How are you feeling?"

Cami lifted a shoulder. "About the same. The morning sickness is a little much and I'm tired, but you know, first trimester problems."

Tara shook her head. "I'm here for you if you need anything. Have you told Zachary yet?"

"No, not yet. I'm waiting until first trimester's over because that's when most things go wrong. If I survive this trimester, then yeah, I'm going to talk to him." Cami picked at a napkin.

Tara sighed. "I'm sorry you're going through this." Cami and Zachary had gone out for a while, but it wasn't serious for him, while their relationship had been very serious for Cami. Apparently, a condom had broken one time, and Zachary had panicked and ended things. Afterward, Cami discovered she was pregnant.

"I'm here for you, no matter what. You know that, right?"

Cami smiled. "Yeah, I know. Even if Zachary is not involved, the dumbass, I'm excited about this baby. A little nervous. But I don't know. Kind of excited." Her smile softened. She glanced at her watch. "Ugh. I can't stay for dinner. I need to get to the coffee shop."

Tara leaned back. "You're working too hard." The woman worked every day from five to eight at the coffee shop, eight to five at the bank, and then another five to eight at night at the shop. She was trying to save up enough money to buy the whole shop from her partner, who wanted to retire.

"I'm fine," Cami said. "I just need a little rest. Right now, I'm going to go push coffee on people who should have tea, and then I'll go home."

"Sounds good," Tara said, her gaze catching on the man in the back booth. "He's here, again?"

"Oh yeah," Cami said, eyebrows rising. "Ask Sandra about it." She scooted from the booth and stopped at the counter to say something to Sandra before heading out.

Sandra hurried over with a Diet Coke. "Are you eating tonight?"

"Yeah, I'm starving. What do you have?" Tara's stomach growled.

"Special's veggie lasagna."

"Perfect," Tara said, nodding toward Ford in the far booth facing them. "Does he pretty much live here now or what?"

Sandra frowned. "He's around a lot. Ever since the robbery last month, he's here every night. He comes in right around dinnertime, eats dinner, and then works on his laptop until I close. It's like he's appointed himself the guardian of the diner."

More like the guardian of Sandra, but Tara didn't say so. "That's sweet. Has he asked you out or anything?"

"No," Sandra said. "He hasn't made any sort of move. He just comes in and eats."

Three weeks ago, two bank robbers had moved through town, and they'd tried to rob the diner. Sandra had shot at them but didn't hit anybody.

"I heard they caught those guys up in Colorado," Tara mused.

"Oh yeah. All three are dead," Sandra said. "I should be sad or whatever, but I'm not. They kidnapped another woman and were killed during her rescue. We don't have to worry about them coming back here."

Relief filtered through Tara. "Good. For now, you seem to have a bodyguard."

"Or a statue, I'm not sure," Sandra said. "I'll put in your dinner order."

"Thanks." Tara took out her phone and sent off texts to friends in her book club. She'd forgotten to print off the questions and was hoping somebody else would do it for next Wednesday night. She still had time, but she'd probably forget—she had too much going on. The door jingled, but she didn't turn around.

Suddenly, Joe Kingsley was in her space and then sliding into the booth across from her, his cologne thick between them. "What the hell, Tara?"

She'd been avoiding this confrontation but forced herself to stare at him. "Ask Sharon Simpson."

He blew out air, looking handsome as ever, with his sandy blond hair askew and his tie slightly off center. "I can't believe you went and married Simpson just because I got together with Sharon. Are you nuts?"

"I didn't marry Simpson because you got together with Sharon. I married him because I wanted to," she said. "You should have told me you were seeing Sharon. You were cheating on me."

He threw up his hands. "How could I have been cheating on you? You and I never got together."

"We may not have had sex, but we kissed and we were dating," she said. "You know you cheated on me."

"Then you should have been there for me," he retorted, his brows drawing down. "It's your fault that you were all prude, and it's not like we were engaged or anything."

All of a sudden he didn't look so handsome anymore. She was glad her eyes had been opened. "I think you should probably leave, Joe."

"I'm not going anywhere," he said.

A hand descended on Tara's neck, curling around her nape. Heat rushed through her entire body. She knew who it was without looking.

"I believe *my wife* asked you to leave," Greg Simpson said.

How'd he come into the diner without even ringing the bell? The man moved as silently as death. She shivered and not just from surprise. Some of it was fascination that sped up her heart rate as well as her breathing.

Joe looked up. "I'm not . . ." And he stopped. Whatever he saw in Greg's eyes had him gulping. "Fine. She is your wife." Rolling his eyes, he scooted from the booth and then made a wide berth around Greg to get out the door. This time it did jingle.

"You okay?" Greg asked.

"I'm fine," she said.

Releasing her nape, he moved around and sat facing her, taking up most of the other side of the booth. "It looks like we have a dinner date." His smile was charming with the hint of a wolf.

CHAPTER 9

The weeks settled into a routine in which the kids went to school and practice, Greg worked the ranch, while Tara taught at school. He still wouldn't let her help around the house, and it was driving her crazy. He said he felt like he'd imposed enough.

He also hadn't kissed her again since that first time, and she found herself not only wondering why, but hoping that he would, which was ridiculous because she knew their marriage was temporary. She had to get her head on straight. She was fantasizing about domestic bliss when reality would come crushing down in a month; she'd be back home alone while Greg would be with the kids, figuring out their lives.

In fact, he'd taken two more mysterious calls from whoever the Master Sergeant was, excusing himself each time to leave the room. He was definitely returning to the military.

Hannah had mostly stayed out of trouble for the past week, although Tara had seen her talking to Roland Kingsley at school. Well, they couldn't exactly make her stop talking to people.

Lucas had been fantastic, working on his grades, playing football, and doing his best. Nonetheless, she was worried about him. He seemed to be tightly wound, and she wondered when the explosion would come.

Jordy was as sullen as ever, and even though she tried to talk to him daily, he didn't want anything to do with her, and frankly didn't want anything to do with Greg. All he did was go to school and practice with the junior varsity and not talk much. The counseling wasn't working very quickly for the kids, but possibly that was normal.

Today was Monday, and it had been a rough one. The kids had all overslept, and she and Greg had had to rush to get them to the school. Devastating storms were hitting the ranches hard, and Greg was working from dawn to dusk in horrible weather, but he wouldn't let Tara help.

She left school right before supper to see that the storm outside had gotten much worse. The clouds were black and the rain and hail devastating. She yelped and ran to her car, jumping inside and watching golf ball–size hail hit the windshield. Her phone buzzed with a text from Greg: STAY IN TOWN UNTIL THE STORM IS OVER. I'LL COME GET YOU IN AN HOUR.

So he could help her, but she couldn't do the same? She'd been driving in Wyoming weather her whole life. He had no right to tell her what to do.

She started the car and carefully drove out of the lot. It wasn't the worst storm she'd driven through. It was slow going for a while, but she kept her car on the road and soon reached the ranch house.

The rigs were in the drive, so apparently football practice had been canceled, which wasn't a surprise. She walked inside to find the kitchen blown apart. Every once in a while Jordy decided to cook, and apparently this was one of those times. Spilled salt, chunks of mango, and burned pots and pans littered the counters. A half-finished soda was on its side, spilling its contents across the counter and down the cupboard to create a sticky pool on the tiled floor. She sighed.

Greg walked in from the garage, shaking water and hail out of his thick hair. He took one look at her. "What are you doing here?"

She paused. "For now, I live here."

"I told you to stay at school until the storm passed."

Her chin lifted as her temper stirred. "It would seem I don't take orders from you, Simpson."

His eyes darkened and she almost gulped. Instead, she held her ground.

Greg took one look at the kitchen and bellowed for the kids to make an appearance. Now.

Lucas hurried out of his room. "What? I was doing my homework."

Jordy more slowly emerged from his with a bowl of cereal in his hand. "What?" His knuckles were bruised and battered yet again.

Hannah finally lolled from her room, holding a physics textbook. "What?"

Greg looked at all three. "Who made the mess in the kitchen?"

None of them answered.

He waited.

Tara started to move to the kitchen, and he held up one finger. "You stay there."

She paused, surprised.

"I'm not going to ask again," Greg said.

Jordy rolled his eyes. "I did. I cooked. I made something. There's probably extra in the fridge."

One of Greg's eyebrows rose. "Were you going to clean up your mess?"

Jordy flushed and gestured toward Tara. "No, she'll do it. She doesn't do anything else around here."

Lucas's mouth dropped open and Hannah gasped.

Greg remained still and then pointed at Jordy. "You, outside."

Jordy didn't move.

Greg's expression didn't change and his voice didn't rise, but when he quietly added the word "now," all three kids jumped and so did Tara.

Warning shot through her, and her body went on full alert. "Greg, I—" His dark gaze moved to her, and the words dried up in her throat. She couldn't speak.

"Don't even think of cleaning up that mess," he said quietly.

She gulped.

His gaze flicked to the other two kids. "You either."

Lucas nodded and Hannah held her book closer to her chest.

Jordy stomped out the back door to the deck and Greg followed him, sliding it closed. Then darkness swallowed them both.

The storm had cleared, leaving clouds wafting across the sky. The wind continued to whistle eerily, pushing them away to reveal a crescent moon.

Greg drove the UTV with Jordy in the passenger seat, arms crossed, staring solemnly out the window. He drove past the two closest barns and turned left toward the summer field, where they'd pasture the cows for another month or so.

"Where are we going?" Jordy finally asked, not looking at him.

"I want to check on the bottle-fed calves," Greg said. He had reunited the bottle-fed calves with the main herd a couple days ago, but sometimes they didn't assimilate very well. After the storm, he wanted to see how they were doing. "Didn't you name a couple of them?" he asked.

"Yeah. George and Lula," Jordy said, his body relaxing a little in the seat.

That's right. George's mama had died calving, and Lula's mom was an old heifer who wouldn't take her. So Greg and the kids had bottle-fed them until just last week.

Greg increased the power of the headlights to see the road through the pasture better. He knew where the cows were, but he was going to take the long way so he could talk to Jordy. Another storm wasn't forecast until the morning, so they had time.

"Your coach called," Greg said.

Jordy stiffened. "So?"

"He wants to start you tomorrow with the varsity team."

Jordy shrugged. "Yeah, but he wants me to play defense."

"That's because you're an excellent nose guard. You have a chance to start in a varsity game. Why wouldn't you?"

Jordy just looked out the window.

Greg sighed. "Listen, I'm done with this. Done with you punching walls, done with the bruised knuckles, done with you hating football."

"I don't hate football," Jordy said, jerking toward him.

Greg slowed down as a cow rambled in front of them. "Then what's your problem?"

"I want to play quarterback."

"Because your brother does?" Greg asked.

Jordy hunched his shoulders. "No. Because my dad did."

Realization smacked Greg hard in the head. His chest ached. "That's what this is all about?"

Jordy turned back to the wide pasture outside.

All right, there had to be a way to get through to this kid.

Greg looked ahead at where the herd was milling around. The moon illuminated the entire pasture now. The temperature was supposed to drop, so he had figured the cloud cover would soon drift away, and he'd been right. They needed a night without hail and lightning and thunder. It still hurt to talk about his brother; he couldn't imagine the pain Jordy was in right now. But they had to keep moving forward. "Listen, bud. Your dad played quarterback, but that's not who he was on the team."

Jordy rubbed his bruised knuckles. "What do you mean?"

"Your dad was the heart of our team. Always. I was a sophomore and he was a senior and yes, he was the quarterback. But his role was to look out for the whole team. He was a great leader." Greg's throat clogged. God, he missed his brother.

Jordy pushed his hair out of his eyes. "He loved being quarterback."

"No, he loved being *on a team*," Greg corrected. "It was important to him. He would've played any position in a heartbeat. He just happened to have an arm like a bullet."

It had been something to watch Chris play. He'd gone on to play in college before coming back to the ranch and starting a family. A family that was now Greg's to protect.

Jordy flexed his hand and looked at his bruised knuckles.

Greg looked out at the pasture, noting the two calves that he was looking for. He'd recognize them anywhere. They were hanging out with the other cows, and that was all he wanted to see. He didn't even need to get out of the UTV.

"I remember one time we were playing Titan, and I was

starting as nose guard. Chris was quarterback, and I had something else on my mind."

"Like what?" Jordy asked.

"A girl. She went to a different school. Her name was Julie."

Jordy snorted. "You lost your concentration over a girl?"

"Heck yeah, I did," Greg said.

"Was this before Tara?" Jordy asked quietly.

Greg nodded, his chest aching even more. "Yeah. Anyway, I was struggling to concentrate during the game. I came off the field, and your dad grabbed my helmet, smacked it into his, and started yelling at me."

Jordy gasped. "My dad yelled at you?"

"Oh yeah," Greg said, chuckling. "Not only that, he clipped me on the side of the head, and he said the team needed me. That I had to decide whether I wanted to play football for this team, or if I wanted to go do something else and worry and whine by myself. Told me right then and there to choose either the team or myself."

"That sounds like my dad," Jordy whispered.

Greg swallowed over a lump in his throat. "Yeah. It hit me then that it was the team, that I had a role to play, and I wasn't doing it. It took my big brother smacking me on the head."

"I'd love to see film on that," Jordy snorted.

"That could be arranged." Greg eyed a couple of large cows in the distance. "Then Chris leaned in and said, 'I know you're angry. You've been angry. Show the other team how angry you are,' and then he pushed me, releasing my helmet."

Jordy resettled his seat belt. "What happened after that?"

Greg grinned, the memory now a good one. "Well, it

was fourth down. They had the ball, and I sacked that quarterback so hard he lost it. We picked it up and scored."

"Yeah?" Jordy asked.

"Yeah. And you know who was the happiest person on the field?"

"My dad?"

Greg slowed down and then turned around on the narrow road. "Definitely, your dad. My big brother."

Jordy studied him for several long moments. "I guess I forgot."

"Forgot what?" Greg asked.

"That you lost him, too. He was your big brother and now he's gone." Jordy wiped at his eyes. "I can't imagine losing my big brother."

Greg jerked as if hit, allowing the pain to spread throughout his torso. "I miss him, Jordy. I know you do, too."

"I really do. I'm sorry I've been difficult and not part of the team."

"You're doing your best, bud. I know it, but I could use a little more team-first mentality." Greg flashed him a grin.

Jordy nodded. "Yeah, I get that." He was quiet until they'd almost reached the house, and then he cleared his throat. "Um, maybe you should let Tara be part of the team, too."

Greg shot him a look. "What do you mean?"

"At school she's always doing something or helping somebody and is always busy."

That was the entire point. "Yeah, exactly," Greg said. "I figured she should rest when she's at home. I don't want her to feel obligated to pick up after us or cook or anything."

"Yeah, but that's not her. You're kind of, I don't know, squelching her."

Greg cut the engine, the hair on his nape prickling. "I'm squelching her?"

"Yeah. She likes to be busy, and she likes to do a lot of stuff. But you're not letting her. Maybe you should let her be her and also be part of the team. Just a thought."

CHAPTER 10

Hannah Simpson snuggled under the Redemption Wolf fleece blanket next to Tara, as she had the last few weeks. Attending the football games as a family had become a tradition, and she wondered if maybe Tara was going to stick around. Sometimes she looked at Uncle Greg with a softness in her eyes that had to be love. Other times she looked at him like she wanted to throttle him.

So it was hard to tell.

Hannah turned back to the game and winced as Jordy tore through the offensive line of the other team and sacked the quarterback for the third time. The crowd roared, and Tara yelled wildly next to her. Greg sat on the other side of Tara eating popcorn, his gaze intent on the game.

Hannah cleared her throat. "I'm going to go sit with my friends for a while—is that okay?"

Tara patted her leg. "Sure, sure. Is everything okay?"

"Yeah," Hannah said. "I just want to see my friends. Also, you're kind of loud." She'd had no idea the quiet school-teacher could get this rowdy. It was kind of funny, but also her right ear was hurting. She could only take so much yelling.

Tara jolted. "You know, I've heard that before, but I

don't think it's true. I'm not too loud, am I?" She looked over at Greg.

"You're definitely exuberant," Greg said, his voice calm. His gaze remained on the field.

"Huh," Tara said. "Interesting."

Hannah patted her arm. "I'll see you after the game." Her ear was still ringing. She jogged down the bleachers and ran to the students' section, waving at her friend Carly.

"Hey, Hannah," Roland called out. She turned to see Roland Kingsley sitting on a brick wall near the row of outhouses.

Excitement ran through her veins. She turned and jogged down the stairs and across the weeds to reach him. The smell of popcorn, hot dogs, and dirt wafted around her.

"What are you doing here?" she asked.

"Just having fun." He held up a coolie cup.

She could smell the beer from where she was standing. "Roland, you're going to get in trouble if you're drinking at a football game. Remember when they suspended Monty Jones?"

"Yeah, I was there," Roland said. "Monty and I are friends, remember?"

Oh yeah, she had forgotten they were good friends.

"Why don't you stop being a pain and have some?" He held out the cup.

"No, thanks." She really wasn't in the mood for beer. Plus, Greg would smell it on her for sure. "I don't know why you like it. I think it's gross."

He hopped down from the wall and stood way above her. "In that case . . ." He was probably the best-looking boy in high school. He had thick blond hair and light blue eyes and a wide chest. He'd probably make a good football player if he ever gave the sport a chance.

"Have you been watching the game?" she asked as people milled around them, headed for the outhouses.

"Not really. Football's stupid."

"Don't let my brothers hear you say that."

He pulled out a wrinkled paper baggy. "Like I care what your brothers think," he muttered. "If you don't want beer, do you want one of these?"

She looked down at the gummies. She'd never tried one, and now wasn't a good time to start. "Um, no, thanks."

His gaze softened, and he ran a finger down her face.

Sometimes he was so sweet, she just didn't know what to think.

"You sure look pretty tonight, Hannah," he said.

Heat rose up her face, burning her cheeks. She wanted to be cool and act like it was no big deal, but she couldn't help smiling wide. "Thanks."

He'd called her pretty before, and each time she loved it. But his eyes were a little glassy.

"How much have you had to drink?" If Greg saw him like this, she'd never get to see Roland again.

He tugged on her ear as if they were boyfriend and girlfriend. "Have you decided? Are you going to come to Denver with me?"

The idea was thrilling and a little scary. "I wish. There's no way Greg will let me go to Denver with you."

"Then we'll just go. Aren't you tired of being told what to do? You don't even know that guy."

She kicked a rock out of the way. "Yeah, I do. He's my uncle."

"Right. He's a guy who came home once every other year for Christmas."

She shuffled her feet. "Well, yeah, I guess so."

Roland leaned in and kissed her forehead and then slid an arm over her shoulders. A couple of senior girls walked by and glared. Hannah snuggled into his side, her heart soaring. He was actually acting like they were dating. She'd been dreaming of this forever.

He leaned in again and kissed her temple. "You know you won't get in trouble if you come to Denver for the weekend. I mean he'll be mad, and he'll probably yell at me, but he won't do anything to you."

That was probably true. Even so, she was kind of liking it at home with both Greg and Tara there. Even Jordy seemed better after he and Greg had checked on the bottle-fed calves to make sure that they'd become part of the herd. When they'd returned, they'd cleaned the kitchen together and had joked the entire time. She hadn't heard Jordy laugh in way too long.

The crowd roared as Lucas threw fifty yards for a touchdown. She wished she was back with Tara and Greg celebrating, but this was pretty great, too.

"Come on," Roland said. "It's not every day that I ask my girlfriend to go to Denver for a weekend. I promise it won't take long. We'll just go, meet up with my friends, including Monty. You remember? He's been living there since he got kicked out of school last year. He's also dating a really cool chick."

Johnny Larrabee walked over from the concession stand, chewing on red licorice. He looked at Roland's arm over her shoulder. "Hi, guys, what's up?"

Roland leaned in and nuzzled her ear, giving her butterflies in her stomach. "We're just talking about the Denver trip."

She shivered and smiled. The idea was awesome, even if it couldn't happen.

Johnny was tall and cute with shaggy brown hair. Sometimes she wondered if he liked her, but then he wouldn't talk to her for a while. She didn't know if he was shy or just thought she was dumb.

He frowned. "You can't take her to Denver. She's a freshman and her uncle will kill you."

"Yeah, whatever," Roland said. "I'm not scared of that jerk."

"Then you're a moron," Johnny said. "He probably knows about fifty ways to kill a guy and not get caught."

Hannah looked beyond Johnny to see Greg at the edge of the bleachers. He was staring at her.

Her stomach dropped, squashing all the butterflies. "Um, I have to go." She pushed away from Roland. The last thing she wanted was for Greg to make some sort of scene. Well, she knew he wouldn't make a scene, but he might threaten Roland again, and she didn't need that. She ran toward Greg and then climbed the bleachers. "Are you looking for me?"

"Yeah, I was," he said, still watching Roland across the distance. "Come back and sit with us. I told you to stay away from that kid."

"I know, but he's actually a nice guy if you get to know him." But even as she said it, she was surprised to realize she actually wanted to go back and watch the game with Tara and Greg. Then she remembered that Roland Kingsley had called her his girlfriend. She giggled. It was a good night.

Roland Kingsley retook his seat on the old brick wall and watched as the Marine eyed him and then disappeared around the corner with Hannah. Roland wasn't a guy who got angry, but he was definitely a guy who got revenge, and Hannah's uncle deserved it.

Johnny watched them go. The kid had it bad for Hannah, that was for sure. "Do you really like her?"

Roland rolled his eyes. "Sure. She's pretty."

Johnny turned back to face him, his eyes dark. "She's more than that. She's smart and funny, and I know you're seeing other girls, but she doesn't. I think she's too young for you."

Roland snorted. "But the right age for you? You're pathetic." The kid lived next door in the trailer park with his parents, and he was lucky Roland had taken an interest in being his friend.

"Whatever." Johnny shoved his hands in his pockets and strode away, no doubt looking for somebody throwing away half a burger or something.

Roland tugged his phone free of his pocket and dialed a number.

"Yo," Monty said by way of answer.

"Hey, bud, everything going as planned?" Roland reached in his pocket for another gummy. He could use some mellowing out.

"Hey, buddy," Monty said. "Yeah, if you're not full of it."

Roland chewed thoughtfully. "Nope. I've got the girl, though I kind of like her."

Monty snorted. "Well, keep her or bring her. I told you that we can make some serious money."

"I need serious money," Roland said. Plus, he'd love to stick it to that arrogant Greg Simpson. Who was he to pull a gun on Roland? "Are you sure you got the connections?"

"Definitely," Monty said. "Are you sure she's a virgin?"

"Absolutely," Roland said. "I can promise you that." It didn't surprise him that Monty had connections to people who would pay top dollar for a virgin, although it all seemed unreal. Was he really going to do this? "Are you sure there's enough money involved?" He would need it to stay off Greg Simpson's radar for a while.

"I'm positive," Monty said. "I know a guy, and we'd make a lot of money, but you're the one taking the risk; so make sure you're good with it."

Roland took a drink of his beer and thought the matter through. "Do you know somebody who could get us fake IDs so we could lie low for a little while?"

"Of course," Monty said. "I've lived in Denver for two years. I know everybody."

Everybody who was a criminal probably, but then again, Roland couldn't talk. His mom had just gotten out of jail, and he'd never met his dad. His family was living in the trailer park on the other side of town, and he was tired of it. His uncle was the only guy in their family who had any coin, and he was stingy. Roland wanted money, and now he knew how to get it.

He took another gummy. "All right. I'll bring the merchandise to Denver next weekend. We'll leave here on Thursday. Okay?"

Monty laughed, and the sound was grating. "That's fine. Just don't sample the goods on the way." He clicked off.

Roland chuckled and shoved his old phone back in his pocket. First thing he'd buy was one of those new smartphones with the good cameras.

He looked over at a group of girls vaping near the gymnasium and then jumped off the fence to saunter in their direction. There had to be somebody who'd be up for a party tonight.

CHAPTER 11

Tara and Greg took the kids for pizza after the team won the game. Tara was enjoying the small family and pushed aside the knowledge that she wouldn't be with them much longer.

She'd miss all of them.

Greg then sent the kids home and met Tara at Piney's Pub; she'd driven to the game after work, and they had two cars. At the pub, adult celebrations were in full force. The place had been built at the turn of the twentieth century and still had the original hand-carved wooden bar and floor. The rest of the building had been updated with cedar log walls, glass shelves for alcohol, and a very modern sound system. Tall tables were placed throughout, with several pool tables and dart boards at the far end. To the right, a dance floor on a raised dais was packed on this busy Friday night. The whole town usually turned out for football games, and when the high school won, everybody celebrated.

The heat from the crowd washed over Tara as she walked inside with Greg behind her, his hand firm at the back of her waist. She was getting accustomed to being around him, but that would only lead to heartbreak and she knew it. He'd just finished a phone call with somebody from his unit before joining her outside. But despite the warning voice in her head, she enjoyed these moments.

Cami and Sandra caught her eye from across the bar and waved.

She moved through the crowd, saying hi to many people on the way, and reached the four-top the girls had secured. "Howdy. Nice table." It was difficult to get one on game night.

"Hi." Sandra's eyes were bright, and she had what looked like a margarita in front of her.

"Good game," Cami said, sipping what appeared to be club soda with a lime slice.

Greg leaned down to her ear. "I'll hit the bar, what would you like?"

The heat from his breath shot through her entire body, and it took her a second to answer. "Just a soda. I'm not drinking."

"All right, I'll be back in a minute." He turned and moved through the crowd, his big body easily parting people.

Sandra grinned. "What is going on with you two anyway? I mean, besides being married and all that."

Tara shook her head. "I don't know. It's weird. Sometimes I feel like we're making this whole odd situation work. Then other times I remember that he'll be gone the second Hannah turns eighteen. I don't want to get caught up in his family and then end up alone again."

Losing Brian had nearly destroyed her, and she didn't want to go through that again. Tara looked around at the busy bar, spotting Ford at a far corner with a couple of the Cattle Club men. "Is your bodyguard still on duty, Sandra?"

Sandra shrugged. "I don't know. Maybe they're out for a good time, but he sure seems close." He was seated in a darkened corner, so it was difficult to see if he was looking at them.

Tara squinted but just couldn't determine Ford's focus. Maybe the guy was out just having a drink with buddies. "Have you ever asked him what he's doing?"

"Yeah. He says he is eating dinner at the diner." Sandra frowned. "He's really quite the mystery. But I have to be honest—I do feel safer when he's around."

Cami snorted. "That's a guy who has a wolf for a pet. You might want to rethink your idea of safe."

Tara chuckled. "You've got a point." She scanned the room again. "I take it Zachary is nowhere to be found, Cami?" He'd always seemed like a good guy to Tara, at least the few times she'd met him, so maybe Cami should tell him the truth sooner rather than later.

"No," Cami said. "I don't think he leaves the ranch much. He does like his parties out there, though, doesn't he?" Frowning, she took another big drink of her club soda.

Tara was bumped from behind and almost spilled Cami's drink. She turned to see a collared shirt with a tie. "Oh. Hi, Joe."

Joe looked her over head to toe. "It's good to see you out and having fun."

Just then, Sharon Simpson moved up from behind him. She slid beneath his arm and placed a hand over his flat abdomen, her fingernails a screaming red. "Well, hey, Tara. How's wedded bliss?" Sarcasm coated the woman's tone.

Tara swallowed.

"Here's your soda." Greg placed a soda and a longneck beer bottle on the table, almost casually stepping behind Tara and pulling her up against his body with his arm an iron band across her abdomen. He dropped a kiss to her head.

Her body did a slow roll and shiver while heat flashed

through her veins. She swallowed. The possessive stance was all Greg, and her body wanted to relax back into him as if she belonged right there.

"Wedded bliss is great," he said calmly, resting his chin on Tara's head. "Any other questions, Sharon?"

Sharon's eyes spat fire. "You know I'm going to appeal the judge's decision, don't you?"

"Sure," Greg said. "You're going to lose, but feel free. I have the time and money to deal with it. Do you?"

Joe edged slightly away from Sharon and pulled his arm free. "Tara? Can we talk? I mean, just for a few minutes, maybe outside."

"No," Greg answered before Tara could.

She jolted, but his arm around her ribs kept her right in place and flush against the hard angles of his body. She could feel every ripped muscle, and her breathing turned shallow. Her thighs trembled and her knees weakened.

Smoothly, he turned her, grasped her hand, and started to move toward the dance floor. "We're going to dance."

She nearly tripped as she followed him, but she regained her balance as he swung her into his arms. "What are you doing?" she asked, trying to ignore the heated desire rushing through her.

"Dancing." He pulled her close, set one hand across her entire lower back, and snuggled her into him. "Just relax."

Relax? The guy was sex on a stick—how was she supposed to relax? The heat from his body warmed her right through, and she turned her head, listening to his heart. They moved together as if they'd been doing so for years. The slow song ended, and she looked back at him. "This is mad."

"I know." Then his mouth took hers. Slower this time, more gentle. As if he was seeking, looking for something, or maybe just trying to tempt her.

So she returned his kiss, letting fire rush through her. The kiss turned carnal, and then he slowly pulled away. Heat flared into her cheeks. She had forgotten they were on the dance floor.

He simply stared at her, his dark eyes appraising. His phone buzzed. Keeping her close, he reached into his back pocket and pulled it free. "Just in case it's the kids." He read the screen. "Oh, I've got to take this." His thumb slid across to accept the call. "Hey, Master Sergeant, what's up?"

Tara blinked and started to step away. He'd already talked to the man earlier. Maybe he was going back sooner rather than later.

He listened for a moment and then nodded. "All right, give me a second." Retaking her hand, he led her back to the table. "This is going to take a while. You should head home before it gets too late. But if a storm comes, stay in town until I come get you. Got it?" Without waiting for an answer, he turned and quickly strode out of the bar.

"Whew," Cami said. "What was that about?"

"Reality," Tara said. "Somebody from the Marines just called." Her heart sank. Her body was still alive for him, but this was a good dose of cold water over her silly daydreams. Greg Simpson was always going to choose the military over Redemption or even her.

He had never hidden that fact.

Hours after Greg had deserted her at the pub, Tara stifled a yawn and pushed her empty glass away. "All right, I need to be getting home."

Thunder ripped the world outside as lightning zapped. She turned and peered over her shoulder. It was after midnight, and the bar had pretty much cleared out, so she could easily see outside.

Cami followed her gaze. "That's a pretty bad storm. The hail will be next. Why don't you come stay with me tonight?" Sandra had already gone home with her bodyguard on her heels.

"No. I can make it out to the ranch. I've driven that road a million times, and I haven't had anything alcoholic to drink tonight. I'm fine." She glanced down at her phone; Greg had texted earlier, reminding her to let him know if she was staying in town or if he needed to come get her. It was after midnight and the guy was probably asleep, so no way was she calling him.

She could stay with Cami, but she wanted to celebrate with the kids in the morning. After each football game they made a big breakfast together the next day. "I'll be fine. Why don't I give you a ride up to your place?"

Cami shook her head. "No, it's only a few blocks away, and I don't mind the walk."

"Too bad," Tara said. "It's raining and it's dark out and you're pregnant. Get in my car."

Cami rolled her eyes. "You are so bossy. I see why you became a teacher."

Tara led the way out of the bar. "I became a teacher because I love kids and I love art." She grinned. "Though it's kind of fun to be bossy sometimes, too."

They ran through the rain to her car, ducking inside. "Whew. This is a storm," Cami said, wiping off her face. "Thanks for the ride."

Lightning zipped down close by and lit the entire area. The smell of ozone filled the car.

"You bet." Tara drove Cami the several blocks to where she lived above the coffee shop and waited until she ran inside and shut the door before making a U-turn and heading toward the archway out of town. Hail barraged the car, and she flipped on her windshield wipers. Visibility wasn't good, so she drove slowly out of town, around several bends, and through meadows and tree stands until she reached the old road that led to several farms. Her car was slipping in the mud by this time, so she white-knuckled it, leaning forward to see better.

Oh, this was not good. She should've stayed in town.

Thunder rolled high and loud, and she jumped. Her car began to skid in the mud. She clutched the wheel and tapped the brakes, trying to pull out of the spin. Her stomach lurched as she spun right off the road into a marshy, muddy area.

Silence descended for a second, and then the rain beat against the windshield with harsh splats. Lightning zipped again, and she looked around, seeing there was no way she was getting out of this meadow with her car.

"Oh, man." This marsh was different from the one she'd driven into a month or so ago, but the mud was just as thick and the weeds as rough.

She swallowed and reached for her phone. Unlike last time, this area had cell service. "Thank goodness." She considered calling the twenty-four-hour hotline maintained by Mac's Garage in town, but she didn't feel right asking Mac to pick her up. Taking a deep breath, she dialed a different number.

"Hey, are you staying at Cami's?" Greg answered.

"Um. Not so much," she murmured.

Silence ticked by for a moment. "Clarify that statement."

Tara wiped rain away from her chin; her hair was still dripping from the mad dash to the car. "Um, I may have spun off the road near the third oak down the dirt road."

"You drove?" His voice had lowered several octaves, and it was already low.

She winced at his tone. "Yeah. Could you come get me?

I'll call Mac in the morning to pull out the car. I can start walking to meet you."

"I swear to God, Tara, if you take one step out of that car, you will not sit for the next two weeks. Got me?" His voice was all command.

She gulped. "Um. Yes. Gotcha." She didn't want to get out of the car, truth be told. She'd be up to her knees in mud. "Though I don't appreciate the threat."

"Then keep your butt in the car until I get there," he snapped. The line went dead.

CHAPTER 12

Greg was known in his unit for keeping calm under any situation. But as he drove too fast down the muddy country road, his temper was fighting everything he had to get out. When he saw Tara's small car in the meadow just mere feet from a stand of dogwood trees, his ears started to heat. She could've been seriously hurt. And why? Because she was determined to show him her independence?

He stopped his truck on the road and jumped out, letting the rain smash against him and cool him. He'd purposely left his cowboy hat back home.

The mud came up past his ankles as he picked a path between the road and her car. She was already opening the door. With quick, deft movements, he pulled her out, reached for her purse, and turned around, trying to shield her from the pelting rain.

"Um, I . . ."

"Not a word," he said. She fell silent.

He gently put her in the passenger side of the truck and shut the door calmly before walking around and getting in the driver's seat. "I'll retrieve your car tomorrow when the storm has passed," he said, flicking on the headlights. The rain was beating so hard, it was difficult to see anything, but he knew the road by heart, so he went slow and steady.

"I'm sorry about this," Tara said.

Irritation clawed down him. "Sorry about what?" He cut her a look and then turned his attention back to the road.

She frowned and flattened her hands on her jeans. "Sorry that . . ."

"What?"

She audibly swallowed. "Sorry you had to come get me in the storm. I know you were probably asleep."

"Wrong answer, Tara. Try again."

She held her hands up to the blowing heater. "I don't know what you're asking."

Did he really have to spell it out? "You should be sorry you put yourself in danger. You should be sorry you disobeyed a clear order."

At his statement, her head snapped up, and her slightly damp hair flew back. "Order? Obey?"

"Yes," he said through gritted teeth. "I'm done. I'm done with trying to play the nice family guy. Things aren't working. I finally have Jordy figured out, but Lucas is still off, Hannah doesn't listen, and now you've put yourself in danger doing exactly what I told you *not* to do? We're done with this mild-mannered approach. It's over. Things are going back to the way they should be."

She pulled back. "What does that mean?"

"It means what I say goes. I'm the head of this family. I'm the one holding it all together, and my word is law. Tell me you understand me." Hearing her scared voice earlier had been like ice shooting through his veins.

The woman snorted. She actually snorted. "Your word is law? Oh, buddy. You're not in the Marines anymore, or at least you're not right now."

"I'm well aware of that," he said. "That doesn't change the fact that things are going to change around here. The first thing that's going to change is you're not going to put yourself in danger. Tell me you get me." He was responsible for her, and she could've been seriously injured if she'd hit that stand of trees.

He'd meant what he'd said earlier. He had no problem enforcing her safety with a good swat to the butt.

Oh, he did not. Tara barely kept her temper in check as they pulled into the driveway at the ranch house. The rain continued to beat down on them with an occasional barrage of medium-sized hail, but she didn't care. She jumped out of the truck.

"Hold on a second." He cut the engine and stretched out. "I have an umbrella."

"I don't need your umbrella," she yelled back, turning and striding toward the house. "You're an arrogant jackass, Greg Simpson."

He caught up to her in a second. "What the heck's your problem?"

She whirled on him, not caring that she was getting drenched. "You're my problem. You don't tell anybody your plans and now you go around bossing everybody around. I don't think so." She poked him in the chest as hard as she could. "I'm not one of your soldiers."

He grabbed her wrist before she could poke him again, his hold firm but gentle. "I didn't think you were one of my soldiers. For one thing, you would've obeyed if you had been one of my men." Outside lights from the garage lit the area, highlighting the sharp angles and deep planes of his rugged face. Anger glowed in his eyes, and it appeared as if steam rose from the rain hitting his body. "But you know what? When it comes to safety, you are going to listen to me from now on."

She couldn't help it. She just couldn't help it. She smacked him right in the chest.

He lifted one eyebrow. "That all you got?"

She curled her fingers into a fist. "I am not a violent person," she snapped, "but you bring me close."

"That's it." He grabbed her shoulders and pulled her in for a kiss. His mouth was hard and demanding, and he bent her back to take her lips. Lust rode through her on the heels of her anger, and she grabbed his wet T-shirt with both hands, kissing him back. Finally, she wrenched her mouth away, panting heavily. The last weeks had been lonely without touching him. Part of her wanted to smack him again, and the other part wanted to kiss him.

"Let's go inside," he said.

Tara put both hands on his chest. "No, we're going to talk this out now." Lightning zipped and illuminated the nearest field.

"You don't learn." He ducked his head and tossed her easily over his shoulder, clamping a hand on her thigh to hold her in place. His long strides ate up the path to the door as the thunder rolled high above them. He kicked it open and walked inside, unerringly headed straight to the master bedroom. One quick motion and Greg dumped her on her back on the bed. She started to sit up.

"Stay down. I'm not done talking to you yet," he said.

Oh, that was it. That was just plain it. Using a move she'd learned long ago, she swept out with her feet and nailed him right behind the knee. He was supposed to go down completely. Instead, he went down on one knee, manacled her ankles, and yanked her toward him. She yelped and then struggled to sit up. Even though he was on his knee, he was still taller than she was sitting on the bed.

"Are you about done being a brat?" he asked.

"If I'm not?" she returned, balancing herself with her hands on the thick comforter.

His head tilted just enough to be threatening. "Oh, baby. You want to stop pushing me now."

She remembered his bossy side well. Even in high school he'd commanded any room he entered, and she'd kind of liked it. Not in an everyday sense, but more like when it was time to kiss. She'd forgotten how well he could kiss. "I'm not afraid of you," she murmured, sliding her hands up his chest.

"That's a good thing. Although you might want to at least be cautious." He levered himself up and sat, pulling her around to straddle him. Then he tunneled both hands through her thick hair, holding her face in place. "I'm not kidding about the danger, Tara. We live in wild country, and a lot of things can go wrong. I need you to try to be safe."

His gaze was intense and his words soft. But the body bracketing her was harder than steel.

Desire made it difficult to speak. "I thought I was being safe earlier. The storm was worse than I realized." His powerful legs warmed her thighs, forcing her to clear her throat to concentrate. "And you're not the boss."

His eyes darkened and something unidentifiable glittered in them. "I am while you're here. Period." He took her mouth again, hard and deep.

She was tired of living alone and tired of not taking chances. Worse yet, she was tired of thinking that life had passed her by. She kissed him back, giving him everything she couldn't put into words.

He pulled away, his expression harsh with desire. "You sure?"

"Yes," she said on a breath, kissing him. They were married, and she wanted it to be real. Even if he had to leave. She'd wait for him this time.

He returned the kiss, holding her in place, taking his time. When he finally released her, she could barely breathe. He made the whole world disappear in a way that seemed impossible. It was amazing. Her lips tingled.

He stared at her—big, broad, and solid.

He rolled them on the bed until he covered her. Then he kissed her deeper and stronger than ever before. The man was hot and he was wild and he was all Greg. Nobody in the world could kiss like Greg Simpson.

Fire swept through her, and she felt more alive than ever. His pull was irresistible, and she was done fighting it. Finally, she had what she wanted and what she needed. She should have known that he'd be the same Greg in the bedroom as out, wild and sexy, demanding and bossy.

He was hot and fierce and now . . . all hers.

CHAPTER 13

Tara handed the rest of her veggie burger to Jordy and sat back, completely stuffed. He sat to her left in the booth with Greg and Lucas across from them. Hannah sat at the head on a wooden chair adorned with lovely hand-stitched cushions.

Sandra had outdone herself on Sunday night dinner with the veggie burger special. Tara might never be able to eat again.

Greg had finished his and had moved on to eating the rest of Hannah's fries while Lucas sipped a strawberry milkshake and Jordy munched happily on onion rings. They looked like any family out for a Sunday night dinner, and Tara couldn't have been happier. She was still a little off-center after her weekend with Greg. Was there a chance they could make it work with her at home and him back with his unit?

She'd been in love with the boy he'd been at seventeen and was even more in love with the man he was now. She wondered if a part of her should feel guilty about finding somebody else to love after losing Brian, but she knew that Brian would have wanted her to be happy.

Did Greg love her? She knew he cared about her, but was that enough?

He reached for more of Hannah's fries, and the girl slapped him. "Knock it off," Hannah said.

Greg looked up and a grin tugged at the side of his mouth. "You said you were done."

"Yeah, well, I changed my mind." Hannah snorted and took another fry.

Tara's friend Laura Jones emerged from a table in the back, tugging a sparkly blue purse over her shoulder. She paused. "It looks like you guys took advantage of the veggie burger special."

"They were delicious," Tara said. "How about you?"

Laura looked toward the back booth. "Oh yeah, we definitely did. The boys ate two each." Laura taught ninth grade history at the school and had four sons, aged eight to fourteen. Her husband was one of the ranch hands out at the big McKelvey Ranch far north of town.

Greg partially stood. "How are you doing, Laura?"

"Oh, sit down, Greg. It's good to see you. I was only two years older than you in high school, you know."

Greg smiled. "I know. It wasn't that long ago."

Laura sighed. "You know, sometimes it feels like it was." There were small streaks of gray in her thick brown hair, and her blue eyes sparkled as always. She was tall at almost six feet and had always been athletic, running marathons for fun. She leaned over and patted Hannah on the shoulder. "I hope you're feeling better."

Hannah coughed on a fry.

Tara frowned and patted her back. "Are you okay?"

"Yep. Yep. I'm feeling much better," Hannah said, taking a big gulp of her water.

"Oh, good," Laura said. "I'm so glad. You can retake the test on Tuesday if you want. I have time right after school and before you have volleyball."

Red burst across Hannah's face.

Greg cocked one eyebrow. "Makeup test?"

Laura looked from him to Tara and then frowned. "Well, yeah. You all had the flu, didn't you?"

Greg narrowed his gaze at Hannah. "Care to explain, kid?"

Hannah shifted uncomfortably in her seat.

Tara looked up at Laura. "I don't understand. She wasn't in class?"

"No," Laura said. "There was a note at the front desk from, well, you Greg, saying that she had the flu and that the boys were probably coming down with it."

"Interesting," Greg said. "I hadn't realized I wrote a note."

Hannah stared down at her food.

Laura winced and took a step back, amusement barely tilting her lips. "Well then, I'll let you all talk." She winked at Tara behind Hannah's head, her eyes sparkling. "I'll see you later." With that, she motioned for her family to get moving, and they soon exited the diner.

The booth was silent. Jordy and Lucas both eyed their sister and then went back to attacking their onion rings.

Greg looked at Hannah. "Where were you Friday morning?"

The girl shifted her shoulders, looking cute in a pink T-shirt and white jeans with her mass of hair in a ponytail.

"I'm not going to ask you again, Hannah."

Hannah looked up at Tara as if seeking support.

Tara just patted her hand. "You need to tell the truth."

Hannah crossed her arms. "Fine. I wasn't ready for the test, so I went and got some coffee in town for the first two periods."

"First two periods?" Tara asked.

"Fine, all day," Hannah said.

Greg shifted his weight in the large booth. "You need to quit lying to me, and you need to do it right now." His voice was soft, but a thread of steel went through it. He sure did have that Marine command thing down.

Tara wanted to help the girl, but they also needed to hear where she had been. "You were gone all day, Hannah. Where were you?"

"Nowhere, really," the girl burst out. "I went to get some coffee and then stayed there for quite a few hours. After a couple of cups, I went to the bookstore. Later on, I just went and hung out."

"With whom?" Greg asked.

Hannah didn't answer.

Tara took a sip of her soda. "Were you with Roland Kingsley?"

"What if I was?" Hannah said, looking up. "I wasn't doing anything wrong."

Greg set his napkin down. "Except for skipping school, forging a note, and then going off on your own without telling us. You mean besides doing that, Hannah?"

She glared at her uncle. "Yeah, besides doing that, Greg."

Lucas drew in a sharp breath, and Jordy looked from one to the other, wincing.

"Were you with Roland Kingsley or not?" Greg asked.

"Yeah, I was. We had coffee and we did go to the bookstore to find a book I wanted, and then we hung out at his place, just watching movies."

Greg had an intimidating way of not moving at all. It probably had something to do with his training. "Were you drinking?" he asked.

"No, I wasn't drinking. I don't drink, except for that one time I tried beer and didn't like it," Hannah said, crossing her arms.

"Was he drinking?"

The girl pressed her lips tightly together.

"That's what I figured. What else happened?" Greg asked.

"Nothing," Hannah muttered. "I mean, he kissed me, but that's all, I swear."

Greg didn't change outwardly, but something shifted.

Even Tara's breath heated in her chest. "Okay, so maybe we should talk about this once we get home," she murmured.

"No," Greg said, holding out his hand to his niece. "Give me your phone."

Hannah's jaw dropped. Even the boys looked surprised. "What?" Hannah said.

"Your phone, now," Greg said.

Mumbling, Hannah drew it out of her purse and slapped it onto his palm. "Now you won't be able to get hold of me."

"Sure I will," Greg said. "Considering I'll be taking you to school and picking you up for the next two weeks. You're home, you're at volleyball, or you're at school. That's it. You're grounded."

Shock filled Hannah's eyes. Even Tara jolted. "Grounded?" Hannah sputtered.

"Yeah," Greg said. "I've tried to take the gentle approach with you. I've tried to be the fun uncle. But when you put yourself in danger, like going to that idiot's trailer in the middle of the day, by yourself, when he's drinking? I'm over it. Your freedom just ended."

Hannah whirled on Tara, facing her. "Don't you have anything to say? You're part of this family now, too, aren't you?"

Tara gulped.

Hannah looked toward Greg. "I mean, right? She is? You're married and you're sleeping together, so, I mean, she has to weigh in, doesn't she? Or are you just the dictator of the house?"

Tara barely bit back a smile, because dictator of the house really did seem to fit. "Honey, I—"

"No," Greg said. "She's right. I've asked you to stay. We're married, and you have every right to weigh in on this. What do you think?"

Hannah looked hopefully at Tara.

Tara reached for her hand and sighed. "I think Greg's right." She would have backed him no matter what, because they needed to present a united front to deal with the three teenagers. "You did put yourself in danger, possibly, and that's terrifying to me. We need to know where you are, and if something had happened, we wouldn't have known."

Hannah jerked her hand away. "You two just don't get it. I will never forgive you for this."

Amusement lit Greg's eyes for the briefest of seconds, and Tara caught it. Fond memories played through her mind. She remembered having the same conversation with her father when she got caught sneaking out with Greg, of all people. "It'll be okay, Hannah," she murmured. "I promise."

Greg walked into the ranch house, noting how much it felt like home these days. Hannah stomped off to her room and slammed the door while Jordy followed a little more slowly, saying, "I've got a test tomorrow, got to study." His door shut much more quietly.

Tara looked up at Greg. "Since you still won't let me help out around here, I'm going to sit on the deck and make lesson plans." Lifting her head, she strode through the living room and outside.

Lucas faltered by his doorway and then paused. "You know Hannah's not that bad, right?"

Greg nodded. "I think Hannah's fine."

"You just grounded her for two weeks."

"I'm well aware. She deserved to be grounded, don't you think?" Greg asked.

Lucas hesitated and then shrugged, turning and shutting his door. Greg stared at the doorway for several moments. Something was off, but he couldn't place it. Going on instinct, he walked across the living room and then knocked.

"What?" Lucas called.

Greg figured that was an invitation to open, so he did. He found Lucas standing by the window, looking outside. "What's going on with you?"

Lucas shook his head. "Nothing."

"I'm not leaving until you tell me."

Lucas turned and fury burned in his eyes. For a second he looked so much like his dad that Greg could only stare. "Get the fuck out of my room! I don't need you telling me what to do right now."

Greg paused. "This is new," he muttered. "What's going on, Lucas?"

"I'm done with the counseling. I'm not going to counseling anymore. And you can't make me."

Actually, Greg could make him, but instead he leaned against the door frame. "Why not?"

"Because I don't want to. I'm tired of talking about feelings. I'm tired of waiting for everything to go wrong. I'm just tired of holding everything together." He looked like a kid again. Greg remembered Lucas as a youngster, exhausted after opening Christmas presents all morning. Lucas had only been three, but he'd been dedicated even then.

Greg needed to know what was wrong so he could find the right words to help. "What are you holding together?"

"Everything," Lucas said, throwing his arms out. "At

least I'm expecting to, the minute you leave. All of this is my problem. So when Hannah gets in trouble or Jordy gets in trouble, I'll have to handle everything."

Shock kept Greg immobile for a minute. "I really do need to learn to communicate better." Maybe he was the one who should attend counseling. He'd forced the kids to go and perhaps he should have set a better example. "I'm not good at talking about feelings and all that kind of thing."

"No kidding," Lucas said. "What's your point?" He seemed to calm down.

Greg shook his head. "I should have told you. I've never been clear with any of you, though that certainly wasn't by design. I just figured if you saw I was here, then you'd know I was here."

Lucas frowned. "Huh?"

Yeah, Greg really did suck at this. "Let me try again. I'm not leaving no matter what you guys do, no matter what kind of trouble you get in. No matter what we have to deal with, we're going to do it as a family. I am not leaving."

Lucas swallowed, looking much younger than his sixteen and a half years for a moment. "You're not going back to the Marines?"

"No," Greg said. "I should have explained it better. I'm home for good. All three of you are going to college, but you'll have a place to come back to when you're done, and for every vacation and every summer. This is your home. I'm your home now."

"And so is Tara?" Lucas asked.

"I don't know about that yet," Greg said, being honest with his nephew. "If you want to come back here and ranch, you can. If you want to do something else and live on the ranch, you can. Your world is wide open, Lucas. But this is your home, and it will always be here, and so will I."

The kid shocked him when he rushed across the room and hit him hard in a hug. When had his nephew gotten so tall and so strong? Greg hugged him back, holding him tight. "I've got you, bud. I really do." And he did.

CHAPTER 14

It had been four days without her phone, and Hannah was pretty much dying. She walked outside after volleyball practice, wishing she could text everybody she knew right now. There was a big volleyball tournament this coming weekend, and the coach had just informed her that she was going to start as setter. She'd been trying to earn that position for a while and finally, here she was. She looked around for her brother, seeing his Jeep in the student parking lot. He must still be watching football film.

A blustery fall breeze smashed into her and ruffled her hair. She shivered and dug her team sweatshirt out of her bag to throw on. Lucas should be done anytime, so she'd just wait. Greg had been taking her to school and picking her up, but he was having problems with the northern pasture and said that Lucas could bring her home tonight.

It seemed when her uncle got something into his head, there was no getting it out. She had no doubt she wasn't getting her phone back for the two weeks he had said. She had to give him props. She'd wondered how long she could push him around; apparently, it hadn't been as long as she wanted. She grinned and couldn't wait to tell him that she was going to start on Saturday.

"Hey, Hannah," a male voice called out. She turned

slightly to see Roland over by his car, leaning against it. Guiltily looking around, she picked up her bag and walked toward him.

He lounged against his beat-up car wearing worn jeans, big boots, and a long sleeve green T-shirt with a marijuana plant on the front. His hair had gotten a little longer, and he looked better than ever. "You still grounded?"

"Yeah," she said. "I can't believe how easy it was to get caught."

"Here in a small town, they know everything. Sorry about that. It was my fault," Roland said, leaning over and kissing her on the nose. She basked for a moment. It was all too good. The more Greg and Tara didn't want her to see Roland, the more she wanted to spend time with him. She understood that he was a bad boy, but it didn't make him any less sweet. They'd had a good time watching movies together the other day, and he had kissed her, and that was all. It had been a great kiss; now she could see what everybody was talking about.

"Guess what?" she asked.

"What?" he asked, tugging on her ear.

She loved it when he did that. "I'm going to start as setter at the match on Saturday. We have a two-day tournament, Roland. You should come."

He straightened away from his car. "What do you mean? I thought we were going to Denver for the weekend."

Her jaw dropped. "I can't go to Denver. I got in trouble just leaving school with you the other day."

"Oh, come on, Hannah. It'll be fine. We'll have a fun weekend and we'll see Monty, and then I'll bring you back. You're already grounded. What more can your uncle do?"

She didn't want to find out. It was bad enough not having her phone. What if he took volleyball away or something? "I don't know. Greg's not a guy you mess with." Which actually, she kind of appreciated. She missed her dad more than anything, but she felt safe with Greg in the house. Now they had Tara, too, and they'd become an odd little blended family. It was working out for them. "Why don't you come to my match? It's a whole weekend tournament."

His face hardened in a way it never had before. "No, you're going to come to Denver with me."

"No, I'm not," she said.

He grabbed her and pushed her against the car.

Pain flared along her hip. "What are you doing?"

"I said you're coming with me. You promised you would, and you are."

"I never promised," she said, pushing him with both hands. He grabbed her hands and shoved her hard against the car again, and the metal hit her rib cage this time. Pain flared both up and down her side. "What are you doing, Roland?"

He opened the back door. "I'm taking you to Denver like we said."

Panic ran through her as she started to struggle, but he was too strong.

"Hey," somebody yelled. They both turned as Johnny ran out of the building with a backpack over his arm. "What's happening?"

"Nothing," Roland said. "We're going to Denver. You're not invited."

Johnny skidded to a stop next to them. "Hannah?"

She shoved her hands against Roland, but he held her wrists tight. "I don't want to go to Denver. You're about to get kicked, Roland."

Roland released her.

Johnny dropped his backpack on the ground. "Leave her alone."

Roland's smile wasn't pretty. "What are you going to do?"

"I'm going to make you," Johnny said, preparing to fight.

Roland threw back his head and laughed. "Yeah, I out-weigh you by about fifty pounds, scrawny. Get lost, Johnny."

"Johnny, don't leave me," Hannah said, panic rising through her. There wasn't anybody else in the parking lot. Not yet anyway.

"I'm not going to leave you, Hannah." Johnny flicked a glance at her, his brown eyes serious. "I promise."

Hannah looked wildly around. Her brother should be coming out any minute along with some of the football players. Even so, she wasn't going to let this guy man-handle her. "You need to leave me alone, Roland." She started to move past him, and he shoved her hard. Her neck hit the door opening and she fell inside, sitting.

"There you go," Roland said. Johnny rushed him, and they smashed against the open door. Roland punched Johnny in the stomach and then the face, and Johnny fell back onto the asphalt. Then Roland pulled out a gun from the back of his waist.

Everything inside Hannah went cold. "What are you doing?"

Roland pointed the gun at Johnny. "Get up."

Johnny, his gaze on the gun, slowly stood. "What are you doing, man?"

For an answer, Roland grabbed Hannah by the hair and yanked her out of the car. "This way." He went around to the trunk, the gun still leveled at Johnny. "Open the trunk."

"Wait a minute, man," Johnny protested.

"Now, or I will shoot you," Roland snarled.

Johnny hit the button and the trunk opened.

"Get in," Roland ordered.

"No, wait. Roland, don't do this," Hannah said, panic engulfing her.

"You shut up." He pointed the gun at Johnny. "One."

Johnny glared at Roland, then looked at Hannah. "It's going to be okay, Hannah." He got in the trunk.

Roland then turned and shoved Hannah in, smacking her in the face so she fell back onto Johnny. She barely had time to duck her head out of the way before Roland slammed the lid shut.

Tara had just finished packing up for the day when her phone buzzed. She yanked her heavy laptop bag and her massive purse over one shoulder before lifting her phone to her other ear. "Hello."

"Hey, it's Greg."

Little tingles zipped through her at the sound of his voice. "Hi." Man, she had it bad.

"Would you do me a favor and bring Hannah home?" he asked. "Lucas was supposed to bring her, but the coach wants him to stay and go over extra film for the game tomorrow night, and I don't want him to miss out."

"Sure," Tara said. "Volleyball must be over, so she's probably waiting outside. I'll head out there now."

"Great. I appreciate it." He paused. "Um, how was your day?"

She groaned. He really was terrible at small talk. "My day was just fine, Greg. How was your day?"

He coughed. "I wrestled in the mud with cows all day. So, not bad."

"You're really taking to this ranching life, aren't you?" she asked, her chest warming.

"You know, I am. As a kid, I didn't really appreciate it and just wanted to get out of here. But now I'm having fun. It's not easy, but I can see why Chris loved it so much."

She still had whisker burn on various parts of her body

from him. Was it possible he'd stay, after all? Her face heated at the memories of the weekend. She opened the school exit door and stepped out into a tumultuous fall day. There was definitely another storm coming. She looked around and saw Lucas's Jeep; then her gaze caught on Roland Kingsley standing beside his car. Was that Hannah's backpack? She ducked her head and hurried toward the student parking lot. "I think I see Hannah's backpack," she said into the phone, "but I don't see her."

"Are there a lot of people around?"

"No, there's no one around except . . ." She hated to say the name. "Roland Kingsley. I think she might be inside his car."

Greg hissed out a breath. "Are you kidding me right now? Just exactly how long does she want to be grounded?"

"I don't know." Tara shook her head and increased her pace. "I'll call you back in a minute." She clicked off and soon reached Roland. "Where's Hannah?" She craned her head to look inside the car, but nobody was there.

"Heck if I know," Roland said. "I came out and found her backpack here." He handed the backpack to Tara.

She looked around the empty lot. Perhaps Hannah had gone back inside because it was cold, or maybe she'd forgotten something. But why would she leave her backpack out here?

A noise caught her attention. She looked toward the trunk and could barely make out a muffled shriek. "What in the world? Is that—"

Roland grabbed the phone out of her hand and threw it across the parking lot.

She took a step back. "Roland, what are you doing?" Scrambling, she ran around the trunk and pounded on it frantically. "Hannah. Hannah, are you in there?"

Hannah screamed, but the sound was muffled. A male voice bellowed as well.

Tara frantically pushed the button to open the trunk. Something heavy came down on her head, and stars flashed behind her eyes. Everything went blurry as she started to fall. In the distance, she heard somebody yell her name. Her face smashed onto the asphalt, and she turned her head to see Lucas walking out of the gym with a backpack over his shoulder. He yelled her name again. She lifted her head but couldn't scream.

"Roland. You are in so much trouble," she whispered, trying to scare some sense into him. She had to somehow get Hannah out of the trunk. Something warm coated her face, and the smell of copper filled her nose. "Did you hit me?" Everything was fuzzy and groggy, and she couldn't quite grasp what was happening.

Lucas started to run toward her. Almost in slow motion, Roland lifted his arm and pointed a silver gun at Lucas.

On the ground, she finally found her voice. "Lucas, run!"

Roland fired three times and then looked down at her. He kicked her hard in the jaw and agony detonated in her face. Then unconsciousness took all the pain away.

CHAPTER 15

Greg leaped over the fence and dialed Tara again. Nothing. Why wasn't she answering? He shoved his leather gloves in his back pocket. His phone buzzed. "Tara?"

"Greg, it's Lucas." Panic rose high in the kid's voice. "There were bullets. I don't know—"

Greg went stone cold. "Calm down and talk to me. Where are you?"

"At the school. I don't know what happened. One second she was there and then she was gone and I—"

"Whoa, whoa," Greg said. "Hold on and take a deep breath. Who are you talking about?"

Lucas coughed wildly. "Tara. I came out of school to look for Hannah, and Tara was on the ground."

Greg's head jerked up. "Tara was on the ground?"

"Yeah, and then Roland shot at me," Lucas said as he wheezed.

Greg was already on the move, running full force for his truck. "Are you okay?"

"Yeah, I ducked. The bullets hit the building, and then he grabbed Tara and threw her in his car and drove away. I ran toward them."

Greg settled into calm. "Wait. You ran toward a guy shooting a gun?"

"Of course. He had Tara."

Greg jumped into his truck and was already peeling out of the driveway. What the kid had done was very brave. "Lucas, are you sure you're okay?"

"Yeah, I am."

He had to get to Tara. "Which direction did they go?"

"They went east."

That made sense. The punk was driving away from town. "What about Hannah? Where's Hannah?"

"I don't know. She's not here. I haven't seen her anywhere."

Greg's gut turned over. Did Roland have both Hannah and Tara? Why? Where the hell did that kid get a gun? "Okay. I want you to stay where you are, inside the building. Got me?"

"No, that guy has Tara. He may have Hannah. I'm not staying here."

Greg took a blind corner at top speed. "I understand what you're saying, but we don't know which way they've gone."

"Yeah, we do." Through the phone line came the sound of a vehicle door shutting and an engine igniting.

"Hey, what's going on?" Jordy said on the other end of the line, and there was the sound of another door shutting.

Fear slapped Greg hard. "Jordy, I want you to get out of that car and go inside the building," he ordered.

"Oh, hey, Greg," Jordy said. "You're on speakerphone. What's happening?"

An engine gunned loudly. "We're getting Tara back," Lucas yelled.

"Dude, slow down. Lucas. Lucas!" Greg snapped.

"That guy has Tara. She's family. If he has Tara, he might have Hannah," Lucas said grimly. "I'm following them, Greg."

Greg couldn't breathe for a minute, and then he dropped back on training. "All right. Let me know if you spot Roland's car, but do not approach him. Got me?"

"Yeah. We'll call you as soon as we find him."

The line went dead. Greg punched the gas pedal and dialed another number.

"McDay. I mean, Sheriff McDay," Austin answered.

"Hey, there's been a kidnapping and a shooting at the high school."

Something rustled as Austin moved. "Was anybody hurt?"

"No, Roland Kingsley shot at Lucas and then kidnapped Tara." He wouldn't think about Tara being unconscious right now. He had to focus.

"Was she hurt?"

"Yeah. Lucas said she may be unconscious. Roland threw her in his car and drove away. And I don't know where Hannah is."

A door slammed loudly. "Which way were they headed?"

"Lucas said they were headed east out of town."

Austin's voice was muffled as he shouted out orders and then returned to the phone. "All right, I'll get the deputies on it. I'm calling the Cattle Club men in, too. We can converge from different areas. I have people everywhere."

"I'm headed to the barn now and can cut them off by horseback." If Roland was driving on the road headed east, he'd soon be turning north, right through the mountain pass. Greg could get there quick. He jumped out of his truck and ran for the stables and his horse.

"I'm at the club and will ride horseback from here. I'll send the *all call* right now. We'll get her back, Greg."

They'd better. He couldn't lose her now.

Pain careened through Tara's head and down her neck. So much agony. She slowly opened her eyes and then winced as more pain shot through her entire brain. What was happening? The world around her was rocking slowly. She forced herself to focus on the dashboard lights in front of her. "What?" she murmured.

"I have a gun, and I'll shoot you. Don't scream," came a voice to her left.

Slowly, trying not to hurt her head any more than she already had, she turned to see Roland Kingsley in the driver's seat. She jerked and agony washed through her brain. "What is happening?" She tried to move and looked down to find a seat belt tightly binding her arms to her torso. The side of her face felt sticky, and memories came rushing back. "Roland, what are you doing? Wait a minute, you shot at Lucas."

"He shouldn't have run after me," Roland said, his knuckles white on the steering wheel.

She swallowed and tried to clear her mind. "Did you hit him? Was he okay?"

"I don't know. I don't care," Roland said grimly, the gun in one hand resting on his jeans while the other was on the steering wheel. "I will shoot you, Mrs. Webber. I mean, Mrs. Simpson."

She blinked. Greg had to be coming for them. "What are you doing?"

"I'm getting out of this stupid town, and I'm going to make some money at the same time."

"Is Hannah in the trunk?" She tried to turn her head, but the seat belt kept her in place. She jerked on it.

Roland lifted the gun and pointed it at her. "Don't make me shoot you."

She stilled. He sounded like he meant it. "Is Hannah in the trunk?"

"Yes, and so is Johnny. I'll probably have to kill him," Roland said quietly. "I don't want to, but I doubt I could sell him."

"Whoa, what? Sell him? Wait a minute. You're going to sell Hannah?"

Roland shrugged, looking uncomfortable for a moment. "Yeah, she's a virgin, you know. Apparently, we can make a lot of money on her."

Tara's stomach rolled, and she swallowed down bile so she wouldn't throw up. "You're involved in human trafficking?" How had she read him so incorrectly?

He frowned as if he hadn't really considered the ramifications. "I guess so. I mean, Monty has sources, so I guess that's what we're doing? I hadn't really thought about it in those terms. I'm sure it won't be that bad."

"Greg's going to kill you. If he doesn't, I will." She tried to lift her arms, but the seat belt was too tight. "You know, you could be killing them both in that trunk. This is an old car."

Roland paused. "Nah, I heard them screaming and yelling and trying to kick their way out a few minutes ago. They're still alive."

She looked around for any way to get herself free. Everything was still fuzzy. How hard had he hit her? "You have to realize this is a bad idea. Come on, Roland, you're better than this." She looked outside. Dusk was falling, and a bright pink and gold sunset was filtering across the mountains. They'd only been gone probably half an hour.

If Lucas hadn't been shot, he would've gotten help. But what if he'd been hit? A sob rose in her and she tried to bite it back. "What's your plan for me?" She had to figure out a way to escape. She pulled on her wrists, trying to loosen the seat belt.

Roland flicked her a glance. "I don't know. You're not that old. Maybe we could sell you, too."

Her stomach lurched and she gagged.

He jerked back. "Don't puke in my car, lady. You've already got blood on the window."

Tara wiggled her shoulders so she could lift her hands. If she could just move one to the side she could unbuckle the seat belt, but she had to keep him preoccupied. "You know, the entire town of Redemption will come after you."

He snorted. "Yeah. Like I'm afraid of a bunch of ranchers and farmers."

"Don't be obtuse," she muttered. "Not only is Greg a former Marine, but there's Sheriff McDay and the entire Cattle Club men. You don't for a second think they're all ranchers, do you?"

For the first time, the kid blinked. "Hadn't really thought about it, but I guess I'll make it to Denver with no problem."

"Does your uncle know about this?"

He snorted. "I'd already forgotten you'd dated Uncle Joe. No. He's useless to me."

At least there was that; she hadn't dated a human trafficker. Just a jerk. She inched her hands a little bit farther and her pinky touched the seat belt release. She was almost there.

He sped up. Cattle and hay crops were visible on either side of them, while the Wyoming mountains rose high above. "You know, Ms. Webber, I always thought you were pretty. Maybe you and I can have some fun on this ride."

He looked at her and winked, looking much older than his eighteen years. "What do you think? Maybe I won't have to sell you."

She strained a little more and then got two fingers on the release button. She looked around. There were no trees nearby. If she caused a wreck, they'd just spin into a fence. She didn't want to take the risk with the kids in the trunk, but Roland had a gun, and she had no doubt he'd use it on Johnny when they stopped.

They were approaching the marshland only known by locals. Right where she'd spun off the road after church. It was the safest place to stop Roland, even if it was a little risky.

So she took a deep breath and depressed the seat belt button. It released with a click, but she coughed loudly. Then in one smooth motion, she threw off the seat belt and lunged for the steering wheel, yanking it as hard as she could toward her. Roland yelled and something exploded.

Pain burst through her leg, and she shrieked. The car spun off the road and twirled in the mud, smashing through a fence and nearly hitting an Angus steer.

Then silence.

CHAPTER 16

Greg came over the rise at full speed, his horse surefooted and fast. He caught sight of Roland Kingsley's car just as it spun off the road and careened through a fence. Panic gripped him, and he yelled out Tara's name.

The sheriff rode over a hill on the other side of the road. A blue truck barreled from the east road, and Lucas's Jeep careened into view from the west.

Greg held up a hand to halt Lucas, and the kid stopped his truck, blocking the way back to town.

Greg rode down the mountainside just in time to see Roland pull Tara from the vehicle by the hair and press a gun to her neck. She had blood on her face and her left leg. Everything inside him went cold. He reached the road and dismounted, his Glock at his waist and a shotgun in his hand. "You're surrounded, Roland."

The kid backed away toward the solid form of a bull who wasn't moving. "Get out of here, or I'll kill her."

"You're not going to kill anybody. So far, you haven't hurt anybody. Let's just get you out of this." Greg edged closer.

Two of the Cattle Club men, the twins Zeke and Zachary, jumped out of the westbound truck, both armed. Sheriff

McDay dismounted from his horse to the right of the bull, and they all started to surround Roland.

Somebody screamed in the back of the car. Greg blinked. Was that Hannah?

"Is she hurt?" he asked Roland.

Roland pulled Tara farther away from his car, which was definitely stuck in the mud. His hand shook on the gun.

Tara's eyes were wide and blood coated the side of her face, but she was calm. Her hands were held in front of her, and her skin was raw.

Greg shoved anger down. "You're going to be okay. I need you to stay calm."

Austin cleared his throat. "Roland, you haven't hurt anybody yet. Let her go, and we'll see how we can fix this. You need help, kid."

"I don't want help," Roland yelled. "I want you all to get out of here. I'm going to take that truck, and we're leaving."

Greg stepped closer. "You're not going anywhere. Let her go so I don't have to kill you."

"Kill me?" Roland's eyes widened, and his lip curled. "I have a gun to her neck, and you're talking about killing me?" He shoved the muzzle even harder against her. Tara winced and tried to move away from the gun.

There was only one way to handle this. Greg jerked his head slightly to get Tara's attention. She blinked, and he mouthed the words "dead drop." Instantly, she went limp and fell.

Roland yelled, but he wasn't strong enough to hold her up. She kept going down, and he turned the gun. Greg fired instantly, hitting him in the arm. The gun flew across the road.

Tara jumped back up and kicked him in the knee, and the kid went down. Then she ran toward Greg, limping slightly. Greg caught her and held her, everything inside him settling.

"You okay?" he said, leaning back and looking at her face.

"Yeah, I am. The kids are in the trunk," she gasped, her chest heaving wildly.

He'd been afraid of that. Taking a deep breath, he turned and hurried over to open the trunk. Both Hannah and Johnny popped up. They were bruised, and Johnny had a split lip. "Are you guys all right?"

They both nodded. Greg grabbed Hannah and pulled her out, holding her tight. She hugged him and put her face into his neck, crying. "I'm sorry. I'm so sorry."

He palmed her head with his hand and held her tight, his heart warming and his chest settling. "You're okay. None of this is your fault. You're all right, okay?" He sat her down and checked her over, careful to look in her eyes. "Are you sure you're not hurt?"

She turned and helped Johnny out of the trunk, hugging him tightly. "Johnny was so brave. He tried to save me." She looked up at the kid, stars in her eyes.

Greg sighed. He'd worry about that tomorrow.

Lucas and Jordy ran up, sandwiching their sister between them in a fierce hug that had her laughing.

Greg looked over to where Austin had cuffed Roland Kingsley, who was bleeding from the shoulder. It wasn't a bad wound; the kid would probably be fine. He was now sobbing uncontrollably.

Greg walked to Tara and held out his hands to her. Her wrists were a mangled mess. Then he leaned down and looked at her leg. It was bleeding, so he tore the denim away from the wound. She'd been shot? Anger flashed through him. He turned toward Roland.

Austin stepped in front of the kid. "No, sorry. We're taking him to the hospital, and then we'll book him."

"For kidnapping," Hannah yelled.

Tara leaned into Greg's side. "Not only that . . . human trafficking." The story she then told him chilled him to his bones, and even Austin looked furious.

"Well, then," Austin said, shoving the cuffed kid toward his truck. "It looks like you have some interesting news for the FBI."

"I ain't saying nothing, man," Roland said as Austin loaded him into the back of the truck.

"We'll see about that," the sheriff drawled.

Greg put one arm around Tara and the other around Hannah. "You're both going to get checked out at the hospital." He looked closer into Tara's eyes. "I think you have a concussion, and while your wound looks like the bullet went through, you're gonna need stitches."

She gingerly wiped at the dried blood on her temple. "And pain meds."

Greg looked at the two women in his life and drew them both in for another hug. The boys crowded in, and Greg took a second to hold all of his family. They were safe and he'd keep them that way.

He grinned and kissed Hannah on the forehead before everyone stepped back. She turned away and returned to the Larrabee boy to take his hands and look up into his face.

Lucas snorted and Jordy rolled his eyes.

Greg groaned.

Tara chuckled and rested her head on his chest. "Can we worry about that tomorrow?"

"Oh, we'll definitely worry about that tomorrow." He set his knuckles beneath her chin and lifted her face, wincing at the dried blood on her cheekbone. "You're going to get better."

"I know," she said.

He gently kissed her nose and then lifted her against his chest. He was going to be so careful with her that she'd never want to leave. It was his only hope for them all.

A week after the kidnapping attempt, Tara's heart was heavy as she drove home from school. Light rain splattered on her windshield, but other than that, the autumn weather had finally calmed. There was only a week left in the two months she'd promised to stay married, yet she didn't think she could make it. It was just too much.

She pulled into the ranch house driveway and parked, seeing both Greg's and Lucas's rigs parked there. She stepped out of the car and dragged her heavy bag with her. The sound of horse hooves caught her attention as she turned to see Greg barreling up on his tall paint and dismounting before leaping over the nearest fence.

"What the hell are you doing?" His long legs ate up the distance between them.

"What?" She shut the car door with her hip.

He walked toward her, looking cowboy tough in faded jeans, a worn T-shirt, and battered cowboy boots. His Stetson was perched low on his head, and he shoved it back with one finger. "I told you I would come and get you if the weather turned."

She blinked and looked around. The clouds were high above them, but it had stopped raining. "It's not even windy. What is wrong with you?"

He set his stance, looking like any old-time cowboy about to draw a weapon. "What's wrong with me? You've run off the road three times lately, and another storm's coming."

She had looked at the weather app earlier, and the storm wasn't due to arrive for at least a day. "It's fine, Greg."

"It is not fine," he said, sweeping his hands out.

That was it. She just couldn't deal with this situation anymore. "This isn't working."

He paused. "What do you mean?"

"I know I'm supposed to stay here for another week. But I just, I just can't." It hurt too much to be with him when she knew their marriage was only temporary. She couldn't pretend any longer.

He frowned. "What are you saying?"

She owed him the truth. "I can't do this anymore. We're pretending to be married, we're pretending to have this family, and it's going to be over the second you go back to the military. It's too difficult. It's easier to end things now."

He pushed his hat even farther back, his gaze darkening. "I'm not going back to the military."

"Ha," she said. "I know you are. Even if you're lying to yourself, we both know you are."

"No, I'm not."

A light rain started to fall, and they both ignored it.

She settled her bag more securely over her shoulder. "Yes, you are. I've heard you talking to someone named 'Master Sergeant' about fifty times in the last two months."

He swallowed. "Tara, I was talking to him about my replacement in the unit as well as various mission plans. I'm easing the transition." He shook his head. "I'm not going back to the military. I've completely retired. How do you not know that?"

She lifted her chin. "How do I not know that?" Irritation

smacked right through her. "I don't know that because you didn't say it."

His jaw went slack and then hardened into the rock formation she knew so well. "I'm here, aren't I? I've made plans for the ranch."

"Oh yeah. Why were you and your lawyer talking to Sammy Jones so intently at Sandra's Diner? She saw you going over paperwork. You're leasing your ranch to him, aren't you?"

"No," Greg said calmly. "I was trying to buy ten thousand acres of his that border our ranch. The only way to make this ranch profitable is to expand it."

She rocked back on her heels. "Huh."

A muscle ticked in his jaw. "I have not been communicating well, and I'm sorry. I should have said that I was staying. I just assumed that if I was here, everybody would know I was staying."

"Well, I didn't," she said, kicking a pebble. "I figured you'd be leaving when Hannah went off to college in a few years." What did this mean? Her heart rate sped up.

"No. I love the ranch, Tara. I needed to get away for a while and grow up, and I did. But I've always thought I would come back and work the place with Chris. Now it's mine, and I need to grow it and protect it for the kids."

She just looked at him. He was staying? For good?

He scratched the hard whiskers on his jaw. "I haven't really said much, have I?" His tone was thoughtful.

"No," she said.

"Hmm. Well, I'm sorry. I should have. I'd like for you to stay, too."

It wasn't enough. No matter how badly she wanted to be with him, she *knew* that wasn't enough. Instead of being sad, she let her temper fly. "That's just too bad. You don't want a partner—you just want me here briefly so you can get the ranch."

Something undefinable glittered in his dark eyes. "Of course I want a partner. I want *you* as my partner."

"Ha," she said again. "You won't let me do anything. I can't even be a part of this household. I can't go in the kitchen, I can't go in the laundry room, I can't even stain the deck like I want to, not to mention that I'd love to plant flowers."

His chin lowered, giving him a dangerous look. "Seriously?"

"Yes," she snapped. "You won't let me be involved at all."

"That's it," he said. "I'm not the only one who can't communicate." He reached for her and swept her up, striding through the rain to the front door, which he kicked open with a little too much force. It banged against the wall, and she yelped. He walked through the kitchen, by the three startled teenagers, and into the laundry room, plopping her unceremoniously on the washing machine.

He bracketed her with his arms. "There. The laundry room is all yours. Have at it."

She settled herself and dropped her bag on the floor. "What?"

"Yep," he said. "It's all yours. I'll put a sign on the door that says, 'Tara's Special Laundry Room.'"

She gulped.

"The kitchen is all yours as well. You want to stain the deck? You can do whatever you want to the deck. You can plant flowers until they're coming out of our ears. But this room is all yours."

Amusement wandered through her, even though her temper was still boiling.

"While I'm at it," he said, "I love you, completely and utterly."

Everything inside her stilled. "You what?"

His gaze softened. "Tara, I've loved you since we were seventeen years old. I never once stopped. It was your face I saw every time I needed something to give me peace all those miles away. I should have said the words, and I'm sorry."

The three teens popped up by the doorway. "What's going on?" Lucas asked.

Greg turned only his head. "You kids know I love you, right?" All three nodded. "Do I have to say it all the time?"

"No," Lucas said.

"Ew . . ." Jordy added.

Hannah nodded. "Yeah, you should say it a lot."

"Oh," Greg said. "In case I haven't been absolutely clear, I love all three of you, and I'm staying here at the ranch for however long we have a ranch, which is going to be a long time. You'll always have a place to come home."

Something eased in the kids then. All three visibly relaxed.

Greg looked around. "From now on, Tara's in charge of the laundry room. She wants it—it's all hers."

Jordy slipped behind Hannah and then disappeared.

Lucas ripped off his practice football jersey and tossed it on the floor. "Great. This thing reeks. The coach said if I didn't wash it before the next practice, he was throwing me in the shower with it. But I'm telling you, it's been good luck, man."

Greg kicked it to the side. "I can smell it from here."

Hannah yanked a duffel bag from the side and took out twin knee pads. "These are mine from volleyball, and they stink. I've tried to wash them in bleach like five times, and it just doesn't work. Good luck, Tara."

Tara watched them sail across the room to land near the football jersey. Humor bubbled up.

Lucas looked over his shoulder and started laughing before stepping to the side, and Jordy walked in holding a wire clothes hamper that was stuffed so high the clothes reached his chin. He set it down, and it immediately fell over, spilling clothing all over the floor.

"Whew," he said. "I'm so glad someone's taking this over."

Greg frowned. "Those are all your clothes. What have you been wearing?"

Jordy shrugged. "I've been just wearing them inside out once in a while, and then rotating them."

Tara smacked her forehead. "Please tell me that's not true."

Jordy smiled. "Yeah, no one's complained. But I've got to say, a couple of the girls in my botany class have asked to move away from me."

Greg turned and looked toward her. "This is what you wanted, right?"

She smiled, her heart warming. "Yeah. This is exactly what I wanted." Then she reached for him. "I love you, too, by the way."

He stepped back, his eyes softening even more. "Yeah, okay. I guess the words are good." Then he leaned in and kissed her.

"Gross," Jordy said, stomping away.

Lucas groaned. "I mean, old people kissing. Ugh."

Hannah laughed. "Yeah, they're old, but they're cute. Why don't we go grab dinner while they start the laundry?"

The door closed, and Greg looked up. "Are you sure you're ready for this?"

"Yeah," she said. "I am, more than anything."

"Great," Greg said as the Jeep sounded outside. "Why don't we break in this laundry room?"

She smiled and then shook her head. "Are you kidding? I can smell those clothes from here. Let's go anywhere else."

He lifted her again, laughing as he went. "It's going to be an adventure."

EPILOGUE

Mother Nature finally cooperated and gave them a decent autumn day. The leaves were falling faster now in clumps of their familiar scarlet and gold, and the wind held a chilly bite, showing that winter was going to be early this year. Today the sun was out, the sky was blue, and the world smelled like gardenias.

Tara stood on the deck of the Simpson ranch house and looked at her friends and family seated at tables spread over the wide lawn. A dance floor had been placed over to the far left beneath a series of pine trees, and the local band was keeping the younger guests dancing. Her father was entertaining some of the Cattle Club men with stories of her youth, and she couldn't help but notice how uncomfortable a few of them seemed to be in crowds. Someday she'd learn their whole story, but probably not today.

Sheriff McDay was strumming a guitar and helping the band out. The guy seemed to have multiple talents. She searched the crowd for Zachary and Zeke. While she didn't see Zeke, Zachary was sitting over on a fence post drinking a beer, focusing intently on something across the way.

Tara craned her neck to discover that the *something* was actually *someone*. Cami stood in a pretty pale blue dress by the punch bowl, chatting with friends from town. Interesting. Maybe the mysterious Cattle Club member wasn't as indifferent as he'd appeared.

A hand curled around Tara's nape and pulled her back against solid muscle. She tilted her head way back to look up at her husband. "Great party," she said. They'd decided to have a wedding reception, and the whole town had turned out.

He looked around. "Yeah, we have more friends than I thought."

She couldn't help but chuckle. When he stiffened slightly behind her, she looked again and followed his gaze to the dance floor, where Hannah and Johnny were dancing a slow dance. Greg let out a short whistle, and Lucas came from out of nowhere to tug his sister away and pull her into a fast dance.

Tara laughed. "That's not cool. We can't have all of you ganging up on the poor kid."

"If we were ganging up on him, he wouldn't be standing," Greg said. "They were dancing too close. He needs to learn to dance much farther away."

Tara asked, leaning back against her husband, happier than she'd been in way too long, "How far?"

"I don't know, a county away," Greg muttered. Her husband was adorable.

She shook her head. "Johnny's a nice guy, and he probably saved her life."

"Like I said, he's still standing." Greg leaned down and kissed the top of her head. "How's your leg?"

Her leg was just fine. The stitches had already dissolved. "I'm good. Stop worrying."

"Huh."

Mark walked up to them with a beer in his hand. "Sharon dropped the appeal."

Tara looked at their lawyer. "Why?"

Mark snorted. "Not as a wedding present." He shrugged. "My guess is that her lawyer told her she wouldn't win and then gave her his bill. Either way, it's over."

"Good," Greg said. "Have you heard anything about the Kingsley kid?"

Mark nodded. "His uncle bailed him out, and they're still working on a plea agreement if the kid tells all he knows about his buddy in Denver. My guess is that he'll do some time at a youth ranch and get scared straight. Hopefully." Mark looked over at the buffet table. "Oh. They brought out more steak." He moved away.

Greg laughed and flipped Tara around to kiss her on the nose. Then he looked at the refreshment table. "We need more water. I'll be right back." He tugged her close one more time and then hustled toward the garage.

Perfect. She began walking toward Cami, only to be intercepted by Judge Maloney. "Judge." She slid her arm through his. "Come sit down. We have some new chairs on the deck."

The man was stooped over and looked like he was struggling. "Sure thing," he said, allowing her to lead him to one of the many brightly colored chairs she'd talked Greg into buying for the party. "Oh, that's much better. Thank you."

She made sure an umbrella was near in case the sun was too much for him. "I heard you're retiring."

He rolled his eyes and lifted a gnarled hand to his thinning hair. "Yeah. Everyone thinks I'm old." His eyes twinkled. "But I sure did the right thing by you, didn't I?"

She sat in a similar chair. "What do you mean?"

"Well, come on. You were never going to make a move. Simpson was never going to make a move. Somebody had to do something."

Her jaw dropped. "Wait a minute. You were matchmaking?"

The judge laughed, throwing back his head and patting

his dark jeans. "Of course, I was matchmaking. Do you really think I would've let you two get away with that fake we're-getting-married nonsense in my courtroom? Come on."

She couldn't help the smile tickling her lips. "Judge, we actually got married. You married us."

"I know," he said proudly. "It was one of my finest days in the courtroom. I figured I'd have to retire soon, so it was a good way to end things. You two have always belonged together."

She gulped. Apparently, the elderly man was much sharper than any of them had understood. "What's your plan now?"

He shrugged. "I was thinking about seeing if Cami would let me work at the coffee shop for a few hours every day. I don't just want to go home and fish, you know?"

What a fantastic idea. "Cami could actually use some help."

"Excellent. Consider it done." He sat back and studied the tree line. "Not sure about that wolf."

Tara followed his gaze and spotted Harley sitting next to a birch tree, watching the festivities. "I think he's as much of a matchmaker as you," she murmured.

The judge grinned. "Maybe he's a kindred spirit. For now, I think I'll just rest for a few minutes."

"All right," Tara said, patting his hand. "I'll have one of the kids bring you some lemonade."

He scoffed. "Lemonade? Have them bring me a beer, would you?"

"Sure," she said, standing and moving toward the refreshment table, where Greg was already tossing more bottles of water into the big metal bucket. "You're not going to believe this," she murmured, "but I think the judge set us up."

Greg finished and then looked toward the judge. "No kidding?"

"Yes," she said.

"Guess I owe the old guy." Greg took her hand and pulled her toward the dance floor, where the band was playing a slow ballad. "This is our party. We should dance."

She moved into his arms. "I know."

"Good." He leaned down and kissed her, going deep in that way only Greg Simpson could. Then he leaned back. "I love you, you know?"

"Yeah, I know," she said. "I love you, too."

He smiled and pulled her even closer. "You're right. The words do matter."

A COWBOY KIND OF ROMANCE

DELORES FOSSEN

CHAPTER 1

"Brenna, don't stop for Jolly Ranchers!"

Captain Brenna O'Sullivan frowned and did a mental double take when she drove by the handwritten poster-board sign that had been staked into the ground on the side of the road. A trio of gold Mylar balloons bobbled from it, and the hot June breeze slapped at them and the matching streamers on the bottom.

"What the heck?" she muttered.

Brenna had expected signs along her route to welcome her back to her hometown of Loveland, Texas, but she seriously doubted the message was a warning for her to breeze right past any actual ranchers who just happened to be jolly.

No, it had to refer to the candy with that name.

A candy she had indeed planned on stopping for before she headed home. Willy Joe's In and Out gas station on the edge of town would almost certainly have a stash of them.

The sign and the message had to be her mother's doing. Anyone else would have added a "please" or a little winky face to let her know it was meant to be lighthearted. But her mom had probably ignored Brenna's request that there not be a homecoming party and had not only planned one but had also made a ton of food for the partygoers. If Brenna had stopped for a candy fix, then Willy Joe or one of his employees might have spilled the beans about the party and ruined the surprise that wouldn't actually be a surprise.

She slowed down when she spotted another sign ahead. "Brenna, go straight to Willow Creek Ranch." In parentheses, someone had added, "And don't stop for a Coke first, either."

Brenna did some more frowning because she'd planned on a Coke purchase as well, but being deprived of her favorite caffeine hit was only a minor annoyance. The bigger annoyance here—and it was a whopper—was that the Willow Creek Ranch was owned by the Cameron family, and it was where Theo Cameron lived and worked. Brenna certainly hadn't expected to have to see Theo on her first day back.

Theo, hot cowboy, rodeo star, and breaker of hearts.

Well, breaker of *her* heart anyway.

However, Brenna had figured she would run into her former high school flame at some point. It'd be impossible to avoid him in a town as small as Loveland, since Theo, too, had apparently moved back for good. Still, she'd need to steel herself a bit to face him, considering he had crushed her six ways to Sunday when they'd been eighteen. That had happened when he'd essentially run away from home, and her, to go on the rodeo circuit.

Brenna reminded herself that she'd recovered just fine from that heart crushing. She had gone to college and joined the Air Force so she could do her own version of running away to have some adventures. Now that the adventures had been had with back-to-back assignments in England and Germany, she was ready to come home and settle down so she could spend more time with her parents and kid sister, Mandy. Something she'd start as soon as she got this surprise party, and apparently seeing Theo, out of the way.

There was another balloon-and-streamer-decorated sign at the entrance to the sprawling Willow Creek Ranch. "Turn here and don't stop to chat with Rafe or anyone else."

Brenna didn't see Rafe, Theo's brother, but even without the warning she wouldn't have stopped, because Rafe wasn't the stop-to-chat-with sort. However, he might have given her a heads-up that there was a party waiting for her, so, of course, her mom would have wanted to nip that possible heads-up in the bud.

As the sign had instructed, she turned off the main ranch road and onto a much narrower one, driving away from the Camerons' massive three-story house and toward . . . Brenna didn't know where exactly. When Theo and she had been an item, she'd come to the ranch plenty of times, but other than Theo teaching her to ride horses in the front pasture, she hadn't gone beyond the main house or the trio of barns. She had heard, though, from Mandy that Theo had had a house built on the ranch, so that was likely her destination.

Brenna slowed to a stop when she saw another sign, except this one was different from the others. No balloons or streamers. It was a life-size cutout poster of Theo and her at their senior prom when they'd been elected king and queen twelve years ago.

"Good grief," Brenna grumbled.

In the cutout, she was in a lace dress that had been pale yellow, but here it appeared white. Like a wedding gown. Theo was in a tux. Partially anyway. He had on the tux jacket with jeans and his usual black Stetson.

The picture looked like a cowboy wedding, complete

with her all starry eyed, gazing up at Theo as if he were the cure for all ills and the source of true happiness. Clearly, he hadn't been, but the disturbing image told her loads. Her mother wanted her to remember those happier times and do something to bring them back.

Like reconnect with Theo.

Brenna assured herself that pigs had a better chance of becoming Top Guns before that happened, but that particular thought trailed off in her head when she got distracted.

By Theo himself.

The cowboy breaker of hearts was standing in front of a log and stone cabin, and she was pretty sure he was waiting for her since he didn't look the least bit surprised that she had just arrived.

"Good grief," she repeated, but this time her voice was packing some breathy heat. A smidge of the heat was from anger at herself for her reaction, but the bulk of it was of the lust variety.

The hot cowboy label definitely still applied to Theo. Man, did it. Tall, dark, and dreamy, he no longer had his rangy teenager's body but had instead filled out in all the right places. Places that his jeans and T-shirt showed off in, well, just the right places. He could give those buff calendar guys a serious run for their money.

Clearly, she'd failed in the steeling-up department and had seemingly developed selective amnesia about how Theo had stomped on her heart. Sadly, she'd succeeded in remembering why she'd been attracted to him in the first place, why he'd been her first lover, and why she'd once told him, "I love you." That made Theo an emotional minefield. Ditto for this situation that her mother had obviously set up by directing her here.

Brenna parked her car in the driveway and glanced around, looking for her mom. No sign of her or anyone else.

Just Theo.

That likely meant her mother wanted Brenna to spend a little alone time with Theo in the hopes that his hotness would facilitate a reunion. It was just as likely, though, to bring about a rehashing of why they'd never reached that happily-ever-after finish line.

Dragging in a deep breath that she was sure she'd need, Brenna got out and faced her heartbreaker. She went closer and got what she called the Full Theo. Not naked as in the *Full Monty*, but the total impact of a man so hot that she felt her pulse jump and her stomach quiver. Just like old times. With one huge exception, of course. She was no longer a teenager and could make herself immune to this heat that was coming off him in waves.

She hoped.

"Brenna," he said in his usual drawl, which seemed to be coated in testosterone. "Welcome home."

She nodded and had to clear her throat to respond. "Thanks."

Fortunately, she'd managed to make that sound perky, an emotion she definitely wasn't feeling at the moment, but it was better than him seeing or hearing the lust reaction she was having. She continued with the perkiness vibe.

"So this is your place?" she asked, and once she had the confirming nod from Theo, she added, "How many people are waiting inside to jump out and yell *surprise*?" She glanced toward the barn, figuring the guests had parked in there or behind it.

"A few," he admitted, "but the party will have to wait."

She shook her head in puzzlement and more than a little frustration. Brenna had known her mom wouldn't obey her no-party request, but she had no idea why there'd be a delay. She preferred to get this over so she could head home and get out of the uniform. The dress blues looked good, but underneath the thick layers, she was roasting.

Brenna was distracted from her discomfort when she noticed Theo step to the side to motion for her to go through the gate. He was limping. From his rodeo injury, no doubt. Her mother had emailed her about it when it'd happened around three months ago and had told Brenna that Theo would be hanging up his bull-riding-championship titles and retire from the rodeo circuit.

The limp wasn't that pronounced, and it must not have interfered with his ability to run the ranch, or her mother would have emailed about that as well. Still, Brenna wondered if he was in pain.

"I obviously saw the signs as I drove in," she commented. "And the stand-up poster of us at the prom. Was that some kind of joke or my mother's idea of matchmaking?"

He frowned. "What poster?" But he immediately waved that off and must have mentally filled in the blanks. "Matchmaking," he confirmed.

Great. Her mother had been around when Brenna had cried buckets after the breakup with Theo, and she just couldn't understand why her mom would want her to reconnect with the guy who'd been responsible for generating those tears.

"So you're officially out of the Air Force?" he asked, his gaze flickering over her uniform.

"Not yet. In three weeks. I'm on what they call terminal leave. I wore the uniform for my flight from Germany."

Brenna had used a military transport flight to get to a base in nearby San Antonio and had asked her family to hold off on seeing her until she'd arrived home. Thankfully, they'd listened to that part of her request, and it had given Brenna a chance to finish up some out-processing paperwork along with picking up her rental car, all without having to deal with the distraction of being with her folks and Mandy.

"And what about the job Sheriff Caldwell offered you?" Theo added a moment later.

It shouldn't have surprised her that he knew about her being offered the deputy position at the Loveland PD. Everyone in town had likely heard, and since she'd told her mom she would be taking the job, plenty of folks probably knew that as well.

"I pin on the deputy's badge after my three weeks of leave are up," she said.

She was about to ask why the signs had directed her here, but then Brenna's mouth froze as she spotted the items on the porch. Bottles of water, two Cokes, and a family-size bag of Jolly Ranchers graced the white wicker table squeezed between two rocking chairs.

Her gaze fired to Theo's. "What's wrong?" she demanded. Because she couldn't think of a good reason for him to have her favorite junk snacks out here when there was supposedly a party waiting for her inside the house.

He didn't answer. Theo just led her to the porch, where a trio of overhead fans were making lazy turns with their whitewashed blades. He motioned for her to sit.

"Just say it fast," Brenna insisted.

Theo complied. "Your sister and my brother are getting married in two weeks."

It took more than a moment for those words to register in her head. She'd braced herself for something pretty darn bad, but this seemed like a joke. *Had to be a joke*, she amended.

"For real?" she still had to ask as she sank down onto one of the rockers.

"For real," Theo verified as he took the other chair.

Brenna shook her head. Mandy was twenty-three and had proudly accepted the Prissy Pants label that some teasers had bestowed on her in elementary school. Her sister was known to be overly romantic, and Mandy's latest job as one of the mayor's assistants was organizing a PR campaign to put Loveland on the map as a romantic destination.

Rafe, on the other hand, was as cowboy as they come with *ruggedly* handsome looks. Emphasis on the rugged. He hadn't accepted the teasers' label of Sourpuss and had told the teasers to shove the label where the sun didn't shine. Even though Rafe was twenty-nine, just two years younger than Theo, Brenna hadn't heard any gossip about Rafe ever having any serious relationships.

"When did they get engaged?" Brenna asked, and then tacked on some other questions. "How did they even get together in the first place? And why are you the one telling me and not Mandy or my parents?"

"The *when* happened two weeks ago; Rafe and Mandy announced to everyone they were engaged and would make a quick trip to the altar. As for the *how*, that's sort of connected to why I'm the one spilling all of this." He paused a heartbeat. "Mandy is pregnant, and Rafe is the baby's father."

The shock slid through her, head to toes. Oh, mercy. Her baby sister was pregnant. That wouldn't have gone over well with her parents one bit. They were traditionalists, and even though they adored Theo, Brenna didn't believe that adoration extended to his brother.

"While this isn't a shotgun wedding, your dad strongly

suggested that Rafe marry his daughter," Theo added. "Rafe and Mandy say they're both fine with that."

"Are they fine with it?" she pressed.

Theo shrugged. "Mandy seems over the moon about the baby, the engagement, and the marriage, but then again, over the moon seems to be your sister's default setting." He paused a heartbeat. "She has been crying a lot, though, about how you'll take the news."

Brenna groaned. Even though Mandy was prone to crying and overreacting, too, it bothered Brenna that she was the reason for these specific tears. Well, some of them anyway. Brenna figured her kid sister was also troubled by their parents' opinion of this situation. Pregnancy hormones could be playing into it, too.

Hearing all of this was a start as to why the signs had directed her out to the ranch, but still didn't explain why Theo was the messenger. It didn't explain a lot of things, and Brenna figured she was going to have to get some of the details from Mandy, like, for instance—was she madly in love with Rafe? How the heck had she started dating him? And why hadn't she come out and told Brenna?

"Did you lose a bet or something?" she asked Theo.

"Yeah," he readily admitted. "Mandy, Rafe, and I drew straws on who would fill you in on everything, and I lost." He stopped, cursed under his breath. "Also, like I said, Mandy's somewhat shaky, and I figured I could break the news and give you a couple of minutes for it to sink in before she has to face you."

It twisted at Brenna to think of her kid sister worrying over how she would react to the news. Yes, it was a shocker, but Brenna's own default setting was to support Mandy in any way she could. However, she did appreciate the couple of minutes of sinking-in time so she could compose herself.

"Mandy thinks you'll be upset because she has this notion that a younger sister shouldn't get married before an older one," Theo added.

Brenna rolled her eyes. "This is Heath Ledger's fault."

Theo blinked. "Excuse me?"

"He was in an old movie that Mandy loves. *Ten Things I Hate About You.* It's based on Shakespeare's *The Taming of the Shrew* where an older sister, the shrew, is pursued in courtship to clear the path for the younger one to be romantically involved." She stopped, did some under-the-breath cursing of her own. "Mandy could have been the one to set out that poster of us at the prom."

He repeated her eyeroll and followed it with a quick sound of agreement. Brenna only hoped her mom and Mandy hadn't joined forces to try to orchestrate a Brenna-Theo reunion.

"How are my parents and yours dealing with all of this?" she asked.

Theo didn't jump to answer, and he seemed to choose his words carefully. "It was a shock." He paused again. "They've had a lot of shocks recently," he added in a mumble.

Even though he didn't spell out what he meant by that last part, Brenna knew one of those shocks must have been his injury. Her mom hadn't blabbed a lot of the details, but Brenna knew there'd been surgery involved, followed by some physical therapy.

Theo looked at her then. Their gazes met, held, and just kept on holding. She got more stomach butterflies, more heart flutters, and the fantasies just steamrolled into her. Maybe that's the way it was with a woman's first. After all, the heat had been intense enough for her to want to choose him as her first lover. They'd fumbled their way together on the seat of his pickup truck, and while it hadn't been textbook-perfect sex, it had hit the amazing mark.

Her body reminded her of that now.

Thankfully, her brain was still functioning just fine, so Brenna could recall the breakup that had followed the amazing sex only a couple of months later. Best for her to hang on to that and finish getting some details so she could see Mandy and try to assure her that no shrews needed to be tamed so that she could marry the father of her baby.

"If the engagement happened two weeks ago, then why didn't anyone tell me before now?" Brenna wanted to know.

"Your mom insisted that you hear both the pregnancy and wedding news in person when you got back home from the base in Germany," Theo readily answered. "She thought it could cause you to be distracted from your job."

Ah, the distraction fear. Brenna couldn't totally dismiss it. Cops should never go on the job while distracted, but her mother had always taken that worry to the nth level, perhaps believing that her daughter spent 24/7 chasing down bad guys. On the rare occasion Brenna had done that, but the bulk of her job wasn't so different from a civilian cop's duties right here in Loveland.

"You okay?" Theo asked, drawing her attention back to him.

"Yes," she assured him. Though Brenna would indeed have to work her way through the news that her baby sister would soon have a baby of her own.

"Good," he muttered. "Because there's more. Mandy has it in her head that you and I are destined to be together."

Brenna did another mental double take. "*Destined?*"

Theo took another deep breath. "Yeah, it has to do with these rocks over by the Marrying Tree."

Brenna was well aware of the Marrying Tree. It was on the edge of Willow Creek and was considered one of the oldest oaks in the area. One of the biggest, too, at six feet wide and fifty feet tall. The town legend was that some of the first citizens of Loveland had proposed to their significant others under the tree and that the subsequent marriages had all been happy and long. Brenna figured it was just a big oak, period, but over the years, dozens of people had made treks to the tree to make their proposals and carve their initials inside heart shapes.

It was also the spot where she'd lost her virginity to Theo.

They'd gone there because it was the town's hot make-out spot, and on this particular night of making out, they had done the deed in his truck only yards from that blasted oak.

"What were Mandy and Rafe doing at the Marrying Tree?" she asked.

Theo dragged in a long breath. "Mandy was doing a photo shoot there with some models for this campaign to sell Loveland as the romance capital of Texas, and Rafe happened to be riding by just as she needed help rounding up a horse that got spooked. Rafe and she had apparently already started dating, but while he was there, Rafe and she found identical rocks. Mandy took that to mean they were supposed to end up together."

Brenna gave him a flat stare, but that was so like Mandy. The woman was a hopeless romantic with a skewed sense that the universe would supply signs and such to direct her on the right romantic path. Brenna knew it was one of the reasons Mandy hadn't pressed for something more serious with other guys she'd dated over the years. Mandy just hadn't seen any signs that one of those guys was her destiny.

Apparently, a pair of rocks had done the trick, though.

"And how specifically do you and I play into that being destined thing?" Brenna asked. "Did she find rocks for us, too?"

The corner of his mouth lifted into a dry smile. Dry and incredibly sexy. "No. She just considered it to be a natural progression of things since she somehow knew that's where you and I had been together."

Brenna wanted to curse. "She got that from my blasted diary. Mandy would have been about ten at the time, and she sneaked into my room and read it." She paused. "Does this mean Rafe and Mandy are going to try to matchmake us?"

"Definitely," he confirmed without a moment's hesitation. "In fact, it's already started. Mandy put our initials in permanent marker on her soul mate rock. She feels eventually we'll get our own signs that we're meant to be together."

Theo opened his mouth, no doubt to add other examples of her sister's matchmaking, but the front door opened and Mandy stepped out onto the porch. One look at her sister, and Brenna got confirmation that Mandy had indeed been crying a lot. Red, puffy eyes, wadded up tissues in her hand, and an unsteady bottom lip.

"Please don't be disappointed in me," Mandy muttered, her voice trembling. "And don't be mad that I waited until you got home to tell you."

Brenna went to Mandy and pulled her into her arms. That brought on a sob and more crying from Mandy, but Brenna thought these tears were of relief. "I'm not disappointed or mad," Brenna assured her, and she added, "Pinkie swear."

Mandy's tears kept coming, but when she eased back so

they were face-to-face, Brenna could see that Mandy was trying to smile. It was thin and plenty uncertain, but it was a start.

"Theo told you about the rocks that Rafe and I found," Mandy continued a moment later. "They were identical and had heart shapes on them. Can you believe it?" Her eyes brightened, the tears stopped, and she gave a dreamy, romantic sigh. "*Hearts*. That's the ultimate sign of destined love."

She didn't pooh-pooh her sister's conclusion. Not verbally anyway. Over the years Brenna had accepted that Mandy was, well, just Mandy. She was a rose-colored-glasses kind of person with some romantic woo-woo thrown in.

Brenna's opposite.

She figured she'd been born with a cop's skepticism, and even though she was thirty-one, she'd never been in love. Not as an adult anyway. That probably had something to do with growing up around her parents and grand-parents, who'd had strong, loving marriages. In hindsight, that had been a blessing and a curse. Brenna was glad to have had such ideal examples, but it had left her with the worry that ideal was something she'd never have.

Or feel.

The front door eased open again, and Rafe stepped out. With his head hung low, he looked nervous, uncertain, and willing to accept any verbal bashing she aimed at him.

"Mandy wanted to talk to you first," Rafe said right off the bat. He took hold of Mandy's hand and brushed a kiss on her cheek. His voice was still gruff, his expression still a little sourpuss, but there was warmth in his eyes when he looked at Mandy. "She was worried about how you'd react and about our wedding hijacking your homecoming. I know this day should have been your celebration, and I'm sorry it won't be."

Well, heck. It gave Brenna's heart a little pinch to hear the emotion in Rafe's voice.

"It's okay," Brenna managed to say just as she heard the sound of a vehicle turning into Theo's driveway.

Theo mumbled some profanity and stepped around Mandy and Rafe to take Brenna by the shoulders and look her straight in the eyes. "I'm supposed to give you another message," Theo said. "It's bad, Brenna."

Confused, Brenna looked at the approaching vehicle and realized it was her mom's. "What do you mean? What's bad?" Brenna asked as her mom stepped from the car.

Before Theo could answer, his front door opened, and at least a dozen people poured out. Theo's parents, Brenna's friends, and even her soon-to-be new boss, Sheriff Zack Caldwell.

The group yelled, "Surprise!" at the same time her mother called out, "How'd Brenna take the news?"

Brenna was suddenly engulfed in hugs and people gushing about how happy they were that she was back in Loveland for good. There were also some murmured condolences and a few sad puppy-dog glances. Brenna could have developed whiplash what with volleying her attention between her guests and her mother.

"How'd Brenna take the news?" her mom repeated. "Is she really upset?"

"Is Mom talking about Rafe and Mandy's engagement and the pregnancy?" Brenna asked Theo.

The partiers fell quiet as if they were collectively holding their breaths, and all gazes became fixed on Brenna.

"That's part of what your mom is talking about," Theo

confirmed, "but there's more." He looked her straight in the eyes again. "Your parents have split and are getting a divorce." He lowered his voice and added in a sarcastic grumble, "Welcome home, Brenna."

CHAPTER 2

Twenty-seven steps.

That's how far Theo had to walk before he located another section of the pasture fence that needed repair. Putting some muscle behind the hammer, Theo smacked the loose nail into the wood fence post with far more force than required. This wasn't his first fence repair of the morning. More like his fifteenth, and with each one, he'd hoped the nail bashing would ease some of the frustration he was feeling.

It hadn't.

Then again, that was asking a lot of mere fence repair.

In the three months since his injury, he hadn't been in the best of moods and figured that was to be expected what with his having to give up the job he'd loved. His life had turned on a dime in the couple of seconds that it'd taken him to land on the ground after the bull named Butt Buster had tossed him into the air.

Even before his surgeon had given him the bad news that his shattered knee was fixed but would never be anywhere near strong enough for him to compete, Theo had known he would be forced to retire.

Thankfully, he'd had a place to come back to, but it had been a major adjustment to spend night after night in the same bed instead of whatever hotel was near the rodeo venue. An even bigger adjustment to lose the adrenaline rushes from the rides. He'd been a winner, a champion, and here on the ranch, he was the co-heir to the place that had become his family's legacy. Not a bad calling . . . if he hadn't been dealing with the total upheaval of his life.

Now there was another upheaval with Brenna's return, his brother's unexpected fatherhood, and both Mandy and Brenna's mom asking Theo to "be there" for Brenna. Her parents' split had no doubt soured the homecoming that Brenna had expected to be a happy celebration.

Yeah, she knew all about lives turning on a dime.

But Theo knew something else. Brenna wouldn't want any "being there" from him. She'd likely want to deal with this in her own way, and Theo was hoping that the past two days since her homecoming had given her some perspective. Exactly what perspective, he didn't know; it was as if Brenna had been tossed off a metaphorical Butt Buster bull and was now having to deal with the aftermath.

He was almost certainly part of that aftermath, too.

Maybe a big part of it. Twelve years ago, he'd broken Brenna's heart when he'd told her he was leaving Loveland, and he hadn't exactly finessed the breakup, either. When he'd started to tell her he was leaving, that he just couldn't stay and be tied down to this place, that he needed to give the rodeo every part of himself he could give, she had started to cry. The tears had rattled him. Hell, they'd knocked the wind out of him. Instead of the explanation he'd planned, he'd ended up hugging her and walking away.

In hindsight, that hug had been a big-ass mistake. It'd had a "let's just be friends" vibe to it, and Brenna and he had been way more than friends. Lovers. Heck, maybe they'd been in love as much as two eighteen-year-old kids could be.

No way could that love still be around after all this time, but the heat sure as hell was. He'd felt it the moment she'd stepped from her car in front of his house. Brenna had looked so stiff and polished in her uniform. Stiff in her expression toward him, too. She'd definitely been giving him an "I'm hands off now" vibe. Yet, the heat had come and come and come.

It couldn't keep coming, though.

Brenna and he had enough fresh wounds to deal with right now without opening up old ones, and both of them were going to have to go through enough adjustments without adding lust to the mix.

His phone dinged, yanking his attention off Brenna and lust, and Theo saw the text was from Rafe.

New bulls arrive tomorrow afternoon at three.

Rafe didn't add that Theo should be the one to accept that shipment and start the training routines to turn them into the prime rodeo bulls the ranch was known for. Theo had grown up around the bulls and the trainers, and he'd gotten bit by the rodeo bug early on. Now he was one of the trainers, the top dog one. He just hadn't expected to step into that particular role for another year or two.

You still in the east pasture? Rafe had added to the text.

Theo sent him a thumbs-up emoji.

Then you'll be getting a visitor soon, Rafe replied. **Brenna's on her way out to you.**

Theo didn't send a reply this time, but if he had, it would have been a string of question marks because he had to be at the very top of Brenna's list of people to avoid. It didn't take him long, though, to spot Buttercup, one of the ranch's palominos.

Brenna was the rider all right.

No stiff and polished uniform for her today. She was

wearing jeans and a blue shirt that was almost the same color as her eyes.

Even though it was barely ten in the morning, it was still plenty hot, so he was glad to see that someone had loaned Brenna a hat. She could ride well enough, no surprise considering he'd been the one to teach her, but he doubted she'd thought to bring a cowboy hat for this trip.

As she got closer, he could see the rosy glow from the heat on her face. Not actual sweat, more like a glistening. She'd pulled her shoulder-length brown hair into a ponytail that swished with the movement of the horse.

"Well?" she asked when she was still a few yards away. "What's so important that you had to see me?"

Theo was sure he blinked. Sure, too, he had a puzzled look on his face.

"I was just going to wait for you in the barn," she went on, reining in and staring down at him, "but Rafe said you might be out here awhile, and I didn't want to hang around, waiting for you to get back."

"Why would you think I had to see you?" he asked.

Now it was her turn to give him a puzzled look. "Because you told Mandy that we needed to talk about the reason for my parents' split."

The moment the words left her mouth, the puzzled expression morphed into frustration tinged with anger. Yeah, Theo was right there on the same page with her.

"You didn't tell Mandy any such thing," she concluded on a huff.

"I didn't tell Mandy any such thing," he confirmed, adding his own huff.

"Matchmaking," Brenna grumbled like raw profanity. "This has to stop. Romance is not the cure for all that ails me. Or you," she added when her gaze slid down to his bum knee.

"Agreed," he couldn't say fast enough. "My mom's in on it. She keeps texting me old pictures of us when we were in high school."

"Yes!" She stabbed her index finger at him. "My mom's doing the same thing. Well, not texting because she sucks at that, but she left a whole bunch of them in my room and insisted on showing them to me. Pictures and other stuff," she tacked on in a mumble.

"What other stuff?" he immediately wanted to know. "You mean like magic rocks?"

Brenna didn't smile, but her mouth quivered a little. "No rocks. But she kept the flower from the wrist corsage you gave me for the prom. And that tacky rhinestone tiara the prom committee put on me after we'd been elected king and queen."

The silence came, not a companionable one, either. This was awkward as hell, and Theo had no doubt that Brenna was recalling that night, those times. Brenna shook her head as if trying to get rid of the memories. It seemed to work because she regained some of her mad.

"And that whole deal about you drawing the short straw so you'd be the one to tell me the bad news—they cheated," she insisted. "I don't know how, but they did and pulled one over on you."

Theo frowned because he could see now that it was true. At the time, he'd just been so caught up in the crap news that Brenna would be getting instead of a hero's home-coming, he hadn't seen the straw drawing for what it was—a ruse to get Brenna and him face-to-face.

"Did Mandy and my mom think I'd just go flying into

your arms and French-kiss you?" she went on, her anger building once more.

It was building some for Theo, too, but he was also feeling that dang heat at the mention of a French kiss. Something Brenna and he had done a lot of way back when. Apparently, there was still plenty of leftover fire.

"You'll need to have a talk with your mom, and I'll have one with Mandy and my mother," she insisted. "No more matchmaking, period. If we present a united front on this, they'll have to back off."

"Maybe," he said, and then paused to think this through. "But if we come on too strong, they might see it as a 'the lady doth protest too much' kind of thing."

Her mouth quivered again, but not in anger this time. He thought Brenna was fighting a smile.

"What?" he wanted to know.

"A cowboy quoting Shakespeare. That blows some of the stereotypes about your profession."

He shrugged, but Theo had to admit it unknotted his stomach some to see that lighter expression on her face. He'd hurt her, bad, and he deserved any venom she had for him. However, he also didn't want her to spend another single second hating him. Brenna should be happy, she deserved it, and likely would be once she got over these latest hurdles that life had thrown at her.

"What can I say?" He went with a lighter tone, too. "I paid attention in Mrs. Carmichael's eleventh-grade English class when we read *Hamlet*, and that line stuck with me. Not that it applies to us then or now," Theo quickly assured her.

"No, it doesn't apply," she agreed, but when their gazes connected, she quickly looked away.

The silence came again, and while still in the saddle,

she glanced around the pasture. "So, do you actually have any clue why my parents split?"

Theo had been expecting this question and wished he had a better answer. Something to ease the hurt he knew Brenna had to be feeling.

"No. There weren't any rumors they were having marital troubles. No gossip about affairs or public arguments or such." He paused. "Rafe is worried, though, that he's part of the reason for their breakup."

"Mandy's worried about that, too," Brenna agreed. "She thinks there might have been underlying problems in the marriage and that the pregnancy was the straw that broke the camel's back."

He had to shrug. It was possible, of course, but Theo figured that news of a grandchild would be more likely to hold a marriage together. Both Brenna's and his parents had had their kids later in life, and they were now all in their mid to late sixties, and both moms had made it clear they wanted to be grandparents while they were still young enough to take an active part in their grandchildren's lives.

Maybe they hadn't wanted to earn that grandparent status with an unplanned pregnancy between their two kids who were polar opposites. But still, Theo doubted Rafe's getting Mandy pregnant had caused the split.

"Last night, my mother asked to borrow some of my clothes and makeup," she went on. "And she keeps trying to talk me out of looking for a place to rent. She thinks we'll be happy as clams living in the house together."

Well, it was a big house, and now that Brenna's dad had moved out and Mandy would soon be doing the same, maybe her mom wanted the company. Then again, with her mom's matchmaking, perhaps she just wanted Brenna under her roof so she could leave dried corsages and tacky tiaras around to remind her daughter of what once had been.

"Dad bought a red sports car shaped like a man's genitalia," Brenna continued. Obviously, she had a lot to get off her chest, and since her glistening had turned to a sweat, she eyed the nearby shade tree and started to dismount. "Mandy keeps finding stuff that she says proves you and I should be together."

Theo sighed. "I'm getting the same from my mom."

Brenna gave him a flat look while she stepped down from the horse. "Mandy's latest find was a tomato slice in her salad at Sugar Baby's," she added, referring to the town's diner. "The slice apparently had my smile, and next to it was a clump of romaine with your bunched-up forehead." Her mouth tightened. "I dare you to top that."

Sighing, and yes, with a bunched-up forehead, he took hold of the reins to lead Buttercup out of the blistering sun. "My mother sent me an article she found on the internet about how a man's sperm count declines as he ages, and she added a note that if I wanted kids, I should get cracking. And, yeah, she used the word 'cracking.'"

Brenna made a face. "Okay, you win. So far, I haven't gotten any lectures about my biological clock."

Their gazes met again. Held. And that's when Theo figured it was time for a change of subject. Yeah, he could offer her some kind of comfort. Maybe a hug that would put them body to body, and it would be good. Darn good. But it would mess with her head, and right now she didn't need that, especially since it would bolster Mandy's claims about tomato slices and lettuce clumps.

As a way to unlock their gazes, he led her to the shade tree where he'd left his own horse, and he took out two bottles of water from the saddlebag.

"So I'm certain you've talked to your folks to try to figure out why they split up?" he asked.

"Talked, talked, and talked some more, and it still doesn't make sense." A groan followed her sigh. "Both say they've lost the spark. Whatever the heck that means."

Theo had an inkling, but he didn't spell it out, mainly because the spark that first came to mind was kissing Brenna back in tenth grade. Even now he could recall in perfect detail that she'd tasted like birthday cake, Christmas, and forbidden fruit all rolled into one. But it'd been twelve years now since he'd kissed her. Likely it wouldn't have the same effect now.

His stupid body nudged him to test that theory.

Theo told his body and the stupidity to take a hike.

Brenna groaned again and squeezed her eyes shut a moment. "My parents burst my bubble, Theo. I'm talking bursting and stomping it to dust. I just can't believe it. I always thought I wouldn't be able to live up to the standards of their ideal marriage, and it turns out the ideal didn't even exist."

He was getting a whole lot of mixed emotions here. On the one hand, it felt good to be able to talk to Brenna again. He'd missed this, the connection that had once felt bone deep. On the other hand, the only reason she was talking to him was because she was hurting. Again. At least this time he wasn't the cause of that hurt, but he could sure as heck add to it if he didn't keep his lust for her in check.

"From what I can tell, neither my mom nor dad is seeing anyone else," she went on. "That didn't factor into their decision to split." Brenna paused, gulped some water. "They went to counseling about six months ago, but in the end, they decided to split and not tell anyone about it until I was back in town. Anyone but Rafe, Mandy, and you, that is," she tacked on.

"Yeah, your mom told the three of us right after the engagement announcement. Then, she swore us to secrecy until you could hear the news in person."

"Because I might get distracted on the job," Brenna said with a heavy sigh, and she sank down onto the ground, anchoring her back against the tree. "Instead, now I'm about to face a new job, and the new life I'd planned here isn't what I'd thought it would be."

"It's a sucky homecoming, that's for sure. If you think it'll help, I've got more Jolly Ranchers at my house. Your mom brought over a big bag to help me deliver the bad news. I also have tequila, and I can promise you that I don't have any fruits or vegetables around that resemble us."

She smiled just a little as he'd hoped she would. That smile was both good and bad. Good because it lit up Brenna's already beautiful face. Bad because the lit-up face only reminded him that he wanted to kiss her again. Since the timing for that sucked and might continue to suck forever, Theo offered her a different option.

"Or we can sit under this tree, and you can curse and bash your folks, Mandy, and Rafe, and anything else that's bothering you," he offered.

The smile faded, and she kicked at a clump of grass. "No, because I can't blame them for bursting my romantic bubble. And I wouldn't want my parents to stay together if they're not truly happy. But losing the spark? Why not stay together and try to find it again?"

Theo had to shrug. "I don't know. Maybe this could turn into an 'absence makes the heart grow fonder' deal? That might be how the fresh spark happens."

"If only. I wish they could figure out a way to get back together, and yes, I know that sounds selfish and whiny. I want them happy, too." She paused. "Ironically, they seem happy. Or maybe they're just putting on a front for me."

She kicked at a clump of grass again, but this time a quarter-size rock went flying. A rock that landed right in her lap. Brenna moved as if to knock it off, but her hand froze over the white limestone, and she eyed it as if it were a bug that should be squashed. Theo soon saw why.

It was heart shaped.

The rock wasn't a perfect replica of that particular shape, but Mother Nature had apparently done enough abrading and tumbling to make it easily recognizable.

Her gaze flew to his, and she frantically shook her head. "This isn't some kind of sign."

"No, it's not," he quickly agreed, though he didn't care much for the coincidence of finding such a thing. "Besides, there are all kinds of rocks around this part of Texas. Once, Rafe found one that looked just like a slimy, wart-covered frog, and he put it on Mom's pillow to freak her out."

Brenna looked at him again. "You're not just saying that to make me feel better, are you?"

"Nope. True story, and Mom was so shocked and scared that she threw the pillow across the room, and the rock smacked Rafe right between the eyes. After she bandaged his bleeding forehead, Mom grounded Rafe, and me, because she figured I was in on it somehow."

She released a long breath of what seemed to be relief. Theo got where she was coming from. They didn't need anything that Mandy could interpret as signs of their mutual destinies.

He looked down at her at the same moment she looked up at him, and their gazes collided. Sort of like a lightning strike with lots and lots of heat and sizzle. Oh yeah.

Kissing Brenna could definitely be better than their teenage fumblings.

Judging from the way her face flushed, Brenna had an idea where his thoughts were going, and that fired up the heat even more. Theo might have tossed caution to the wind and followed through on his desires, but Brenna spoke first.

"So what's the deal with your injury? Just how bad is it?" she asked. "Obviously, you can ride and mend fences since that's what you were doing when I rode up."

Her question mentally yanked him back from the kiss and put the chill button on the lust, too. He'd figured Brenna would want to know about what'd happened, but it still wasn't easy talking about it. Well, normally it wasn't, but today the words just flowed out of him.

"My bum knee creates some limits," he admitted, "like competing on a bull hell-bent on tossing me off his back, running a marathon, or kickboxing. But I'm coping. It's all about steps." And he immediately wished he hadn't added that part, because she gave him a puzzled look. "I count or estimate the steps I need to go from point A to B, and I take them one at a time."

Theo wished he hadn't added that, either, because he thought he saw some sympathy pop up in her eyes. No way would he elaborate any further and explain that at first each step had been excruciating, but now he just experienced twinges that felt like victories. Each and every one of them. Some people probably measured out their lives with career successes or even segments of time, but the steps were most important to him.

"Physical therapy has helped, so I'm okay to go for most things," he assured her.

She made a sound of agreement and then paused a very long time. "Good," Brenna muttered.

That simple response packed a wallop, and Theo didn't think it was his imagination that her voice was laced with some anger. He believed he knew the source of that particular emotion, too, and it didn't have squat to do with his knee or the number of steps he'd taken.

"You can curse and yell at me, too," he offered. "I deserve it because of the way I hurt you."

"Yes, you do," she snapped. There was fire in her eyes, but it cooled just as fast as it came. "I probably shouldn't be pouring my heart out to you like this, but it took me a long time to get over you, Theo. A long time," she emphasized. "And I can't do it again. That's why we'll both need to make it clear to our folks and Mandy that you and I won't be an item."

That statement cut deeper than any cursing or yelling would have done. Because it definitely wasn't a case of a "lady protesting too much." It was a quietly spoken decision by a woman he'd hurt. Her words did a good job of cooling down his lust.

Until Brenna looked at him again.

They were close enough for him to take in her scent. Soap and saddle leather. Close enough for him to see when the flash of unwanted heat sparked in her eyes. The old attraction was obviously still there. Man, was it. But he'd heard her loud and clear about not wanting to be hurt again.

"Besides," she went on, her voice sounding a little dreamy now, "we're not the same people we were back in high school. Thank heaven for that," she added.

"Yeah, thank heaven," he echoed, and Theo tried to tear his gaze from her.

He failed.

Worse, his gaze dropped to her mouth. The very mouth he was aching to kiss. Hell, there were a lot of things he wanted to do with Brenna, and common sense had nothing to do with his need.

Thankfully, distraction intervened when he heard the sound of approaching horses. Theo looked up and groaned at the sight of Mandy and Rafe riding straight toward them. Well, hell. So much for riding fence to get away from his troubles. The troubles were obviously coming to him.

"Mandy can't see this rock," Brenna muttered, and she glanced around as if ready to toss it. But Mandy and Rafe were plenty close enough to see such a toss and might even get a glimpse of the rock. Instead, Brenna shoved it into the pocket of her jeans.

"Are we interrupting something?" Mandy called out, her voice filled with giddy glee. Probably because she'd seen Theo looking at Brenna with lust in his eyes.

"No," Theo and Brenna answered in unison.

Unfortunately, their denial came so fast that it sounded as if they were trying to cover up something. Which they were, of course. No way did he want her sister to see the blasted rock, because Mandy would amp up her attempts to prove to Brenna and him that they had some sort of destiny together.

"Are you sure?" Mandy pressed, adding a teasing lilt, but her happy look cooled some, probably because Brenna and Theo managed to keep their stony expressions. "Sorry," she added.

There was no trace of Mandy's smile when Rafe and she dismounted. "We're sorry," Rafe echoed. "It's just that Mandy said she thought Brenna was completely okay with our engagement and the baby—"

"I am," Brenna interrupted, cutting off what would have no doubt turned into another round of apologies. "In fact, I'm happy for you."

"Then, why the sad faces?" Mandy wanted to know.

Brenna waved that question off. "Theo and I were just talking, that's all."

Mandy's gaze slid to Theo's injured leg, and she sighed. "Good. I'm glad you two have each other."

Theo groaned and was about to tell Mandy to stop her matchmaking and to stop looking in salads and such for signs, but Rafe spoke first.

"Look, Mandy and I were planning on just having the Justice of the Peace marry us, but now we're thinking we'd like to have an actual wedding. We wanted to ask if the two of you would be our best man and maid of honor."

Normally, this request would have brought on quick, positive responses, but judging from the fact that Brenna stayed as quiet as Theo, she obviously shared his suspicion that it was another matchmaking ploy.

"I'll be happy to stand up for you at the wedding, but Theo and I aren't getting back together," Brenna spelled out.

"Ditto," Theo put in.

Mandy smiled. "Of course, you aren't," said in a total *I'm not buying it* way. "Yay on being the maid of honor and best man!" She clapped her hands and hugged them both.

Rafe joined in with a thanks and a slap on the back for Theo. When Mandy pulled back, though, she had a fresh glimmer in her eyes. One that gave Theo a bad feeling in the pit of his stomach.

"I have something else to tell you," Mandy went on. "And, no, this isn't about trying to remind the two of you of just how close you used to be. But it is sort of connected to the L-Word campaign."

Theo wasn't sure who looked more confused. Brenna or him. "Excuse me?" Brenna asked.

"The L-Word campaign, that's what I'm calling the PR project I'm doing for the mayor," Mandy explained. "The one to attract lovers and newlyweds to Loveland so we can become a small-town romance destination. I mean, the town already has the perfect name for it, right?"

Loveland was indeed a good name for a romance destination unless you were a local who knew that it had originally been called Bogg to honor the founder's eldest son. Apparently, once that particular given name fell out of fashion, the town had adopted the founder's surname of Loveland.

"So a perfect name and a fun campaign that'll get everyone's attention." Mandy clapped her hands in excitement. "Theo and you will be part of it, too, because you'll soon be a billboard."

Theo borrowed Brenna's "Excuse me?"

"A billboard," Mandy verified, smiling as if this were the best idea in history. "Fourteen feet high and forty-eight feet wide."

The woman was downright giddy as she pulled out her phone and showed them the picture. Yes, that very prom picture of Brenna in a tiara, wearing the wrist corsage and staring up at him. And him staring down at her as if he intended to take her mouth right then, right there.

Mandy squealed with delight. "This will be the first thing people see when they drive into town. You two will be the stars of the L-Word campaign."

CHAPTER 3

Brenna nibbled away at her deluxe BLT with pepper fries, a specialty of Sugar Baby's diner, while her father went on about his plans to expand the inventory at the hardware store. Not exactly riveting stuff, but this was her dad, so she listened with far more interest than "Jiggle No More" toilet repair kits deserved.

Over the past week since she'd returned home and learned her parents had split, lunch with her dad had become the new routine. That was partly because he'd moved into the apartment above the hardware store, and it was right next door to Sugar Baby's. It was obvious her dad was trying hard to make sure she was okay and that she was happy. He wasn't alone in those attempts, either.

A forty-five-minute lunch at Sugar Baby's would often include neighbors' enthusiastic "welcome home" greetings, followed by remarks about the billboard and how fun it was to see Theo and her again. Some weren't as subtle as others.

For instance, just moments earlier, the town's florist, Candy Jean Arnez, had come out and asked her if Theo and she would be making it a double wedding so the town would have their scaled-down version of *Seven Brides for Seven Brothers*.

Brenna had managed a polite enough smile to go with her firm, "No."

She hoped if she kept saying it often enough, folks would back off. Unfortunately, her denial of a prom king and queen reunion wasn't keeping anyone from matchmaking. Especially Mandy and her mother.

"Any luck finding a place to rent or buy yet?" her father asked, yanking her attention back to him.

She shook her head, knowing that anyone in hearing range would start making offers, ones that would likely include reduced rent to compensate for the fact that she was having a hard time dealing with her parents' split. It seemed as if the entire town was either trying to matchmake Theo and her or else pity her into the ground.

"Oh, well," her father went on. "Your mom's no doubt happy to have you with her as long as possible."

Brenna studied his face. Her father rarely brought up anything to do with her mother. She was hoping to see something like regret in his expression, but it simply wasn't there.

"I know you're upset about your mom and me splitting up," he went on, probably prompted by her heavy sigh. "Trust me, though, when I say it was for the best."

"Was it?" she snapped, and instantly regretted it because three people turned to give her sad, pitying looks. "Was it?" she repeated in a whisper.

Her father's sigh was heavy, too. "It was. Neither of us was happy, and we're both coming up on our sixty-fifth birthdays. Retirement age," he added in a mumble. He stared down into his glass of sweet tea. "You've got a lot of years left, so I figure it's hard for you to understand."

"It is hard," she verified, then paused. Even though she'd already asked this question in several different ways,

Brenna went with the direct approach. "Did the split have anything to do with Mandy's being pregnant?"

"No," he quickly assured her. "The news was a shock, of course, but the split was already in the works before that."

Brenna was glad of that. Well, as glad as she could be of anything connected to this separation.

"Did the breakup have anything to do with me?" she pressed. Since she was going for the direct approach, it was something she needed to know.

Her father frowned. "No." Again, his response was quick. "Why would it?"

She had to shrug, and then Brenna groaned and shook her head. "I don't know. But I just don't want it to be because of me."

"It isn't." He patted her hand. "Your mom and I are so proud of you. You got a hard blow when Theo walked out on you. Yes, I know he broke your heart," he added when she lifted her head. "But you picked yourself up and became a hero."

"I'm not a hero," she insisted. "I was a military cop."

"Same thing," her father assured her in a way that only a dad could.

That actually made her feel . . . well, better. Not better about the split or Theo but about things in general.

"Is being apart from Mom making you happy?" She had to know.

"Yes." Her dad's answer was fast and firm, but some of that firmness faded just enough to give her hope that this separation was temporary. "There's an excitement in my life now. I can do what I want to do when I want it. Like buying my new car and watching TV late into the night."

Neither of those things would be particularly exciting for Brenna, but she was trying to find some empathy to go along with the smidge of good feeling she had. "But you're telling me the truth when you say there's no one else in the romantic equation?"

"There's no one else." Again, his answer was fast, and this time none of the firmness faded. "It's not like your heartbreak over losing Theo when you were eighteen. That's probably why our separation is making you hurt all over again. Being apart just feels right, and your mom agrees."

Well, Brenna couldn't argue with that, because her mom did indeed seem to be happy about the split. And at least her dad had said separation and not divorce; maybe they weren't planning on the latter anytime soon.

Brenna would have explained that what had happened with Theo wasn't eating away at her anymore—not much anyway—but she heard the sound of an incoming text. She pulled her phone from her purse, and the rock came out with it.

The heart-shaped stone clattered onto the table, and she silently cursed herself for not just tossing the darn thing. But no, instead she'd taken it from her jeans pocket and put it in her purse to avoid her mom seeing it in the trash, and now her father was eyeing it.

"Hey, what's this?" he murmured, picking it up to have a look.

Brenna didn't even attempt an explanation, looking instead at her phone screen. She saw the text was from Mandy.

Rafe and I are planning a combined bachelor and bachelorette party Friday night, and we want Theo and you to be our guests of honor. Isn't that the best idea ever?

A whole lot of emotions hit Brenna at once. For her personally, this was a sucky idea, but she couldn't fault

Rafe and Mandy for wanting to have a semi-traditional celebration before the wedding. Still, it would be an opportunity for folks to study her every reaction and twinge, looking for signs of her getting back together with Theo. He would get some scrutiny, too, to see how he was coping with his injury.

And her.

Because Brenna wasn't deaf to the whispers that Theo and she had already turned to each other. Depending on who was doling out the gossip, the turning was either for consolation sex or because they simply hadn't been able to keep their hands off each other.

Brenna shoved all those concerns and the gossip aside and went with a cheery reply to Mandy. **Sounds great. How can I help?**

Squeee! Mandy immediately texted back. **So glad you're on board. Check with Theo. He's working out all the details.**

Brenna settled for a thumbs-up response. This was likely another matchmaking ploy, but Brenna didn't care. At the moment, it felt as if Theo was the only person in Loveland who actually understood what she was going through, and he was definitely the only one who'd understand how this incessant matchmaking was wearing on her.

She said good-bye to her dad, gave him a kiss on the cheek, and while she walked back to her car, she fired off a text to Theo. **Mandy told me about the party. I'm on my way out to the ranch.**

I'm working in the big barn, he texted right back.

Brenna got an instant flash of a shirtless Theo and his calendar-worthy body. In this heat, he would likely be a little sweaty in a hot guy sort of way, and he'd . . . She stopped herself from going any further with that fantasy. She was going to Theo for party planning and to whine about all the matchmaking, not for any ogling or fantasizing.

She drove away from the diner to the edge of town, where Brenna slammed on her brakes as she saw it. The billboard. It was there, right in front of her, and it astounded her to realize just how big the darn thing was. It seemed to take up the entire Texas sky.

The image had been doctored, too. Instead of the cluttered background of a high school prom with tacky amateurish decorations, someone had photoshopped in the image of the Marrying Tree in all its glory. Beneath the massive image was apparently the slogan to go along with the campaign.

Loveland, where you'll find your own happily ever after.

According to the print at the bottom, the sign had been sponsored by Petal after Petal Flower Shop, Sweetly Sugared Bakery (*Wedding cakes are our bread and butter*), Snap You Up Wedding Photography, and O'Sullivan's Hardware.

Brenna wasn't surprised that neither her mom nor dad had mentioned becoming a sponsor. They had to know this wouldn't please her. And if they had brought it up, they would have no doubt claimed it was to support Mandy.

Since she'd seemingly run out of sighs and groans, Brenna went for an eyeroll and continued her drive to Willow Creek Ranch. Considering that just a week ago, she'd mentally vowed never to come here, she was certainly coming here a lot. This would be her third visit since her homecoming.

She parked her car and began walking toward the barn, but she stopped and looked up when someone called her name. Brenna soon spotted Theo's mom, Audrey, in one of the second-floor windows.

"You're here to see Theo?" Audrey asked, all smiles.

Brenna nodded. "It's about the party."

"Well, have fun," the woman said as if Brenna had just announced Theo and she were going on a date. "And FYI, I love the billboard. It's double-sided, you know, so people can see it coming and going."

Brenna hadn't known, but she still scrounged up a smile. "It's something, isn't it?" And while that definitely wasn't a compliment or approval, Audrey took it as such and continued to smile, giving Brenna a good-bye wave.

As she started walking, Brenna wondered if Theo had gotten around to having a chat with his mom about match-making. If so, it didn't seem to be working.

She threw open the barn door, and her tongue nearly landed on the floor. There was Theo only a few feet away, and he was in full fantasy mode. A body-hugging shirt, a little sweaty, his jeans riding low on his hips while he hefted up a hay bale. All sorts of muscles flexed and re-acted to the lifting, which meant all sorts of dirty thoughts started flying through her head.

Oh, mercy.

Talk about one hot cowboy.

He turned his head, glanced at her, and then did sort of a double take. Probably because she was standing there looking like a lust-filled teenager. No way for her to shut off the lust, but Brenna tried to put on her cop's face to minimize it.

She failed.

The corner of Theo's mouth lifted in the damnable smile that no doubt seduced lots of women. Including her. She hated that he still had her hormonal number, but it was hard not to enjoy the cheap thrill of all of this. Dirty thoughts, lust, and a hot cowboy all worked together to give her body a nice sexual buzz.

Brenna allowed herself just a moment more of that buzz

before she cleared her throat and tried her cop's face again. "Uh, Mandy said you might need help with the party . . ."

Her words trailed off as she looked around. Theo had distracted her from seeing the decorations. There were twinkling lights hanging from the rafters. Hundreds of them. Rows of folding chairs were neatly arranged, and even a makeshift aisle led to the very spot where Theo plunked down the hay bale.

Brenna's gaze shot to him when she heard him grunt. Not from exertion but rather pain.

"I'm okay," he quickly assured her. "I just get twinges. It's only about thirty steps to bring the hay bales from the flatbed out back into the barn."

That wasn't the first time he'd mentioned steps, and his reaction seemed like more than a twinge to her, but Brenna didn't push. Instead, she continued to look at the decorations. Considering the ceremony had been more or less slapped together, the barn would turn out to be a beautiful venue for the wedding.

"Will the party be in here?" Brenna asked.

"It will." He put his hands on his hips and glanced around. "We'll move out the chairs for that. We put them in place right now just so we could get a feel for the space."

Theo had no sooner finished that explanation than the door opened, and Rafe came in with another stack of chairs. He, too, was wearing a snug shirt and was sweaty, but Brenna didn't get that kick of lust the way she had with Theo.

"Oh, hey," Rafe greeted when he saw her.

"Hey back. I'm here to help," she responded with as much enthusiasm as she could manage.

"Yeah, Mandy said you might be dropping by. She's at work today, but she'll be here later, too." He set down the chairs and volleyed glances at both Theo and her as if trying to suss out whether there'd been any hanky-panky going on before he'd come in.

"I've only been here a couple of minutes," she settled for saying.

Rafe nodded but looked about as comfortable as a steer's rump beneath a branding iron. "Look," he said as Theo headed to the back of the barn. "I know you must think Mandy and I are spending too much time trying to get you two together—"

"You are," Brenna interrupted.

Rafe chuckled and nodded again. "I try to rein her in, but that's hard to do since we're so happy. We are happy," he emphasized. "Mandy and I are big-time opposites, but I want you to know I love her."

There was no doubting his sincerity. She could see it all over his face, and that made Brenna ease back on the defensive vibe she was likely sending off.

"Mandy loves you, too," she said.

Rafe smiled and flushed a little. "Yeah. Don't ask me why, but she does." He shook his head as if he couldn't believe his luck at finding her. "Mandy's just so positive, you know. So hopeful." He looked Brenna in the eyes now. "And that's why she wants you to be happy, too."

Best to spell this out in case Rafe could actually get through to Mandy. "Theo and I aren't getting back together."

"I know. And Mandy really doesn't mean to push so hard."

Brenna raised an eyebrow. "Have you seen the billboard?"

Rafe winced a little. "Yeah, but I can promise you that Mandy went through hundreds of old photos of town events, and that one of Theo and you best captured the heart of the L-Word campaign."

She didn't ask him to explain that. Brenna remembered the way she was looking at Theo in that photograph, and if it wasn't her face on the forty-eight-foot display, she might indeed have thought it was a good example of "Loveland, where you'll find your own happily ever after."

Theo came back from wherever he'd gone, and he was hauling in a huge barrel. She moved to help him, but Rafe beat her to it. Not to Theo's approval, though. He scowled at Rafe and then together the brothers placed the barrel to the side of what she assumed would be the altar. She was guessing the scowl was because Theo didn't want help that reminded him of his injury.

"I'll get the other barrel," Rafe muttered, and headed off.

"So what do you need me to do?" she asked Theo.

He turned to her, and his expression softened some. Her own expression probably changed, too, because some of the buttons on his shirt had come undone, and she was getting a peep show of his chest and abs.

"Why don't you figure out the best place to put a hay bale stage for the strippers," he said, glancing around as if looking for a spot.

Brenna had been doing a lot of mental double takes lately, but that suggestion required her to do another. "There'll be strippers?"

Theo nodded, but like her, his expression indicated he'd done a mental double take on it, too. "Mandy hired both male and female strippers for the combined bachelor-bachelorette party. Apparently, their acts will be somewhat toned down, but she wanted this to be a traditional experience."

"A traditional experience," she muttered, shaking her head, but then she had to smile. Mandy obviously had her own interpretation of traditional.

Theo smiled as well, silently sharing his amusement

with her. But it seemed like more than that. Intimate even. Because any positive connection with Theo was capable of breaking down a whole lot of heart-guarding barriers she'd put in place. Barriers that should stay put for a reason. Too bad she was having trouble recalling exactly what that reason was with Theo this close to her.

She forced herself to quit thinking about him and do what he'd asked. Brenna glanced around the barn and spotted an area where there were already some hay bales. It was behind the spot where Theo and Rafe had just put the barrel.

"The stage could work there," she said, pointing to it.

The corner of his mouth lifted again, and she knew why. It'd be a stripper stage for the parties and then would turn into the very spot where the vows would be exchanged. Her sister would no doubt get a kick out of that.

"There's the added advantage of not having to move out all the chairs for the party," Brenna pointed out.

Theo made a sound of agreement and looked at the chairs. Well, he did after he tore his gaze from her. Apparently, she wasn't the only one having trouble with their unspoken "eyes off" rule.

He walked toward the first row of chairs, studying them, and then studied the aisle. "This width might not be right. And there might not be enough space at the makeshift altar since Mandy wants it flanked with barrels of flowers. You and Mandy are about the same size, and Mandy said her dress is four feet wide."

"At least that," Brenna interjected. "I saw it this morning, and it's princess style. A very poofy bottom," she added when Theo gave her a blank look.

She eyed the aisle and chair placement, too, and then held out her arms to simulate the four feet of space. It'd be close. Then, she remembered Mandy wouldn't be walking down alone, that their dad would be by her side to give the bride away.

"You walk next to me and pretend you're my father," Brenna instructed.

In hindsight, she probably should have come up with a different solution. Because of her outstretched arms, it didn't exactly put Theo and her side by side, but the moment he stepped into the aisle, her hand brushed that incredible stomach she'd been ogling.

"Sorry," she muttered.

Brenna adjusted her position and tried to keep her right hand a few inches ahead of Theo's body as they proceeded. She added some music by humming the traditional wedding march, but she'd barely made it to the "all dressed in white" part when she saw that Theo had been right about there not being enough room.

"Either Mandy's going to have to squish against our dad, or she'll risk mowing down guests with her dress," Brenna pointed out.

"Yeah," he agreed, eyeing the chairs again. "We can push them farther apart some, but there might have to be a little squishing, too, with Mandy and your dad."

Theo looked at her again, and he was likely debating the risk of them testing out being squished together. He didn't dismiss it. In fact, she saw the heat stirring in his eyes. Then again, there was almost always heat when their gazes locked.

Like now.

Locked and loaded with a whole bunch of heat.

Brenna felt herself swallow hard. Felt the flush of arousal, too, but she remembered those barriers. The ones she'd put up after getting her heart broken. It was best for her to remember that Theo was the cowboy heartbreaker.

She cleared her throat, her head as well, and got them moving again. Best to finish this test run before she did something she'd end up regretting.

Her hand bumped into him again when they started walking, but this time she'd obviously dropped her arms too low because her fingers swiped the front of his jeans. He grunted. Not from pain. Nope. This was arousal, and while the look he shot her was still heated, it also had a grimace mixed with it.

"Sorry," she repeated, and moved even faster so she could put an end to this torture. Torture not just for Theo but for her, too, since Brenna had some awfully clear memories of touching every part of Theo's body.

When he'd been naked.

Yeah, those weren't good memories to have right now.

"I'll keep my hands outstretched," she said as they approached the altar and stopped. "Rafe will be there." She motioned toward the barrel. "Now, you turn to face me. That way, you'll know where to position the Justice of the Peace so Mandy's dress doesn't knock him off the hay bale podium."

Facing each other was a risk because, hey, she'd be looking right at Theo again, but Brenna intended to make it quick.

She failed.

Oh, mercy. Did she ever fail.

Her gaze didn't just lock with Theo's. It latched on to him and refused to let go. Worse, the heat came with a vengeance as if it refused to be penned in any longer. Brenna wouldn't have been surprised if actual sparks flared up between them.

Theo obviously felt it, too, because he cursed, and for

some stupid reason that made her smile. Not for long, though. Theo pretty much gobbled up that smile by kissing her.

His mouth landed on hers, and in the same motion, he hooked his arm around her waist to pull her to him. Body to body. Mouth to mouth. And as Mandy would add, heart to heart.

But Brenna wasn't thinking about hearts right now. This was a lust kiss, all heat and need. There was a whole lot of both, and it was good. Oh, so good. She remembered his taste and the perfect way his mouth fit to hers. It still felt perfect, and he still tasted like the hot cowboy he was.

She would have gobbled him up as well, but the sound of approaching footsteps had them flying apart. Theo banged into the barrel. She tripped over her own unsteady feet, and her butt smacked down onto the hay bale.

"Should I come back later?" someone asked.

Both Theo and Brenna groaned. Their visitor didn't. Or rather *visitors*. Brenna looked at the barn entrance and saw who'd made those sounds.

Rafe, Mandy, her mother, and Theo's mom.

All four were grinning.

Theo and Brenna weren't.

"I should go," Brenna somehow managed to say, and to a chorus of giggles and Mandy's mumbled "I told you so," Brenna got out of there fast.

CHAPTER 4

While he sat in his office, Theo tried to lose himself in paperwork. A necessary but mundane chore to work out training routines for the new bulls and work schedules for the ranch hands. He was succeeding for the most part, but he kept going back to that kiss in the barn.

The past forty-eight hours hadn't cooled down his body one bit. Nope. He was still burning, still aching to kiss Brenna again even though he knew it was a crappy idea. Brenna didn't need her emotional waters muddied that way. Heck, she didn't need *him*, not after what he'd done to her in high school, but that kiss had made certain parts of his body believe that bygones were bygones and that a fresh start just might be possible after all.

His body was often stupid when it came to such things.

Brenna would certainly agree with that assessment. She'd also likely disagree about the bygones and fresh start. Besides, she had enough on her plate dealing with her parents' separation without adding a messy, complicated relationship with him.

Mentally repeating that last part, he dove back into the paperwork again and vowed to quit thinking of Brenna. Hard to do, though, what with that billboard image of them branded into his memory and the constant gossip about their being back together.

The only thing worse than billboards and gossip was the continued matchmaking. Apparently, Mandy and the two moms thought the kiss needed some more fuel to complete the Theo-Brenna reunion, and they'd gotten the town involved in the refueling efforts.

The local newspaper was running old photos and articles about Brenna and him. The diner had created a heart-shaped cheeseburger with jalapeños, mango, and bacon that the diner owners were calling the Prom King and Queen. According to the description, it was "the perfect mix of spicy and sweet, just like our own prom king and queen."

Theo figured he'd be avoiding the diner for a while.

There was also the added problem of the billboards that were now at both entrances to town, and a third one had just gone up on the road to the ranch. He'd get a daily dose of that one even if he never left his house. Theo wasn't sure how Mandy had talked the mayor into spending the bucks to put one there, where it wouldn't be seen by a lot of people, but she'd somehow managed it.

He was still trying to keep Brenna, billboards, romance-themed cheeseburgers, and the kiss out of his mind when Theo heard Brenna in the hall outside his office, which was located in the main house where his folks lived.

"I'm sure I can find the place on my own," Brenna said, her voice strained.

"No need," his mother quickly responded. No strained voice for her. "These roads on the ranch can be a bit tricky, and Theo won't mind."

Theo opened the door to find his mother's hand lifted and ready to knock. Brenna was right next to her, and she didn't have to say aloud that this was the last place on earth she wanted to be. Her expression conveyed her feelings just fine.

"You won't mind, right, Theo?" his mother asked him.

"Mind what?" His own voice was loaded with caution.

"Taking Brenna out to the cottage. She's interested in buying it."

Theo felt himself frown. First, he hadn't known the cottage that had once belonged to his grandparents was even for sale. Second, it wasn't that hard to find. The ranch roads weren't especially tricky, either.

"I don't want to interrupt your work," Brenna tried again, but his mom quickly pooh-poohed that.

"Nonsense," she said. "Theo's been at it for hours, and he could use a break. Show Brenna the cottage," his mom instructed, "and then bring her back here so we can have lunch together."

With that, his mother moved darn fast to get out of there, not giving either Brenna or him a chance to argue.

"Stating the obvious here, but she's matchmaking," Theo muttered.

"Yep," Brenna readily agreed. She looked up at him. "And I'm sorry about that. Sorry, too, for interrupting your work. I can sneak out through the back and find the cottage on my own."

He considered her suggestion. It would be a way to avoid the awkwardness between them because of the kiss. But Theo soon realized the heat he was feeling had doused the uneasiness, and said heat was now telling him that being with Brenna was a stellar idea.

It wasn't.

If he wanted to avoid more kissing, the way to do that was to keep his distance from Brenna. But apparently, his body had no such plans.

"It won't take me long to show you the place," he heard himself say.

She shrugged, but there was nothing casual about the gesture. The awkwardness might indeed be gone, but he suspected she was trying to wrap her mind around this lust problem just as he was. Either it had to end, period, or they had to figure out where the heck it was going to lead them.

They went out the back and to his truck. If it hadn't been so hot, he would have suggested they walk since the cottage was only about a quarter of a mile away, but driving would prevent heatstroke and get this errand done faster. The problem was he didn't know if "faster" was good or bad.

"Why are you thinking of buying the cottage?" he asked as he drove.

"Our mothers," she readily admitted. "I've looked at every available place in town to rent or buy, and none of them suits me, so my mom suggested the cottage. I suspect she suggested it after talking with your mom. They probably figure it's a way to get you and me together."

"Yeah," he agreed. "That's probably how it played out." He turned onto a road that paralleled the one leading to his place. "FYI, the cottage has been empty for years. We use it for guests, and every now and then a relative going through a tough time will ask to stay there to get back on their feet. It's never actually been up for sale as far as I know."

She nodded. "Your mom said she's been thinking about selling it for a while, but that she wanted to wait for the right buyer since that buyer would be living on the ranch." Brenna paused. "I'm well aware this could backfire. That you and I might always be . . . uncomfortable around each other. That discomfort could skyrocket if we're also neighbors."

"Uncomfortable," he repeated, and Theo purposely drove very slowly to give this conversation some time.

"That's my fault. I broke your heart, and I'm sorry for doing it. Sorry I didn't handle things better. My offer still stands if you want to curse or yell at me. Might make you feel better."

She opened her mouth as if she might do just that, but she waved the invitation off. "Over the years, I've called you enough bad names that I guess it squashed the possible therapeutic benefits of yelling."

Theo winced and hated that she'd felt so much hurt and anger. That was even more reason to tread lightly, or not tread at all, around Brenna. He definitely didn't want to hurt her again.

"So a possible new house and new job," he said to shift the subject as the cottage came into view. "Are you okay with so much change?"

"I am. I wouldn't have been eight years ago, but it's what I want now. I want to be back home even if home has sort of imploded on me." She paused. "What about you? Are you okay with this?" Brenna motioned around the ranch grounds.

Good question, and in some ways, Theo was still sorting out the answer. "It's growing on me. I would have had to retire from bull riding in a couple of years. I keep reminding myself of that. The injury just moved up the timeline for my return home."

"That had to be tough. I've seen your rodeo stats. You sure know how to handle bulls. Well, all except for Butt Buster."

It surprised him that she'd known the name of the bull that had ended his career. Pleased him, too, that she'd kept up with what was going on in his life. "I read about you getting a medal."

Her eyes widened a little, so maybe she was surprised he'd kept up with her life as well. "My folks made sure everyone knew, but that was a team effort. I was the senior ranking officer, so I got the publicity."

He hadn't heard about it from her folks but had rather read about it on the internet. Brenna and some military cops who worked for her had broken up a high-level theft ring on the base.

Theo had been driving at a snail's pace, but he eventually reached the front of the cottage. It was a smaller version of his own house. With a few big differences.

Like the gate.

Brenna frowned when she spotted it. The white metal slats had been cut out as little hearts. Rows and rows of them.

"My grandmother was a serious romantic," he grumbled. "Beware, in the spring, the flower bulbs form heart shapes when they bloom."

Brenna sighed, then chuckled. "Well, at least the house isn't in view of the billboard photos of us."

Theo sighed, too, and pointed across the far end of the pasture where the new billboard had just gone up.

"Oh, for Pete's sake," Brenna grumbled.

He was right there with her in that particular sentiment. "For what it's worth, only one of the windows in the cottage faces that direction."

Hell, he sounded like a Realtor selling a perspective buyer on a home. Something he probably shouldn't be doing since the cottage was so close to his place. Still, if it would make Brenna happy to live here, then he wouldn't balk.

The key for the front door was under the welcome mat, which also had hearts, and he used it to let them inside. Someone, his mother probably, had turned on the A/C and had freshened the cottage up because it smelled of roses.

That's when Theo spotted the bouquet of yellow and white roses on the kitchen island.

"It's not a big space," Theo explained. "But my mom had it renovated after my grandparents moved into the house with her and my dad." That'd happened about five years ago, shortly before both of his grandparents had passed away.

Brenna strolled through the living room, which a Realtor would probably say was cozy what with its fireplace and original wood floors. With the remodeling, it was now open concept, one large-ish area that encompassed the living room, dining room, and kitchen. Brenna kept strolling to the hall, which led to two bedrooms and two baths. One of the bedrooms was small, but the master was ample sized.

"It's perfect," she muttered, but she didn't sound especially happy about that.

He didn't think her unhappiness was because of the heart-shaped gate or the billboard, either, but rather because of the proximity to him.

And what that proximity would mean.

"If you move here," he spelled out, "our folks and the town will see it as a signal that you've forgiven me. For them, that'll only be a short step to believing we can rekindle what we once had. People will amp up the matchmaking even more."

"I'm not sure more is possible," she muttered, then paused. "I don't guess you're dating anyone else to make those people tone down the matchmaking?"

Theo stared at her. "I wouldn't have kissed you in the barn if I'd been involved with anyone else." He stopped, huffed. "Well, I'd like to think I wouldn't have kissed you if I'd been dating someone else, but I wasn't exactly doing the right kind of thinking in that moment."

Another nod from Brenna, and he couldn't read her

expression. She'd gone all cop on him. "So you regret it," she said. Definitely not a question.

Theo went with his gut and answered honestly. "No. But I am sorry if I caused you any regrets."

Their gazes connected for what seemed an eternity or two, and the attraction sparked those lightning flickers between them. Finally, she muttered some profanity as if disgusted with herself and turned to move away. He took hold of her hand, only to make sure she didn't storm off before he had a chance to dole out another apology, but Brenna didn't do any storming.

Not away from him anyway.

She turned his hand so that instead of him holding her, Brenna was holding him, and she pulled him to her. Before he could say a word—not that he was planning on talking anyway—she drew him to her, came up on her tiptoes, and put her mouth on his.

Surprise and pleasure jolted through him, with the pleasure quickly winning out, big-time. This was definitely unexpected but very much wanted, and Theo didn't hold back. He returned the kiss, sliding his hand around the back of her neck so he could draw her even closer. So he could deepen the kiss just the way he'd been wanting to do.

It had only been two days since he'd last kissed her, but Theo felt starved for her. Not good because it made him want to keep deepening, keep pressing himself against her. And when he did just that, the heat intensified.

Brenna moaned, a silky sound of pleasure that brought back memories of other kisses that had led to making out. It was hard to stick with only kisses when your body felt like a powder keg, ready to blow.

"No way should I be doing this," Brenna muttered when she broke for air.

That stopped him because it sounded as if she was ready

to put an end to this. But she wasn't. She went back in for another kiss. Then, another. Until Theo was reasonably sure she was trying to torture him or melt him. At the moment, he was willing for her to do both.

She caught on to his hair, knocking off his Stetson. Without looking down, he kicked it out of their way so they wouldn't trip over it, then dived back into the kiss again. This time, though, he went after her neck because he recalled that had been an especially sensitive area for her.

It apparently still was.

Theo smiled a little when her silky sounds of enjoyment turned to a groan of torturous pleasure. He totally got that sound. He was on fire as much as she was.

Brenna upped the torture by maneuvering them until his back landed against the kitchen island, anchoring him so she could go after his neck as well. Turnabout was indeed fair play because that was his own hot spot, and she exploited it with some clever circles of her tongue. Easy for her to recall that trick since they'd spent hours and hours making out just like this. Back in the day, they'd given each other many, many hickeys along with all that pleasure.

Brenna did something else familiar, too. She pressed herself against him, body to body. They fit in all the right places. He was hot, hard, and ready.

Until he got a jolt of cold and wet.

There was the sound of breaking glass, followed by the cold/wet, and it sent them flying apart. That's when Theo realized they'd smacked against the vase of roses, and it'd tipped over and broken.

Brenna blinked hard and fast as if trying to yank herself out of a dream. She didn't quite manage to put on her cop's face, but he could see her reining in her desire.

"Uh, I'm sorry about that," she muttered.

She couldn't have said anything that would have smacked

him back to reality more quickly. Hell. He didn't want to do anything to cause Brenna any more regrets, and here he'd obviously done just that.

Theo nodded and dragged in some breaths while he tried to figure out what to say, what to do. She'd probably run for cover now and do her best to avoid him. This latest kiss could have blown his chance of being around her again. And in that moment, he realized something.

He wanted Brenna back.

But hell in a handbasket, how was he going to manage to do that?

CHAPTER 5

Brenna was lost. Not literally. She knew her way around the barn on the Willow Creek Ranch. After all, she'd helped decorate it for the combined bachelor and bachelorette party. But she was lost trying to figure out what the heck was going on between Theo and her.

After that scalding kissing session in the cottage, she had needed a whole lot of thinking time, and he'd given it to her all right. That'd been two days ago, and the only contact she'd had with him was a couple of texts about the party prep and a single non-party-related text with two puzzling words.

I'm sorry.

Brenna hadn't been sure how to answer, and that was because she wasn't certain how she felt about all that kissing. On the one hand, it'd been awesome, but it had also been equally troubling because she couldn't continue to kiss and lust after Theo while guarding her heart.

Then again, maybe heart guarding wasn't even necessary, considering that *I'm sorry* text. If she took it at face value, then it could be that Theo believed their kiss to be a mistake that he didn't intend to repeat. That could be why he'd had such *limited* contact with her over the past two days.

Emphasis on limited.

While Brenna had been in the barn for various stages of
the decorating, Theo had popped in and out, and even
though he'd been pleasant enough, he definitely hadn't
launched into a conversation about what the heck was
going on between them.

"Maybe that's for the best," she muttered, watching the
party play out in front of her.

The music was pumping "Boot Scootin' Boogie," and
some of the guests were on the makeshift dance floor
showing off their moves. Others were clustered by the
bars that had been set up in the corners. Frequent bursts
of laughter cut through the music. Ditto for cheers and
whoops for those riding the mechanical bull. Others were
chowing down at the make-your-own-sliders' table or
bringing in plates from the grills that had been set up just
outside the barn. The place smelled of barbequed ribs,
beer, and freshly baked rolls.

This clearly wasn't a traditional way to celebrate a bachelor or bachelorette party, but everyone seemed to be
having fun. Well, mostly. She was definitely feeling lost.

Along with drowning in hearts.

Mandy had made sure they were featured in every inch
of available space. Strings of twinkle lights forming hearts.
Horseshoe wreaths in the shape that'd been nailed to every
wall. Above the dance floor was a "hearted" *Congrats to
Mandy and Rafe* banner. And just in case anyone had forgotten the theme of this particular shindig, dozens of heart-
shaped Mylar balloons floated around, bopping into each
other and anyone who got close to them.

That lost feeling faded some when she caught sight of
Theo again. Even in the packed space, Brenna had no
trouble keeping track of him. Her eyes just refused to quit

looking for him, and unlike her, Theo wasn't hiding next to a stall in the darkest part of the barn. He'd been mingling, chatting with guests, and checking the various food and drink stations. She'd watched as he even made a few minor adjustments to the stripper area. No strippers had shown yet, but Brenna knew that Mandy still had them on the agenda.

"Hey, Theo," one of the ranch hands, Shawn Martinez, called out, his voice carrying above the din of the crowd and music. "You're up next on the bull. Show us how it's done."

An alarm shot through Brenna as she immediately thought of his injury, and she found herself bolting from the stall. "It's my turn," she volunteered just as seemingly everything in the barn went quiet.

All eyes turned to her, including Theo's, and he was looking both puzzled and a little amused. That brought on volleying glances from the guests, who were no doubt watching to see how this would play out. Brenna was reasonably sure how it would end. With her butt on the floor once she was bucked off, but at least Theo wouldn't have to risk aggravating his knee.

Brenna set down her drink and went closer to the bull. And Theo. "You're sure you want to do this?" he asked.

She tried to look a whole lot more confident than she felt, which wasn't hard because she wasn't feeling any confidence at all. "Absolutely," she said. "Uh, how long does the average person last on one of those things?"

"Thirty seconds to a minute, depending on the setting." Theo glanced at the bull. "This one is set on orange for medium."

Brenna doubted there was a setting low enough for her particular skill set in this area, and she was starting to feel a whole lot of nerves. "Any advice from the pro?"

"Yeah, stay on." He chuckled, and despite the indignity she was about to face, that warmed her heart. So did the gentle squeeze he gave her hand.

There was no heartwarming, though, when he put his mouth against her ear. His breath brushed against her cheek, and she took in his scent. "No need for you to volunteer, though. My knee can handle this just fine. The moves are predictable, so I wouldn't have jostled around much."

"Now you tell me," she managed to say, and then got swept away by those ushering her toward the bull.

Brenna climbed on and looked out at the partyers who were already cheering her on. Mandy and Rafe. Her mom. Several of her soon-to-be fellow deputies. Even her dad was at the back of the crowd and was doing some whooping. Brenna got caught up in the moment. Caught up in Theo, too, since he kept his gaze pinned to her as she straddled the bull and assumed the pose of catching on to the rope with one hand and lifting her other in the air.

The operator turned the machine on, and Brenna lurched forward. Then, back. Nothing about this felt predictable.

If she hadn't laughed at the roller-coaster bobble of her stomach, she might have found her rhythm sooner. Soon enough to last more than eleven seconds. Not exactly an impressive ride, but when she went into a slide off the bull, Theo moved in to catch her. The crowd cheered when she landed in his arms.

The moment seemed to freeze, and the place went quiet again. Obviously, everyone was waiting for something, and she didn't have to guess what. They wanted to see if Theo and she would kiss. And Brenna so wanted to do that.

Mercy, did she.

She wanted to take his mouth and keep on kissing, but

talk about a firestorm of gossip that'd create. So she reined in her lust and let Theo steady her enough so she could lift her arms in triumphant fist pumps.

Some of the crowd cheered. Others groaned because they were clearly expecting more. Theo gave them more, but not by doing any public kissing. He eased her away from the bull, climbed on, flipping up the mode to the highest level, then rode and rode and rode as the cheers got louder and louder.

Brenna kept watch on his face to make sure he wasn't in any pain. He didn't seem to be. In fact, he seemed to be relaxed and, well, happy. He might not have completely come to terms with his injury, but he was obviously having fun.

At the one-minute point, he slid off the bull, and unlike her, he landed in a fluid, graceful standing position despite his injured knee. That set off a collective cheer so loud that Brenna wouldn't have been surprised if it had raised the roof.

Chuckling again, Theo slipped his arm around her waist and led her out of the arena and into the crowd. There were congrats and backslaps, but Theo kept threading them through the partyers until he made it to the back of the barn. He grabbed two beers from one of the bars, holding the necks of the bottles in one hand while keeping the other clamped to her waist. He led her to the same stall area where she'd been hanging out earlier.

"You looked mighty impressive on that bull," she told him. Brenna was still feeling a little giddy, and she felt that pull of heat. The pull of other things, too. She'd never seen Theo ride, but the man certainly made a picture while doing it.

"I've had some practice. And it helped that the bull wasn't Butt Buster," he joked.

She had a sip of the beer when he gave it to her and decided to launch right into what was bothering her. "You said 'I'm sorry' in your text."

Theo studied her while taking his own sip and then sighed. "Not sorry about the kissing. Sorry that I pushed you too hard. I was going to give you some space, but then I saw you tonight, and I wanted to be in that space with you."

Brenna stared at him. "You big lug," she grumbled. "I started the kissing. Not you. And I left because I figured if I stayed another second, we'd end up having sex."

"We would have," he assured her in that sexy drawl that messed with her mind again. Messed with her body, too.

"I was more than ready for kissing and such, but I wanted to take a step back and make sure a quick round of sex wouldn't mess things up between us. And you didn't push," she quickly added before he could say anything. "Well, maybe you pressed me against a counter or something. Hard to remember since your kisses turned my brain to mush."

He smiled, just as she had hoped he would. "You have the same effect on me."

Their gazes locked again, and the heat came, washing over her. Brenna would have no doubt kissed him had someone not interrupted.

"I can see it," Mandy gushed, and that's when Brenna realized her sister was only a few feet away. Mandy clapped her hands. "You two are falling in love again."

"It's lust, not love," Brenna quickly corrected. If she'd needed a step back to decide whether sex would happen between Theo and her, then she'd need many steps back to figure out whether falling in love with him was even a possibility.

Theo made a sound of agreement, muttered something

about having to see somebody, and took hold of Brenna's hand to rescue her from her sister's glee-filled eyes.

Once Theo and she had put some distance between Mandy and them, they stopped outside one of the stalls and glanced around. Thankfully, most people had their attention on Rafe, who was now taking his turn on the bull. Theo opened the stall gate and pulled Brenna inside. It was dark, and she was pretty sure it would be somewhat private.

Or rather it would have been had it not already been occupied.

Brenna practically bumped into the kissing, grappling couple, and then she gasped when she realized it wasn't just any couple. It was her parents. Her mom and dad flew away from each other, revealing disheveled clothes and hair. Clearly, there'd been some groping going on.

"Mom," she managed to say. "Dad?" But then it hit her what she was seeing, and Brenna smiled. "You two are back together."

"No," they said in unison, and her father latched on to her mother so they could hurry out.

"No?" Brenna repeated, questioning their answer. "Did you see what I just saw?" she asked Theo.

"Yeah. Maybe they're trying to work things out."

Brenna nearly said it wasn't a smart way to solve their problems, but maybe it was, considering they'd separated because they'd lost that so-called spark. Making out could definitely produce some sparks.

Grinning and feeling even better than she had a couple of minutes earlier, Brenna was ready to duck into the now-empty stall with Theo. But he obviously had something else in mind because he took her into one of the tack rooms and through a door that led outside.

Thanks to a summer breeze, the night air was much

cooler than she'd expected, and no one else seemed to be on this side of the barn. Good thing, too, or they would have witnessed Theo pulling her to him. His mouth came to hers, and the kiss was long, deep, and immediately hit the pleasure mark.

Brenna considered that they'd probably kissed before outside this barn, but it still felt new and exciting. And hot. Sparks indeed were already flying, and they continued to build as the kiss escalated.

Brenna could still hear the thrum of the music inside, the laughter and the chatter, but it was all starting to fade because she was quickly getting lost in the lust haze that Theo was creating.

It's lust, not love, she'd told her sister, and Brenna still thought that was true, but she could also feel something else stirring beneath the heat. Again, it was an old sensation that felt new. And different. Because this feeling seemed to be a whole lot stronger than what she'd once felt for Theo.

She made a sound of protest when he took his mouth from hers, and Brenna immediately felt the loss of his body against hers after he backed away. Her first thought was he was giving her the "space" she no longer wanted, but he took hold of her hand and drew her toward the corral. She soon realized why. A group of partygoers were rounding the corner of the barn, and neither Theo nor she wanted an audience for what they were doing.

"Come on," he said. "It's only about a hundred steps from here to the stables."

There it was again. That reference to the number of steps. "Does taking the steps hurt?" she asked.

"Not anymore, but marking them off is a reminder of how far I've come and where I want to be."

She thought she understood that. A simple way of coping, of mapping out his life, and in this specific case, the mapping was hopefully going to take them to a private place where they could continue making out.

And more.

Brenna very much wanted more, and she hoped it wouldn't take them long to cover those steps. It didn't. He maneuvered her past the corral and into the stables where she'd been just days earlier when she'd borrowed a horse to ride out to talk to Theo in the pasture. That day, there'd been several ranch hands tending the horses, but tonight the place appeared to be empty.

Theo turned to her, pulling her back to him and reclaiming her mouth. Brenna did some reclaiming of her own. The kiss instantly went from hot to scalding, but Theo didn't stand still so she could add some touching to this heated mix. Nope. He circled his arm around her waist and kissed her while they moved.

Brenna had no idea where they were going, and she didn't care. As long as the kisses continued, she figured she'd be content, but of course, the kissing only fired up the heat enough that soon she wanted more.

Theo finally stopped, and he fumbled behind him to open a door. To an office, she realized, when he got her inside. He didn't turn on the light, but there was enough moonlight slanting through the window to give the room a milky glow. He shut the door, locked it, and things skyrocketed from there.

The earlier kisses had already been plenty hot, but Theo took the heat up a whole lot more. And she finally got the touching she wanted when he slid his hand between them and cupped her breast.

Yes! This was what she wanted. Correction, what she needed, and Theo knew just how to fill that need. He touched, kissed, and pressed himself against her so she could feel the hard set of his muscles. She could feel his hardness, too, behind the zipper of his jeans, and that upped the fire even more.

Brenna went after his shirt, peeling it off him so she could get her hands on his chest. He'd definitely filled out in all the right places, and she was reaping the benefits now. She slid her hands over his chest and down to his stomach. When she went even lower, he cursed, and she knew she'd hit the right spot. Then again, anything in that general region would have no doubt been right.

He pressed her against the back of the door, giving her another of those deep kisses that added more fuel to this already blazing fire. But then he stopped again and met her eye-to-eye.

"You're sure about this?" Theo asked.

"Yes," Brenna decided on the spot.

Of course, the heat was playing into her decision, but it felt right to be with Theo like this.

He didn't question her response, maybe because she didn't give him a chance. Brenna launched into another round of kissing and went after his belt. That started a battle for clothing removal, and Theo tackled her loose cotton dress. He pulled it off over her head, leaving her in just her underwear and cowboy boots.

Theo pulled back to look at her, not eye-to-eye this time, just sliding a glance down her body. He must have approved of what he saw because his groan was of pleasure and need. A whole bunch of need.

Since Brenna wanted her own peep show, she put her hand on his belt again. Then, the zipper of his jeans. Not an easy feat, considering how hard he was. Still, she managed to get him unzipped.

And slid her hand into his boxers.

Yes, he was hard and ready, all right. He cursed her again and went after her bra, pushing it down and taking her nipple into his mouth. His hands hadn't lost any of those clever moves, because in the same motion, he went after her panties, pushing them off her and to the floor.

Then he gave her a kiss in the center of her naked body that had her cursing him. Then praising him. Then gasping from the sheer pleasure he was giving.

Brenna felt herself already climbing, climbing, climbing to a peak that would end all of this too fast, too soon. That's why she caught on to his hair to hit the pause button and slid with him to the floor so she could tackle his jeans. She wanted him naked, and she wanted that now.

But then, she was the one to stop.

"Please tell me your knee can handle this and that you have a condom," she said, her voice choppy because of her short breaths.

"Knee is fine. Condom is in my wallet," was all he managed to say before she started up again.

Brenna maneuvered him so his back was on the floor where she could haul off his boots, jeans, and boxers. She did the same to her boots before she straddled him. And she nearly ended up having accidental sex with him when she leaned down to kiss him.

His erection pressed against her center, making her ache to have him right then, right there, but thankfully common sense won out. Together they fumbled around until they located his wallet. Then, the condom. The moment Theo had it on, she took him inside her.

The past seemed to melt away, and she stilled for just a moment to savor, well, the moment. Theo and she had made love plenty of times, but although most of those times had hit the amazing mark, this one seemed to be even better.

Theo notched up the *better* again. Of course, he did. He caught on to her hips, moving her as she began the thrusts that would amp up the pleasure even more. It amped it up and up and up. Until the need built. Until she knew she wouldn't be able to take more. Still, Theo gave her more until she felt her body give way.

There it was. That final kick of pleasure mixed with need. Oh, so much need that brought her exactly what she had to have.

Release.

Theo was right there to catch her, too, as he found his own climax. He pulled her to him, gathered her into his arms, and held her.

CHAPTER 6

"I'm not sure Mandy could have found another place to add more hearts," Brenna muttered as Theo and she studied the barn.

Theo had to agree. Mandy had kept the heart lights and wreaths from the party and had added others, including glittering heart confetti in the aisle and heart bows on the backs of all the chairs.

"Isn't it amazing?" Mandy asked, twirling around on the confetti and giggling as she looked up at the twinkling lights that now spelled out her and Rafe's names. In a heart shape, of course.

"It's amazing," Brenna concurred, and the three of them stood there for what would be the last quiet moment they had in a while.

The guests would be arriving soon. Rafe, too, and Theo would take up position with his brother in the tack room from which they'd be making their entrance for the ceremony. Mandy had decided that Brenna, their dad, and she would be coming down the aisle together. Considering the bulk of her dress, which Theo was pretty sure was wider than four feet, some folks were going to get smacked by the puffy fabric. He doubted anyone would mind.

Not once they got a look at Mandy's bright smile.

His soon-to-be sister-in-law was giddy with excitement and happiness, and since Theo had seen Rafe just minutes earlier in the main house, he knew his brother was feeling the same. So was Theo, but his own giddiness was the result of just being with Brenna.

It'd been only a couple of hours since she'd left his bed so she could hurry home to get dressed for the wedding. That couple of hours still felt like an eternity or two, and he couldn't wait to get her back in his bed again. Over the past forty-eight hours since the party, they'd slipped back into their old ways. It seemed they were starved for each other. Nothing wrong with that. In fact, there was plenty right about it.

But he wanted more from her.

And that wanting could end up ruining everything if he wasn't careful.

"Oh, before I forget, I have this for you," Mandy said, and she handed Brenna a small box she'd been holding.

Brenna opened it to reveal a necklace, which, of course, continued the theme of the day. It was a silver heart. "It's beautiful. Thank you," she said, kissing her sister's cheek.

Mandy tipped her head to the pearl necklace Brenna was wearing. "Why don't you wear this one, and I can wear the pearls? That way, I'll have something borrowed and old since those once belonged to our grandmother. I've already got the blue covered." She gathered up the yards of fabric in her dress to reveal the blue garter she was wearing.

They swapped necklaces, and then Brenna took something from the pocket of her pink maid of honor gown. "I found this, and I thought it could be your something borrowed."

Mandy's eyes brightened even more. "You found a heart rock?"

"I did," Brenna confirmed, "when I was with Theo in the pasture."

Theo nearly groaned, an automatic response to the matchmaking wheels he imagined turning in Mandy's head, but then he relaxed. A little matchmaking might not be so bad after all.

"Don't tell me not to read anything into this," Mandy said to him as she clutched the rock. "Because it's definitely a sign."

Neither Brenna nor Theo insisted that she back off. They didn't argue with her conclusion, though he personally didn't believe in such things. Still, it never hurt to have a little woo-woo working in his favor.

The barn door opened, and Brenna's folks came in. Theo didn't think it was his imagination that they looked sated, as if they'd just had a pre-wedding celebration of their own.

"So many wonderful, happy changes," her mother declared, smiling when she looked around the barn. "Mandy's getting married and becoming a mom. Brenna's buying her own place. That cottage is perfect for her," she added to Theo.

He couldn't agree more, and it had only made the morning more special when Brenna had told him her decision that she would be his neighbor. She'd then joked they could endure the billboard together.

"Is one of those wonderful, happy changes that you two are back together?" Mandy asked, hope and excitement written all over her. Over Brenna, too.

Theo immediately saw the change on their mother's face, though, and he wanted to groan. Because that wasn't a wonderful, happy expression. Then again, it wasn't an especially unhappy one, either. Both of Brenna's parents seemed to have gleams in their eyes.

"We'd wanted to wait to tell you after the honeymoon," her father started, "but your mom and I are staying separated."

"But we're taking a trip to Bermuda together," her mother quickly added. "I know this is hard for you to understand, but for now, we just want to have some fun, and then we'll work on our marriage."

"Uh, isn't having fun the way to work on your marriage?" Brenna asked, taking the words right out of Theo's mouth.

Her father shrugged. "Possibly. We'll just have to see." He winked at his daughters and then hugged them.

Theo figured there was no "possibly" to it; the fun would lead to the couple realizing they were meant to be together. That thought skidded to a stop and stuck in his head like a flashing neon light.

Were Brenna and he meant to be together?

Had the fun they'd been having made her realize that?

Maybe. He hoped it had made her realize a whole lot more.

Her mother checked his phone when a soft alarm sounded. "Oh, I see the Justice of the Peace just drove through the ranch gate. It won't be long now," she added, kissing Mandy's cheek. "Your dad and I will take a quick look around to make sure everything's in place."

"Oh, I want to do that, too," Mandy said. "And I have to check to see how many things my dress might knock over."

Mandy turned, immediately knocking over two chairs and sweeping away a bunch of heart confetti as she followed her parents, leaving Brenna and him alone. Alone-ish anyway. Soon, the Justice of the Peace would arrive. Rafe, too. But Theo didn't need a whole lot of time to tell Brenna what he had to say.

"There are one hundred and sixty steps between my house and the cottage you're buying," he informed her.

She smiled. "Does this mean you want me to visit often?"

"Absolutely. I don't need any rocks to convince me that I want you in my bed for a long, long time."

"I'd like that." She touched her mouth to his in a little peck that still managed to pack a wallop. "No rocks needed for me, either."

Good, and her smile kept him going. "We will have to deal with everyone bragging about succeeding in getting us together," he pointed out.

She sighed, nodded. "But at least the matchmaking will stop."

Maybe. Theo hoped so anyway, but he figured Brenna and he would be under the relationship microscope for a while. He was okay with that. He could be okay with a lot of things as long as he had her.

"Actually, I'd like you in my life for a long, long time," he added.

Her expression froze for a second. One heart-stopping moment when Theo thought maybe he'd pushed too hard, too fast.

"Really," she muttered. "How long is long?"

Because he felt the zing of nerves, he kissed her. It worked. Nerves instantly settled. Unfortunately, the kiss revved up his body. Then again, he was always revved around Brenna.

"This long," he added, deepening the kiss until it turned scalding hot.

She was smiling and looking a little dazed when they finally broke for air. "I'm in love with you," she said. "I know I told you that when we were eighteen, but it's still true."

Now it was Theo's turn to freeze, and her words caused

a fresh zing of nerves. The right kind of nerves, though, and he realized he'd been waiting to hear her say just that. Ditto for him waiting to give those words right back to her.

"I love you, too, Brenna."

Of course, they kissed. It seemed a surefire way to celebrate. He kissed her, held her, and felt everything go right with the world. This moment had been years in the making, but it had definitely been worth the wait. And all the matchmaking.

"So how long is long?" Brenna repeated.

For once, it was an easy answer. "Forever," Theo assured her, and he pulled her back to him for another kiss.

Visit our website at
KensingtonBooks.com
to sign up for our newsletters, read
more from your favorite authors, see
books by series, view reading group
guides, and more!

Become a Part of Our
Between the Chapters Book Club
Community and Join the Conversation